Robby Riverton:
MAIL ORDER BRIDE

by

ELI EASTON

Robby Riverton: Mail Order Bride

Being a fugitive in the old west shouldn't be this much fun.

The year is 1860. Robby Riverton is a rising star on the New York stage. But he witnesses a murder by a famous crime boss and is forced to go on the run—all the way to Santa Fe. When he still hasn't ditched his pursuers, he disguises himself as a mail order bride he meets on the wagon train. Caught between gangsters that want to kill him, and the crazy, uncouth family of his "intended", Robby's only ally is a lazy sheriff who sees exactly who Robby is—and can't resist him.

Trace Crabtree took the job as sheriff of Flat Bottom because there was never a thing going on. And then Robby Riverton showed up. Disguised as a woman. And betrothed to Trace's brother. If that wasn't complication enough, Trace had to find the man as appealing as blueberry pie. He urges Robby to stay undercover until the danger has passed. But a few weeks of having Robby-Rowena at the ranch, and the Crabtree family will never be the same again.

Damn, what a kerfuffle. If only Trace can get rid of the fugitive while hanging on to his own stupid heart.

To the authors I loved in my younger days who wrote historical Americana romances, especially the brilliant Pamela Morsi and Maggie Osborne.

Acknowledgments

This seed for this book was planted at Rainbow Con in Florida in 2015. I was sharing a table with author Leta Blake. At one point Indra Vaughn and Emory Vargas stopped by, and we got on the subject of the older historical Western romances. It turned out we all loved them. We discussed how it would be cool to do a m/m mail order bride story. By the end of the con, we agree to do a series of them set in various time periods. Mine was going to be the Old West.

The idea just sat there for a number of years. None of us started our books, too busy with other things. Once in a while, I'd dust the concept off and mention it someone and the response was always along the lines of "I want to read that, so get your butt in gear and write it."

Hey, guys. I finally wrote the book.

In addition to thanking Leta, Indra, and Emory for planting the idea years ago, I want to thank my beta readers – RJ Scott, Veronica Harrison, Kate Rothwell, Nico Sels, Vicki Locey, DJ Jamison, and Quinn Anderson. Also thanks to my editor, Edie Danford, and sensitivity reader, Nikki Hastings. Also to proofers Belen Tornabell and Becky Condit, and to Rachel Maybury, who organizes all the ARC & blog tour business.

The cover was a challenge. I wanted something that was a spoof of an old time Western mail order bride romance cover. Artist Dar Albert pulled that off and then some. Thank you, Dar!

And, as always, thanks to my husband for helping me survive crunch days.

Published by Pinkerton Road
Pennsylvania, USA
First edition, April, 2018
eli@elieaston.com
www.elieaston.com

Chapter One

March 15, 1860
New York City

"It was from Aunt Dinah's quilting party, I was seeing Nellie home!"

Robby's melodic tenor echoed in the narrow corridors backstage as he made his way to his dressing room. He exchanged winks, grins, or backslaps with everyone who squeezed past him. He was in a damned pleasant mood. The standing ovation they'd just received had put him on top of the world.

"Seeeing Nellie hoooome!" he bellowed in the big finish as he banged into his dressing room. His name, ROBBY RIVERTON, was on the door, and there was a water pitcher and a single rose on the table. This was the good life.

He plopped down at his dressing table. In the mirror Jenny Daley appeared, looking like an exotic flower in her red kimono. She leaned against the doorframe. "How you have a scrap of energy after three shows a day, I'll never know."

"Tis the reward of a pure and saintly heart," Robby said, laying on a thick Irish brogue.

"Bollocks. You're depressingly young. That's all."

Jenny Daley was a huge star of the New York stage. She played Lady Macbeth in their current production, and easily convinced the audience she could bend a man to her will with her raven hair and green eyes. She'd managed to outrun her age so far, though Robby figured she had to be nearing forty.

"You hardly even break a sweat," Jenny complained.

"Nonsense. I'm wet as the Hudson in unmentionable places. Lord, I'm parched." Robby reached for the pitcher. It was vilely hot onstage, especially under the costumes and makeup. He tilted the china pitcher over a glass, but nothing came out.

"Flory!" he bellowed. He went to the doorway, squishing Jenny aside, and stuck his head out. "Flory!"

Jenny stuck a delicate finger in her ear. "And to think I once had excellent hearing."

Flory, a mousy little thing of about fourteen, came running. "Yes, Mr. Riverton?"

Robby ignored the hearts in her eyes. "My pitcher is empty *again*. How many times must I remind you to keep it filled?"

Her face fell. "Sorry, Mr. Riverton." She bobbed a curtsy and ran off with the pitcher. With a huff, Robby returned to his chair.

"Don't be hard on the girl," Jenny tsked. "She's awfully mashed on you, Robby."

Robby began wiping off his makeup. "You forget, I *was*

that girl. I labored backstage for four years, and I always had water ready for the actors."

"Yes, but you are smart and capable," Jenny said gently. "Thank God not everyone is, or we'd have even more competition than we have now."

Robby gave her a smile in the mirror. "You're right. Though how you stay so humble, I'll never know."

She made a face. "I've been set down a peg or two in my life. Now, are you coming out with us tonight? Don't tell me you're working, for I shall despair if you say no."

Robby grimaced. "Not tonight, me bonny lass. I have an audition tomorrow. Need to memorize my lines."

"Oh? What's the play?" Jenny slunk into the room with renewed interest.

"*Nick of the Woods* at the Tripler." Longing shot through Robby's chest. He really wanted this role.

"Ooh! That ghastly thing?" She looked delighted.

"Yes, life in the wilds of Kentucky. It's quite bloody, you know."

"The play is? Or the real Kentucky?"

"Both."

She shuddered. "Lands. You couldn't drag me any farther west than Philadelphia."

"I concur. But *playing* a frontiersman would be loads of fun. Don't you think? All that growling and snarling and . . . hair." Robby made claws with his hands and grimaced horribly at her in the mirror.

She laughed. "Darling, you growl like a kitten. You'd sooner be cast as Nick's wife. Want to borrow my red dress for the audition?" She smiled at him prettily.

"Nick doesn't have a wife. He has animal pelts, and knives, and a vengeful heart."

3

"Pity. You'd be a shoe-in for Mrs. Of-the-Woods."

Robby would never live down the fact that his first big break at Burton's New Theater had been in a female role. He'd been working in costuming when the actress playing Ophelia fell ill with the flu, as did the understudy and several other cast members. *Hamlet* had been his mother's favorite, and Robby had every line of the play memorized. He'd stepped forward and, at nineteen, got his first role on stage. The audience and critics had loved his "tender insanity."

Well, why not? Men played women's roles in the olden days. If anything, Robby considered it a double feat of acting—playing the part of "Miss Angeline Smith" who was playing the role of Ophelia. He was blasted proud of that performance.

"I *can* growl," he said firmly. "When you come see me in *Nick of the Woods*, I shall put you into convulsions of terror."

"Well, good luck, my bene boy. We shall miss you tonight. You know what they say about all work and no play."

She kissed his cheek and glided from the room, a picture of grace.

She didn't give Robby the chance to respond, but what *he* said about all work and no play was that if he were very diligent, and very lucky, he might one day be as famous as Jenny Daley.

Robby finished removing his makeup, thanked Flory and gave her a sweet smile when she returned with water, and put on an undershirt and dressing gown. He settled down with a bottle of wine an admirer had sent backstage, turned up the lantern to its highest pitch, and dove into the realm of the dreadful Nick. He paced and grimaced, shouted and groaned.

He *could* growl, damn it. He needed a role like Nick. He'd been playing pretty boys for five years now, always the son or the young, naive lover. Hence his role as MacDuff's son in the current production and not Macbeth. He needed to prove he was ready for mature roles despite his baby face.

He was so focused on his task that he lost track of time. Then tiredness hit him like a sledgehammer from out of the blue, and he could barely keep his eyes open. He glanced at his pocket watch. It was just after midnight. The unsavory elements would be out and about, and it was a twelve-block trek to Mrs. Grassley's boarding house. He should have left hours ago.

When he exited the back door of the theater, the sky was pitch black and the city was transformed by the flicker and shadow of gas lamps. It was cold, the sort of cold that made the inside of your nose crisp and brought tears to your eyes. Robby pulled on his gloves, struggling with them under the back door's gas light. At least the cold woke him up. If he walked fast, he'd be home in no time.

Only he got no farther than one step. He was suddenly aware that near the opening of the alley were moving shapes. There was a shouted, "No, please," and a barely there *snick* of a knife.

Robby blinked in surprise. His eyes adjusted to the shadows just in time to see the act. Two large men held the arms of a dignified-looking fellow with gray hair, an elaborate moustache, and a three-piece suit. A fourth man, a short bulldog of a brute with thick jowls, a heavy wool coat, and a bowler hat, attacked the gray-haired man, jabbing forward with his right arm. The victim's face contorted with agony as the knife plunged. Bowler-Hat stabbed again and again until the man with the gray hair slumped, lifeless. And still the knife moved once, twice.

Robby was so close, he could see the sticky glint on the blade.

He only realized he was panting in terror by the rapid cloud of condensation that formed in front of his face and faded, formed and faded. Then he made an involuntary sound, a sort of lowing, and the three men snapped around to look at him.

"Don't stand there, you nimenogs. Get him!" Bowler-Hat bellowed.

The men who were holding the victim let him drop to the cobblestones. It wasn't until they'd taken a step toward Robby that he found the sense to move. He briefly considered going back into the theater, but the door had locked behind him, and there was no time to muck around with keys now. He dove to the right. The alley wasn't a dead end, thank God. He came out on Centre Street, the sound of his pursuers loud in his ears. He ran harder and faster than he'd ever run before in his life, on and on, street after street, turning as often as he could. He finally turned onto a familiar street and, seeing no one when he glanced behind him, dove into the Long Shoreman.

Jenny and her friends frequented the establishment often, and Robby was not unknown there. The owner, Phil, was a good sort. After no more than a brief plea, Phil stuffed Robby into his private office then vanished again. With his ear pressed to the door, Robby heard Phil's voice and the angry demands of his pursuers. The back door banged as someone rushed out.

For a long moment all was silent, and there was only the pounding of Robby's blood in his ears. Then a light tap on the door startled him. Robby stepped back to let Phil in.

Phil carried a whiskey bottle and two shot glasses, and he filled them. "They're gone. Here, drink this."

Robby took his and swallowed gratefully.

"What the hell was that about?" Phil grumbled. "Is *The Weekly Sun* hiring thugs as their critics now?"

"I saw a murder." Robby's voice was hushed, as if it were afraid to come out. He dropped down onto a settee crowded with coats, the strength leaving his limbs.

"No kiddin'? Did ya really?" Phil didn't sound especially surprised. Murders were far from uncommon in New York City. "Well, we can smuggle you outta here after a bit, and you should be all right. I told 'em you went out the back and off they went.

Robby shook his head. It had all been such a blur. But a heavy, dark feeling was settling on him, a sense of utter doom and dread. "No, they saw me coming out of the theater. Had to have gotten a good look at my face. There's a gas lamp above the door."

"Oh. That's a bit of rum luck." Phil pushed aside some coats and sat down next to Robby. He poured them both another shot.

"And I was so thrilled to have that new poster of me stuck up at the front of the Burton too," Robby said with a bitter laugh.

It had pricked Robby's pride every time he passed that poster. There were five glass frames hanging at the front of the theater, and several were dedicated to the current and next production, so being featured in one of the remaining slots was the privilege of a drawing attraction.

The poster depicted Robby standing with one foot on a stool, a dashing cape cast over his shoulder, his face angelic as he looked toward the heavens. The costume, complete with leggings and puffy pantaloons, was from his recent role as Laertes in Hamlet. His face, unfortunately, was completely bare in the image, without even whiskers to disguise him. *WITH ROBBY RIVERTON* the poster proudly announced.

Yes, it was rum luck. The rummiest. Robby wondered how long it would take the men to trace him to Mrs. Grassley's boarding house. A day? An hour?

"Ah, Robby, I wouldn't worry about it," Phil said amiably. "They're probably some no-accounts who won't even bother to go look at the front of the theater. Why should they? You saw something, they scared you off, end of story. It was dark, wasn't it? You probably didn't get a good look at their faces. They've no reason to track you down."

Robby stared at Phil, that sense of doom settling deeper. Ice crept up his spine and he thought he might cast up his accounts. This couldn't be happening. Dear Lord, his life was ruined. Scorched earth. He couldn't go back to the Burton, or any other theater in New York. He probably shouldn't even go back to Mrs. Grassley's to collect his things.

Because he *had* recognized them, or at least one of them. He'd just seen Mose "The Terror" McCann, leader of the Bowery Boys and the most notorious gangster in New York, murder a man in cold blood. And Mose

McCann was known for being smart, vicious, and very careful to never leave witnesses.

Robby grabbed Phil's shoulders with both hands, like he might grab a life raft in a treacherous sea. "You must help me get out of town, Phil. Because if I don't, I'm a dead man."

Chapter Two

April, 1860
Flat Bottom, New Mexico Territories

Trace swatted at a fly on his arm and peeked out from under his hat at little Carson Meeps.

"A touch faster there, Carson," Trace drawled.

Carson blinked away a sleepy look and moved the fan he was holding vigorously. Trace sighed in satisfaction at the gentle breeze puffing along his face.

It was midday in April in Flat Bottom, which meant nothing much got done. Not that much ever *did* get done in Flat Bottom, at least not on Trace's account. But it was especially quiet in the streets today. From the porch of the sheriff's office where he sat in his chair, boots on the porch rail, Trace had a wide view of Main Street, tip to tail. There was Pete's General Store, the saloon, a smithy shop, the livery stables, the city office, and Mrs. Jones's boarding house, which served meals when she felt like it, and had a few surveyors in residence at the moment. There were another half-dozen private homes. And at the south end of town sat the school house with its big willow tree and fenced-in yard.

Very little moved anywhere. Which was just how Sheriff Trace Crabtree liked it.

"I gotta go muck stalls at the stables at two o'clock," Carson said proudly.

"That's fine." Trace yawned and closed his eyes.

"Can you tell me when it's nearly two? Don't wanna miss it."

"Sure thing."

Trace might have felt guilty about having a boy stand there and fan him, as if he were some fat pasha in a storybook. But Carson, at eight years old, was the most enterprising soul in Flat Bottom. He didn't have a daddy, and his mama took in laundry, including Trace's. Carson helped out doing just about any work he could scrounge up when school was out. And Trace had little else to spend his pennies on, seeing as how meals and board came with his job.

He'd just about dozed off when he heard the rumble of wheels. He slit his eyes open to see who it was. A flatbed wagon lead by two chestnut horses was coming up the street. The driver was a large young man in an old blue coat faded nearly to gray, too-short pants that revealed hairy ankles above battered work boots, and large hammy hands on the reins. His most notable feature was the wild black hair that sprung up all around his head like a cloud and a big bushy black beard. Next to him on the seat were two young ladies, both wan-looking and dressed in threadbare clothes. A baby was in the arms of one of the gals. Likewise, the three children in the flatbed looked like they'd dressed out of the beggar's box at church. The wagon stopped in front of the general store.

Several ladies emerged from the store, tilted their noses haughtily in the air, and offered the family a perfunctory greeting before hurrying away.

With a heavy sigh, Trace pulled his boots off the rail and stood up. He took a dime from his pocket and tossed it to Carson. "Gotta get a move on."

"Gosh, thanks!" Carson ran off toward the stables with renewed optimism. The boy would be president one day, Trace was pretty sure.

He moseyed over to the general store. Up close, he noticed that Marcy had the fading yellow of a black eye as well as the more recent scrape on her cheek. Emmie had some purple discoloring near her hairline. Their dresses were nearly colorless from washing and frayed in spots.

Christ on a crutch. No wonder the ladies in town shunned the Crabtrees.

Marcy gave him a shy smile. "Hey there, Trace."

"Marcy. Emmie." Trace tipped his hat.

"Uncle Trace!" Billy, an eight-year-old dynamo, sprang over to Trace before remembering he was too big a boy to be picked up. Instead he bounced on his toes at Trace's side. Paul, six, and Missy, five, were not as concerned about their maturity and they each claimed a hug.

"How are y'all?" Trace asked, swinging Missy up into his arms and looking her over. She was healthy, her eyes bright. But she was far too pretty for that misshapen brown dress she wore.

"We're fine," Marcy said. "Pa-Pa wanted me to ask you to supper tonight."

"Can't. Gotta work." Trace chucked baby George on the chin. He sat on Emmie's hip, staring around placidly.

"Uncle Trace!" Missy tugged on his sleeve. "Guess what? There's a mess of new piglets and I got to name one. Wanna know her name?"

"Um . . . Bessy?" Trace guessed. "Sunshine? Sweet Cheeks?"

Missy laughed. "No, *Snowbell*. Ain't that a good name?"

"She's a red pig. It's a stupid name for a red pig," Billy scoffed.

"Now come on, children. Let's get the shoppin' done," Emmie urged, bouncing the baby. She looked around the street with some disappointment before herding the kids and Marcy into the store.

Clovis finished tying up the horses. "I could use a drink."

"Lead the way," Trace said.

"Less you're too busy bein' sheriff."

"Well, now, Clovis, you're the worst element in the town at the moment, so I figure keepin' an eye on you is my job."

Clovis punched his arm lightly, and they headed across the street to the saloon.

All of Trace's brothers—Wayne, Roy, and Clovis—worked the ranch with his pa. It was hard work, sometimes grueling, and they gave Trace guff about his sedentary life. And they weren't wrong.

The saloon was mostly empty since it was barely noon. They both ordered a ginger beer. Trace asked about the ranch, and Clovis gave a longer account than Trace wanted—number of heads, a sickness that had worried them but hadn't turn out too bad, the cases of hoof rot and the runs caused by a pernicious spring weed.

That was the world Trace had grown up in, and he'd fought like hell to get out of it, running off and joining the army at sixteen. Now here he was, ten years later, back in Flat Bottom. It was enough to downright discourage a man.

"You should come by tonight for supper," Clovis said, when the list of animal maladies had run dry. "We'll probably wrassle."

"Gotta work," Trace said flatly.

"What the hell do ya do in town at night? Sit in here and drink?" Clovis scoffed. He sounded jealous.

"Just when do you think a town needs sheriffin' anyway? As ya can see, there ain't a whole lot of rowdy goin' on this time of day." He swept his hand at the empty room. "And cattle rustlers don't do business in broad daylight."

"Cattle rustlers would be where there's *cattle*," Clovis muttered.

It was funny, and Trace couldn't stop a smile. "Well, Crabtrees aren't the only ranchers in the area."

"Pa gets testy when ya never come. Then we have to hear him moan about it."

"I'll come on Sunday."

Clovis shrugged and drank his beer.

Trace felt a familiar unsettled itch. He needed to figure out what the hell he was doing. Long before he'd gotten shot at La Ebonal, he'd been unhappy with the army. He enjoyed trick-shooting for sport and felt pride in his ability. But he didn't much like being a sharpshooter for the government, picking off unwary men—

usually Indians—when ordered to do so. It was one thing when they were in a battle, and he was killing men who were attacking his regiment. But it was another thing when he was shooting men at a distance, when they were unaware he was even there. The sound of the rifle shot, the violent jolt of the bodies, the life that was stolen from one breath to the next . . . These things plagued his nightmares.

Then he'd come home wounded and being back here didn't fit either. A few days under the same roof as Pa, and Trace had remembered why he'd run away from home. No sir, he couldn't stay in that house.

The three months it took him to heal out on the ranch had been a misery. Seemed he was always in the gals' way, and he couldn't be out helping the men. He started sniffing around Santa Fe for a job. That's when Flat Bottom decided to hire a sheriff. It was true that the town was growing, and there'd been cattle rustlers in the area. But his pa had been the one to press the town board to act. And he'd pushed Trace to apply for the job. One shooting demonstration later, he'd been handed a badge.

Well, he wasn't complaining. It suited for now. It offered a room in town, peace and quiet, and as little fuss as possible. Or it would, if Pa would quit pestering him about spending more time at the ranch.

Clovis let out a hearty belch just as the saloon door opened. Miss Stubbens, the schoolmarm, walked in. Clovis jumped an inch in his chair, and Trace had to bite back a grin. Poor Clovis. He always did have the worst timing.

Miss Stubbens blushed when she spotted Trace and Clovis. She quickly looked away and approached Stan at the bar. "Have you seen Carson Meeps? I know he works here sometimes."

"Ain't seen him this mornin', Miss Stubbens. Sorry 'bout that."

"Thank you kindly, Mr. Winston."

Trace spoke up. "Carson is over at the stables."

Miss Stubbens turned to face them. She always reminded Trace of a little yellow bird. She was tiny—both in height and build. Her straw-colored hair was tucked neatly back in a bun and her face had a pleasing fragility, Trace supposed. If a man liked that sort of thing.

Clovis lumbered to his feet with the grace of a bear and swiped the hat off his head. "Good morn—um, day, Miss Stubbens."

Miss Stubbens's back stiffened and her face paled. "Good day, Mr. Crabtree. And, uh, thank you, Sheriff."

She hurried out of the saloon like she'd seen a ghost.

Clovis sank back down heavily in his chair, looking like a mighty felled tree. His face, what you could see if it around his massive beard and shaggy hair, was an alarming color.

"You look like a plum I et once," Trace said with some amusement.

"Aw, shut up."

"No sir. I don't think that gal is ever gonna come around to it."

"I know that," Clovis said sullenly. He kicked the floor with his toe.

Trace felt a pang of guilt for teasing Clovis—but only a little. A man had a right to tease his baby brother. It was practically a sacred duty.

"There's plenty of fish in the sea, Clovis."

Despite his words, Trace had his doubts. Miss Stubbens had outright refused Clovis's attempts at courting and her attitude wasn't uncommon. There wasn't a gal in town who'd marry up with the Crabtrees. Marcy had been the first—marrying Trace's oldest brother, Wayne. And she'd been the last too, once the other ladies in town had noted how seldom she'd been seen and in what condition. Roy, the second oldest, had found his wife, Emmie, in Santa Fe. And now, from what Trace had heard, none of the good women there were interested either.

Trace didn't give a good goddamn for himself. But Clovis was all but dying for a bride. Frankly, Trace didn't want to think too hard about why that was, but he supposed Clovis was just plain horny. Living at the ranch with his two older brothers and their wives probably made his lonely bed seem all that much colder.

"Pa says he's got it taken care of already," Clovis said.

"He took care of gettin' ya married up? How?"

Clovis shrugged. "Won't say. He just says I'm already spoken for, and I'm not to talk to Miss Stubbens anymore."

"Doesn't look to me like you'll have any trouble there." Trace smirked.

"Shut up."

Trace rubbed his jaw. Knowing his pa, he'd thought up some crazy scheme. "I sure as hell hope, whatever tricks Pa's pullin' with you, he doesn't try to do the same with me."

"Everyone knows ya don't wanna be married," Clovis said stiffly.

"No, I don't. It'd take a noose around my neck to drag

me to the altar," Trace confirmed. If he said it loudly and adamantly enough, maybe his pa would respect the matter.

Clovis finished his ginger beer. "I'd better see if the gals are ready to go. We got fence mendin' to do."

"You have fun with that," Trace said lazily.

Clovis shot him a look and left the saloon.

Chapter Three

The first few days on the wagon train were every bit as uncomfortable and tedious as Robby would have imagined. If he'd ever given a moment's thought to taking a wagon train. Which he most certainly had not. Wagon trains were for immigrant families, men foolish enough to believe they'd strike it rich in a gold mine, and those out to make a name for themselves.

Robby had *already* made a name for himself. Robby, who'd run away from his Pennsylvania farmstead at the age of fifteen, had beaten the odds and made it in New York City. He'd busted his tail, sewed costumes until his fingers bled, done hair and makeup for impatient and occasionally ill-tempered actors, pushed away roaming hands with a laugh so as not to offend. And when he'd finally gotten his break, he'd thrown everything he had into his stage career, eschewing drink and the libidinous ways so common in the theater. Now all that hard work and sacrifice counted for nothing, his career snatched away in the space of one unfortunate moment, and it galled him to no end.

His first plan had been to hide out in St. Louis for a few months, then make his way back to Boston or Philadelphia where he could rebuild a life. But two Bowery Boys had shown up in St. Louis asking about Robby Riverton and showing around his poster. Robby had fled. He'd taken a coach to Independence, Missouri, picturing a bullet between his eyes the entire way. Once there, he'd joined the next wagon train heading west.

He'd hoped to go to San Francisco. But the only spot he was able to find at such short notice was with a blacksmith named Stoltz who was taking provisions to the army in the New Mexico Territory via the Santa Fe Trail. Stoltz had room for two passengers on his wagon.

The price was steep—two hundred dollars. It was one hell of a price to pay to travel in a direction he didn't want to go, and it took nearly all the money Robby had. But he figured it was head west or give up on breathing. And Robby liked his life, thank you. He intended to keep it.

Surely Santa Fe had at least one theater? Maybe they were starved for talent. Maybe those ranchers and prospectors would think Robby was a hoot and a half. If not, he could make his way on to San Francisco from there.

"Why do you keep watching behind us?" Miss Fairchild asked. "You got someone chasing you, Mr. Smith?"

Robby's fellow passenger in Stoltz's wagon was a young lady. She was statuesque, well-bred, and finely dressed. She had light-brown hair that flirted with the idea of being red and a starry sky's worth of freckles on her nose and cheeks. Her current dress was a green brocade, though she had six trunks filled with gowns and parasols and hats and other folderol. They took up an annoying amount of space. She wore a lacy ecru shawl about her person, always, despite the heat. She sat at the back of the wagon where the tarp was open, enjoying the scenery.

Said scenery was nothing but endless green woods and flies, and Robby couldn't be bothered. Besides, he was still nervous about being seen.

"As a matter of fact, I'm being chased by a Russian countess whose heart I broke," Robby said dramatically. "She sent a regiment of Cossacks to drag me back to her side."

Miss Fairchild stared at him blankly for a second then laughed. "Oh, you! My Aunt Fanny! But I can believe you're leaving behind a broken heart. Or a dozen. You're what my mama would call a bonny lad."

"Ack, would she now, your sainted mother?" Robby switched to his best Irish brogue.

Miss Fairchild grinned with delight. "Lands, that's good. Are you Irish?"

"Not even a wee little bit. Not a blessed hair on me head."

She studied him, amused. "What are you, then? Your clothes, your hands . . . You're no laborer. You don't look stuffy enough to be a preacher or a teacher, and you're too young and handsome to be a politician. Are you a poet, sir?"

Robby laid his finger alongside his nose and then pointed at her and winked. "Close, dear lady. I'm an actor."

"Oooh, I've never met an actor before! Mama took me to poetry readings last summer and the gentleman who did them, Roe Farley? He was exceedingly handsome too. Do you know Roe Farley?"

"Can't say as I've had the pleasure. And what about you? What adventure are you off to all on your lonesome, Miss Fairchild?"

He'd wondered about Miss Rowena Fairchild. At first, he'd assumed she was with Mr. Stoltz. But Stoltz paid her even less mind than he did Robby. Which was to say, he ignored them both, going off to take his meals elsewhere, sleeping out in a bedroll under the wagon, and spending his days driving the team.

Her chin lifted defiantly. "I'm going to meet my husband."

Wasn't it *Miss* Fairchild? Robby blinked in confusion. "Ah. And when did Mr. Fairchild go out West?"

She started to speak, hesitated. A mischievous gleam lit her eyes. "Can you keep a secret?" she whispered.

"I know not a single soul on this wagon train but you. And it's awfully tight quarters for secrets."

"That's true. Besides, there's only so long I can hide this if you and me are sharing this wagon all the way to Santa Fe." Moving her shawl to the side, Miss Fairchild revealed a very definite mound at her waistline.

"Ah," Robby said.

"I told Mr. Stoltz I was going to join my husband. But the truth is . . . Here. This will explain better than I can." She drew out an envelope from her tasseled purse and leaned over.

Robby hurried forward to take the missive, worried about her straining her belly. He joined her at the back of the wagon and, after checking again that there was nothing but a long chain of wagons behind them and no hint of the Bowery Boys, he took out the letter and attached contract and peered at it.

"A mail-order bride?" he said in surprise. "Well, that's certainly adventurous. What do you know about this . . ." He scanned for a name. "This Mr. Clovis Crabtree?"

Miss Fairchild palmed her stomach and relaxed against the edge of the tarp. "He's twenty-five, his family owns a wealthy ranch, and he's clean, godly, and a hard worker. That's what it said in the letter. We're to be married just soon as I get to Flat Bottom. That's a town north of Santa Fe."

"And so ingeniously named. Does Mr. Clovis Crabtree know about your delicate circumstance?" Robby asked, seeing no reason to play coy.

Miss Fairchild blushed, but the way her eyes sparkled, it was more with pleasure than shame. "But that's what's so very clever of me! I have it all planned out. You see, I managed to hide this before I left since I wasn't showing much." She touched her belly which, to Robby's eye, was showing more than a little, but maybe she'd always been round there. "No one back home's the wiser. And at my biggest, I'll be on this wagon train where no one knows me. By the time we reach Santa Fe, I'll have had the baby. I hope so anyway." She frowned slightly. "They say it'll take three months to get there, and that's about right."

It sounded like a horrible ordeal to Robby, delivering a baby on a wagon train. But he figured it would help nothing to say so.

"And then, what I'll do . . ." She looked delighted with herself. "I'll say to Mr. Clovis Crabtree, I'll say, 'Why, sir, it's a downright tragedy! A nice Christian lady on the wagon train died having this babe. And I couldn't leave him to the wolves, now could I?'" Miss Fairchild batted her eyes innocently.

It was bold, Robby had to give her that. "What about the baby's father?"

"What?"

"The good Christian lady who had the babe on the wagon train. Wasn't she traveling with her pious husband? Wouldn't he want custody?"

"Oh shush!" Miss Fairchild gave a dismissive wave. "I'll just say he was eaten by a bear. Anyhow, no man wants to raise a baby alone." She appeared to think better of it though, as she amended brightly, "I have it! I'll say the daddy was struck dumb with grief and couldn't bear to touch the child." She raised her arm dramatically across her brow.

Robby figured any man who didn't suspect a tall tale when his young bride appeared with an infant was a fool indeed. But who was he to interfere? And anyway, there was every chance Miss Fairchild's intended wasn't particularly bright. After all, he lived in the New Mexico Territories. And what sort of man went in for a mail-order bride?

"I even managed to slip my chaperone, Aunt Edna," Miss Fairchild continued. "I told her the wagon train left in the afternoon and snuck out while she snored away in the hotel. That's why no one on this earth will ever be the wiser!"

"Do you plan to kill everyone on the wagon train, then?" Robby asked, just to be contrary.

She gave him a dirty look. "Don't be silly! The West is a big place. Chances of me and Mr. Crabtree ever running into any of the folks I meet on the trail is no bigger than a mite on a flea."

Miss Fairchild was likely correct. Though, by the line of worry on her brow, Robby had given her doubts. He could picture the well-mannered Miss Fairchild going around and slitting all their throats in their bedrolls just to make her "plan" even more clever. The thought amused him.

"Who's the real father?" he asked, before he could think better of it.

Miss Fairchild got a sour expression. "A traveling salesman. He was selling Bibles. Can you believe it?"

"Doesn't surprise me a whit."

"Mamma and Poppa were out making calls and our maid, Drusilla, was sleeping away in the kitchen like most afternoons. When Joseph came knocking, he was so handsome, I let him in."

Miss Fairchild did seem to have a weakness for "handsome," Robby decided. But then, so did he.

"I know it was foolish, but he had such a silver tongue. The things he said to me!" She stared out the back dreamily.

"I know just what you mean."

"And I did everything a sensible girl ought to to keep this from coming to pass," she insisted hotly.

"Oh? What did you do?"

"Why, right after I dallied with that man, I ran up to my room and washed real good. And I commenced to jumping up and down for ages! It was a good hour at least. And then I went to bed, but I woke up twice in the night and fretted, so I got up and jumped around some more."

"I can't say as I ever heard of jumping as a means of contraception."

"Contra-what?" She looked at him like he was teasing her. "No, silly, it's for stopping *babies*."

"Ah."

"Guess this one was just determined to come." She stroked her belly fondly, looking down at it with a smile.

"Well, I wish you the best, m'lady. And if I can assist you in any way, consider me your cohort."

"My what?"

"Your co-conspirator, companion in arms, your fellow seaman on the good ship Deceit." Robby gave her a cheeky salute. "If you ever need an eyewitness account, that is to say. To my eyes you are as slender as a reed."

Miss Fairchild's brown eyes grew sparkly. "Aw. That's the nicest thing anyone's ever offered to do for me! I admit, I was afraid coming on this trip all alone. But now that I've met you, Mr. Nick Smith, I know God's looking out for me, despite the error of my ways."

"Indeed," Robby said uneasily. The false name had been a necessary evil. He hoped the Bowery Boys would finally lose his trail.

"Do you have a sweetheart, Mr. Smith?" Miss Fairchild lowered her eyelashes coyly.

There was no mistaking her meaning. Robby forced a smile. "I'm afraid my heart is not my own."

Miss Fairchild's disappointment was brief. "Oh well. Then we shall be the best of friends!"

"Given our close quarters, I think you shall be my sister in the end," Robby said. He hoped Miss Fairchild had some cards in one of those trunks or at least liked to read aloud. It was going to be a very long three months.

As it turned out, all of Miss Fairchild's machinations were for naught. She fell for Mr. Traymore, a bookish and sensitive young man a few wagons back. He was heading to Dodge City to start up a new bank. Smart girl, Miss Fairchild. When Stoltz's wagon continued west, Rowena, her belly like a full moon, stood next to Traymore at the Dodge City stockyard, smiling and waving.

"Good-bye, Mr. Smith," she called out to Robby. "Good-bye!"

She gave Robby her contract with the Crabtrees, along with a letter to deliver to her intended at the end of the trail. The letter was a poetic treatise on the undeniability of true love with fervent wishes for Mr. Clovis Crabtree's own future happiness.

Robby hoped the ranchers in Santa Fe weren't inclined to shoot the messenger.

Chapter Four

July, 1860
Monday
Santa Fe, New Mexico Territory

Trace hated going to Santa Fe. The two-hour ride south from Flat Bottom was pleasant in good weather, but that was rarer than a white buffalo's moustache. Generally, it was too hot and, sometimes, too cold. The wind could be relentless. The scenery was dramatic in spots, but mostly same-ish. This year it was so dry, as the saying went, that the bushes followed the dogs around.

If he had his druthers, Trace would be sitting right now on the porch of the sheriff's office doing nothing. But Santa Fe was a hub of trading for the West, with goods coming in from the East via the Santa Fe Trail. So, everyone always wanted something from Santa Fe, something Pete didn't carry at the mercantile—rock candy, a bit of Spanish lace, or a New York magazine. The men of Flat

Bottom took turns going, and whoever went gathered lists from the others in town. Trace himself went once a month.

Trace, however, didn't go out of a neighborly obligation to shop. Nope. That was just an excuse. *He* went to slake his lust.

One hardship to living in Flat Bottom was its lack of partners for his particular brand of pleasure. Trace had had the luck, through most of his life, of finding like-minded men who were up for a little mutual relief on the regular. Even in the army. But such was not the case in Flat Bottom. If there was another man who shared Trace's proclivities, he was slunk too low to give any telltale signs. On the one hand, it was a good thing not to be tempted to indulge anywhere close to his family. On the other hand—literally—taking care of himself only worked for so long.

He might have lost his ambition in the war, but it hadn't done a thing to curb his damned libido. When the craving for push and shove, hard flesh on hard flesh, and that fiery feeling only a shared passion could ignite got to be too unbearable, Trace rode south.

In Santa Fe there was a barber named Rafael who invited certain customers into a back room. He was big and surly, and they rarely exchanged more than a few words, but it was good enough for Trace. If there was a hollowed-out feeling afterward, he figured that was his lot. A man like him would never have the kind of cozy life most men took for granted, and he'd made his peace with that. Though he did long for the day when he could have sex without coming away stinking of shaving soap.

Trace left his horse at the Santa Fe livery stables and

started toward the barber shop. He was just crossing the dusty central plaza when a ruckus attracted his attention.

Two men accosted a young lady in a green gown and red shawl in the middle of the street. The men wore black pants, black city boots, red shirts, suspenders, and tall stovepipe hats. Belts around their hips holstered guns and knives. Their clothes were like nothing in these parts. They looked like immigrants or like they were from out East, New York or Philadelphia or some such, and they looked like bad news. The lady was demanding, in a very cultured voice, that they unhand her. Trace scanned the street. There were a dozen men in view and none of them even looked toward the argument. A woman led a small boy by the hand, hurrying along the wooden sidewalk in the opposite direction.

Trace might have ignored the argument too, except for three things. First, goddamn but it chafed his hide when men abused women. Second, there was something about the lady that drew his notice. She was a beauty but in an unconventional way. She was tall and thin with wide shoulders. Her face was striking, long and narrow with a square jawline that would cut glass. Her mouth was full, her nose long and straight, and her green eyes sparked with fire. Dark hair peeked out from under her bonnet. Her words were defiant, but Trace knew terror when he saw it.

The third thing was, he heard her say, clear as day, "I told you, my fiancé lives in Flat Bottom, and he'll be here shortly to escort me!"

Well. Hell.

Gritting his teeth, Trace approached the trio. His hand

loitered gracefully near his gun. "What seems to be the trouble here?"

The two men stared at him flatly. They did not let go of the lady.

She, however, searched his face, her eyes pleading. "Sir, I beg your assistance. I was making my way to the *fonda* to seek a room. I just arrived from Missouri, and I need to send a message to my intended to come for me."

"You'll get your room when you're done answering our questions," one of the men snapped. His accent was hard and flat—definitely an Easterner. It was an odd situation to run across in the middle of Santa Fe, but the wagon trail brought all sorts of garbage west.

"But I *have* answered your questions. Repeatedly!" The lady's eyes swam with tears.

The manhandling of the woman ticked Trace off. But it was the way the two men dismissed him as irrelevant that really lit his fuse. He drew his gun and cocked it. This got their attention. The younger one looked slightly puzzled as to what his problem was. The older one stared, his eyes as cold as ice. He was a big man and he looked danger-ously strong despite being soft around the middle. There was not a speck of conscience in those eyes. Trace *really* didn't like him.

Cold-Eyes shifted one hand.

"*Stop.*" Trace leveled the gun at the man's stomach. "You'll be gut-shot 'fore you can draw."

His voice was calm, but it conveyed all the malice he felt. Cold-Eyes froze. The lady looked at Trace with wide, frightened eyes. She was wearing far too much makeup for a woman who spoke in such a genteel manner. But then,

ELI EASTON

Trace wasn't up on the latest fashions. Beneath all that rouge, her face was white with fear.

"Now," Trace said evenly. "Where did you say your intended was from, ma'am?"

"F-flat Bottom. It's supposed to be near here. Do you know it?" Her gloved hand fluttered near her high collar.

"As a matter of fact, I happen to be the sheriff of Flat Bottom."

The two men exchanged a dark look.

"I have a letter. And a legal contract," the lady said firmly. "I showed it to these men, but they—"

"Aw now, listen, Sheriff," Cold-Eyes interrupted. "We're looking for someone. We're not going to hurt the lady, just talk. So, put that fooking gun away." The man's tone was cajoling now. As if they were all men of the world here.

Trace considered it. He slipped his gun back in the holster, knowing he could have it out again in a second. From the way the men studied the action, they knew it too.

Cold-Eyes signaled the other man with a single look. The other man was in his thirties with a fleshy face, stringy blond hair, and a blue feather in the band of his stovepipe hat. He pulled out a large piece of paper, unfolded it, and showed it to Trace. "We're looking for this man. Name's Robby Riverton, aka Nick Smith, but he could be called anything now. You seen him?"

Trace glanced at the poster. It was a theatrical notice featuring an actor. His prissy, old-timey costume, and the pose with one foot up on a stool reminded Trace of a play he went to once in San Antonio. The actor was a young man with dark hair and green eyes outlined in black like a

32

raccoon. He looked heavenward with the attitude of a martyred saint.

He looked too soft to be anyone in these parts.

"Did you check the saloon?" Trace asked with a dismissive shake of his head. "That's the only place they have shows like this."

"He's on the run," Cold-Eyes said. "He's not going to be putting himself on stage, is he?"

Trace had no clue and didn't care. "Can I see that letter you mentioned, ma'am?"

"What business is it of yours?" Cold-Eyes asked.

"Well," Trace said with exaggerated slowness, "the way I see it, this lady is on her way to Flat Bottom, and I'm the sheriff of Flat Bottom, so she is my business."

"But we're not *in* Flat Bottom," Cold-Eyes argued.

"It is an amazing coincidence," Trace agreed.

The lady tried to open her purse, glaring at the two men until they released her arm. She dug inside and presented Trace with an envelope. It contained a hand-written letter in exaggeratedly careful handwriting and a one-page legal document stating the terms of a pending contract of marriage between one Rowena Fairchild and—good God—Clovis Crabtree.

"Aw hell," Trace muttered.

Pa had done lost his mind completely this time. He'd sent for a mail-order bride! Trace could hardly believe it. And *look* at her—fine silk dress, elegant bearing, high-class way of speaking, and natural beauty to boot. It was like ordering all the way to Washington D.C. for fancy china then putting it in the pig trough. Trace would lay money this gal would run screaming from Crabtree Ranch within a week.

Trace wanted to spit onto the dusty street, but he refrained on Miss Fairchild's account.

"Do you know my fiancé?" Miss Rowena Fairchild asked sweetly.

"Yeah," Trace said grudgingly.

"I thought someone would be waiting for me at the stockyard," she said, clutching her shawl more tightly around herself. "But Mr. Stoltz said we made excellent time, so my intended probably didn't expect me so soon. I'm sure once I send word—"

"Pardon my fooking French, but we was talking," snapped Cold-Eyes.

Miss Fairchild clamped her mouth shut and looked heavenward as if entreating God for patience.

"You sure you ain't seen this man?" Blue-Feather demanded of Trace.

"Never in my life," Trace drawled.

As he said it—*never in my life*—there was a funny tickle in his stomach as if that weren't true. He glanced at the poster again, frowning. There was something about the actor's face that rang a bell. Trace had seen his share of song and dance routines, from Texas to the Arizona Territories and all over the West. He didn't deliberately seek them out, but he liked to drink in places that had that sort of entertainment. The music was nice.

He was pert sure he'd never seen this actor before, though. Usually saloons had gals in fancy clothing. If shows had men who looked like this one instead of pretty girls, he'd have taken more of an interest.

Cold-Eyes nodded at Blue-Feather and the poster was rolled up and put away.

"Well, we're looking for him. Came all the way west

after him. And this lady here shared a wagon with Riverton all the way from Missouri."

"I told you, it wasn't proper for us to fraternize. We barely spoke," Miss Fairchild said prissily.

"For three months? He had to say something about where he was going and—" The man shot a look at Trace. "—what he was running from. Where'd he get off?"

"The only place he mentioned to me was San Francisco, but I have no idea how he intended to get there. He was in and out of the wagon all the while. I didn't realize he'd left for good until yesterday, but if I must guess, I'd say he stayed on at Fort Union."

"We was *at* Fort Union. Riverton ain't there!"

"Well, then, I have no idea." She turned to Trace. "Please. I'm just so awfully tired."

Trace got caught by those sleepy green eyes. They were the prettiest he'd ever seen—clear and intelligent, a soft shade that glowed like pond slime in the sun and deepened to moss where her lashes shaded the iris. Those lashes were thick and velvety, like the coat of a chestnut horse Trace once had. And right now, they were imploring him to take charge of the situation.

He cleared his throat, feeling a little discombobulated.

"What did he say about San Francisco?" Cold-Eyes demanded, grabbing Miss Fairchild's arm hard to get her attention. "The words. Tell me the exact words."

"Ow! You're hurting me!" Miss Fairchild cried.

Trace's patience evaporated in a flash of rage. He put a hand on his gun. "Let. Go."

With a glower, Cold-Eyes released her.

Trace stepped forward and took Miss Fairchild's elbow, getting between her and Cold-Eyes. "The lady's answered your questions. If you're lookin' for someone, I suggest ya talk to the Santa Fe sheriff. The office is that way." He jabbed his finger down the street.

He turned and steered Miss Fairchild toward the *fonda*.

Trace didn't turn around to see if the men followed, but he kept his right hand on the holster of his gun and his ear cocked for the sound of a gun hammer.

Cold-Eyes called out, "We know where to find you, Miss Fairchild! If we decide to renew our conversation."

Miss Fairchild's expression didn't alter, but her arm trembled. Trace's first assessment had been right. She was more afraid of them than she let on. She had a hell of a poker face.

They reached the wooden sidewalk and turned left toward the *fonda*. Trace wondered what the hell he was going to do next. He couldn't take Miss Fairchild back to Flat Bottom with him unless he hired a rig. He'd need a chaperone too, damn it all. A young lady didn't go traveling alone with a man, not even her fiancé's brother. And he wasn't about to cross that line with Clovis's bride and give Pa cause to rant and rave. But what choice did he have? He couldn't leave her in Santa Fe. Those two men would be back to harass her the minute he walked away.

Where was her chaperone, anyhow? Had she really been in the same wagon with that Riverton fellow all the way from Missouri? Something didn't smell right to Trace. But then, nothing about this smelled right.

He glanced at her as they walked past the shops. She clutched her shawl tightly, hiding her figure, so he couldn't see much. But she was tall for a woman—only a few inches shorter than Trace. Of course, Trace had met tall women in his day, so that wasn't unheard of. Her gown was ill-fitting and pulled tight across the shoulders. Her high lace collar and red shawl seemed too fancy for the pale green dress. It seemed odd for someone who owned such expensive pieces not to match them up any better. But then, maybe that was the style in the East.

She looked up at him, her expression wary. "Are you really the sheriff of Flat Bottom?"

"Yes, ma'am."

"Oh. I surely appreciate the rescue. You're my knight in shining armor." She gave him a coy look from under her lashes.

He returned her look with a scowl, and Miss Fairchild looked away demurely. He didn't lay great odds on her working out with Clovis, but if she made a habit of flirting with men, especially as pretty a gal as she was, the whole dang thing could be a nightmare. It was a good thing Trace was immune to women himself.

At the *fonda*, she reached for the front door handle. Trace got there first. She withdrew her hand with an abashed look and let him open the door.

They stepped inside the cool, cream-colored lobby with its pueblo walls and potted palms. It wasn't as grand as a big-city hotel, but it was cooler than the streets and blessedly peaceful. Only a handful of people were lounging in the chairs or at the front desk.

Miss Fairchild shut her eyes for a moment and sighed. She looked truly shaken.

"I'm sorry ya had such a rude welcome to Santa Fe. Perhaps you'd care to sit down, Miss Fairchild?"

She opened those pretty green eyes and turned to him. "I'm fine, Sheriff . . . I'm sorry. What did you say your name was? I'd like to thank you properly." She placed a gloved hand on his arm.

Her direct gaze made Trace feel discombobulated again. "Um . . ." What was his name again? "I—Crabtree. Trace Crabtree. But you can call me Sheriff Crabtree. Or just Trace is fine."

Dear Lord, he was an idiot. Why did Miss Fairchild unnerve him so?

She frowned at him. "Trace Crabtree?"

Make that doubly an idiot. "Sorry. Yeah, I'm Clovis's brother. I had no idea you were arrivin', though. Or even that Pa—our father—had, er, set this up."

"I see." She withdrew her hand, looking uneasy. "Thank you for coming to my aid, kind sir."

"Aw. It ain't no problem at all." He cleared his throat. "I was thinkin'. We can rest here for a spell, then go to the stables and get a wagon. I'll see if the hotel has a woman they can send with us. To chaperone."

Miss Fairchild's gaze shifted back to Trace, her eyes widening. "Oh, no! You don't need to trouble yourself on my account. I'd like to rest for a few days. Perhaps if you wouldn't mind delivering a letter?"

Trace blinked at her. Was she trying to get out of this already? He looked down at himself. He wore his city-going black pants, black vest, and a gray shirt. He thought he was fairly presentable. If she objected to the look of *him*, poor Clovis was really in trouble. Or maybe it was his gun belts that frightened her?

He shook his head slowly. "No, ma'am. It wouldn't be wise for you to stay here alone, what with those two men around."

Her gaze went to the door and she stiffened, but she

put on a forced smile. "I'm sure they won't bother me again. Truly, I'm grateful for your help, but right now, I just want to check in and have some quiet time to myself. I don't want to keep you. I'm sure your father has made other arrangements on my behalf."

Her tone was firm. Yup. She was trying to get rid of him, all right. If that didn't beat all. She really expected him to leave her. Men back East must be spineless creatures if they were this easily ordered about.

Trace pushed his hat back. "I'd like to oblige ya, Miss Fairchild, but that won't work at all. It would be all kinds of wrong for me to leave ya here. I'm afraid you'll have to come back to Flat Bottom with me. Today."

"Nonsense." Her eyes darted to the stairs and then the windows.

"Now, it's a three-hour ride in a wagon," he explained calmly. "So we'll get there before nightfall. There's a boardin' house run by a nice lady named Mrs. Jones. You can stay with her if ya wanna rest up before goin' on to the ranch."

"Excuse me," she said brightly. "I need to find the powder room and neaten up first. If you'll wait right here, Sheriff. Trace. I won't be but a weensy moment." She turned and moved quickly toward the stairs, skirts swishing.

Trace called after her. "Miss Fairchild!"

"Miss Fairchild, is that you?" echoed a voice from behind him.

Trace turned to see Marcy and Wayne coming into the lobby. Marcy was dressed in a tan calico dress and cream shawl, probably the best thing she owned. Wayne, too, was cleaned up. His dirty blond hair was slicked flat on his head like it had died. His large frame was tucked into an uncomfortable-looking old brown suit with a white paper collar. Marcy ran after Miss Fairchild while Wayne strolled up to Trace.

"What're you doin' here?" Wayne asked.

"That's a nice greetin'."

Wayne just looked at him, waiting for an answer. As the oldest brother, Wayne sometimes had an uppity attitude, like he was in charge. Trace hadn't liked it when he was little, and he sure didn't care for it now.

He saw Marcy catch up to Miss Fairchild on the stairs. The two ladies began chatting together.

"I came to town on business," Trace said. "And I happened to run into Miss Fairchild. Did you know about this? About Pa getting a mail-order bride for Clovis?"

Wayne made a face. "Not until yesterday, when he told me to come fetch her."

"What the hell was he thinkin'?"

"That no one would marry Clovis," Wayne said with a shrug.

He opened his chaw packet and put his fingers in. He seemed to think better of it, though, looking around at the fancy lobby. He put it away again with an unhappy frown.

"Well, I can't see how this can fail to be a disaster," Trace grumbled.

Wayne regarded Miss Fairchild warily, a frown between his brow. "She looks like a fancy woman."

"She looks like a *lady*," Trace replied, harsher than he meant to. Though why he should feel defensive of Miss Fairchild was anybody's guess. "I swear, this is Pa's craziest idea yet."

"Guess that's Pa's business."

Wayne didn't seem too worried about it. Maybe Trace was wrong. Maybe Miss Fairchild would be happy as a clam as Clovis's wife. Anyway, he told himself, Wayne was right. It was Pa's problem, not his.

"Well, guess I'm glad you showed up," Trace said, rubbing his jaw. "I thought I'd have to rent a rig to take her to the ranch."

"Nah. I just put our rig up at the stables. Guess I'll go get it out again. Figured we might have to stay here a week waitin' for that danged wagon train, but we lucked out. Pa will be glad to save the money."

"You could spend the night," Trace suggested. "Since you're here. Bet Marcy would like it."

Wayne made a dismissive sound, as if that was the stupidest idea he'd ever heard. "I'll have the wagon here in ten minutes. Tell the gals to be ready."

Without waiting for an answer, he turned and left.

Trace watched him go, feeling all kinds of discontented. He realized he was sort of expecting he'd have a chance to talk to Miss Fairchild on the way to Flat Bottom. Ease her into the situation slowly. Give her a hint of what she was in for. But it was too late now.

He didn't get a chance to say much to her, either, as they waited with Marcy for the wagon. The silence among the three of them was awkward, and Miss Fairchild seemed determined not to meet his eyes. Her trunk had arrived at the *fonda*, so Trace manhandled the thing to the back of the wagon for her while Wayne sat in the driver's seat looking straight ahead. Trace helped Marcy up into the back seat, saw her settled, then turned to help Miss Fairchild.

She placed her hand in his and hiked up her skirt to put her foot on the side board.

She was wearing brown city boots. They were men's boots. As if in slow motion, Trace's gaze dropped to their hands. Her hand was large, her grip strong, and her lacy gloves were way too tight. The delicate fabric had split on the side as if they were a few sizes too small.

Her head was down, watching her footing, but then she looked up at him, those green eyes raised heavenward.

He forgot to breathe.

Somehow, Trace pushed with his arm, and she was up on the bench seat. Wayne started the wagon without a good-bye. Marcy was the only one who glanced back at him.

Sheriff Trace Crabtree stood in the dust and watched the wagon drive away. His jaw was dropped down to his chest, and you could have knocked him over with a sneeze. He was in a state of absolute shock.

Miss Rowena Fairchild was a man.

Miss Rowena Fairchild was Robby Riverton.

Chapter Five

obby fought a desire to panic and do something stupid as the flatbed wagon rolled out of Santa Fe. He had an urge to jump down and run. But with these damned skirts, he'd probably break a leg. Besides, Wayne Crabtree would chase his lunatic future sister-in-law, and then how could Robby explain himself?

No, he couldn't act in haste. He had to be smarter than a rabbit that ran straight at a pack of dogs. He couldn't afford to slip up now, not when the Bowery Boys were hanging around. They'd waylaid him on the street, even in his disguise!

It was the second time in twenty-four hours Robby had thought he was a dead man.

It had all gone to hell yesterday. The wagon train had been moseying along the final few miles to Santa Fe. Everyone was in a good mood, buoyed by the prospect of imminent saloons, restaurant cooking, and whores. Most of the wagon train had stopped in Fort Union, so only eleven wagons remained. Robby, aka Nick Smith, had been riding next to Stoltz as he drove the team. He'd been reading out loud from his volume of Shakespeare—the burly blacksmith favored the bloody, war-themed plays like *Henry V*.

After Rowena departed in Dodge City, Robby spent more time doing chores with, and riding alongside, Stoltz. He'd become friendly with the man. Stoltz was laconic and grim, but he seemed to enjoy the company. Conversations with him where nearly all one-sided, so Robby had come upon the idea of reading out loud to pass the endless miles. It suited them both. Besides, Robby needed to keep his voice in good form.

He missed the stage. Missed the adulation—and challenge—of the audience. But to his surprise, he'd enjoyed the trip. The further they got from Missouri, the more the landscape changed. They'd crossed lush grasslands, lugged the wagons and livestock up and down steep river canyons with ropes, passed gigantic red shelves of rocks and majestic mountains. The land was so wild and so vast. They saw herds of buffalo, comical prairie dogs, and many other animals Robby never imagined existed.

He hadn't heard a peep from his pursuers since Missouri, and he assumed he was in the clear. But that last day, Stoltz made a grunting noise and nodded his head toward the rear. Robby looked back. Two riders on horseback had come up behind the last wagon and were talking to the driver. They stopped the horses and one of the men got onboard, searching for something or someone.

Robby's blood turned to ice. He recognized the stovepipe hats and red shirts with suspenders the men wore. Bowery Boys.

Oh God, no. They found me.

The book of Shakespeare fell with a thud to the floor beneath the bench, his fingers lifeless.

"They after you?" Stoltz asked, his voice even.

Robby nodded, terrified.

Stoltz turned his head to peer back at the men, his gaze hardening. "What're we gonna do?"

We. Stoltz was on his side. Robby was profoundly grateful.

"Tell them I got off a ways back. Maybe, I don't know, Fort Union? Please."

Stoltz nodded once. Robby climbed back into the covered wagon.

He knew exactly what he was going to do. He only hoped he had time enough to do it. After Rowena went off with her beau, Robby had discovered she'd left one of her trunks behind, one they'd covered with a cloth and made into a table. It had occurred to Robby he might use her clothes in a pinch, as a disguise. But he hadn't really expected to need them. Now he hurried to undress.

There was a compartment in the floor of the wagon, and he stuffed his own belongings in there while trying to dress himself at the same time. He wished he'd tried on Rowena's clothes before and adjusted them. It was too late now.

He chose the gown that looked the largest, a pale green silk. But his shoulders were too broad and the sleeves too tight. There was no way he could button up the back. He cast a shawl over himself instead. He couldn't stuff his big feet into her slippers, so he put his own boots back on. The skirts would hide them. There was a large-rimmed bonnet, thank God. Robby used some pomade to slick back his hair, so it would look like he had a bun. He hadn't shaved regularly on the wagon train, so he had to do so now, as fast as he could. Fortunately, he'd never been able to grow more than sporadic tuffs of hair, so it wasn't a time-consuming task. His ears were pricked for sounds. It wouldn't take them long to search these few wagons.

Lastly, he pulled out his tin of stage makeup and applied pale powder and heavy rouge. A shadow pencil hollowed his cheeks and narrowed his jaw, disguising the shape of his face. He used blue paint on his eyelids. Red lipstick made his lips fuller.

He stared in the small mirror in despair. It was way too much paint. But maybe the Bowery Boys would assume Stoltz was traveling with a strumpet. He couldn't risk them recognizing him.

Hooves pounded outside. A man yelled at Stoltz to pull up. The wagon swung off the trail, slowed, and stopped. Heart pounding, Robby did one last visual check and then went forward to put on the most important performance of his life.

He sat next to Stoltz and linked their arms together, eyeing the Bowery Boys with wary curiosity. He recognized one of them, an older thug with a thick waist and cold eyes. He'd been in the alley that night. He didn't recognize the younger man. Both looked capable of gutting him as easily as they'd shuck an oyster.

Thank God for Stoltz's stoicism. He didn't bat an eye at the appearance of "Rowena." He told the Bowery Boys that Nick Smith had gotten off in Fort Union. One of the men searched the back but didn't come up with anything.

It was only after the men rode off, that Robby reacted

to the gravity of the situation. If they'd discovered him, they would have taken him a short way off into this dry, inhospitable landscape, and shot him. Or more likely slit his throat. They would have left his body for the buzzards and coyotes. Robby's too-good imagination conjured up the image for him. Lovely.

Sitting next to Stoltz as the team plodded on, Robby began to shake. Without a word, Stoltz handed him a bottle of whiskey.

Now, sitting in the wagon next to Marcy Crabtree, the shakes began again. Robby fought to rein them in.

"Bet you're real tired," Marcy said. She was a mousy kind of woman, with dull brown hair and eyes, and so painfully drab she hardly existed at all. There was a bruise on her chin that gave her the look of an urchin.

"Yes. I'm weary to the bone." Robby affected a shy air.

"We'll be home by supper," Marcy offered.

"Thank you." Robby looked away over the dust and sage.

What was he going to do? He'd hoped to slip away in Santa Fe. Now here he was, in the middle of nowhere, without a single friend or confidant, riding on to what was surely his doom. His *new* doom, as opposed to that other doom, which he'd barely escaped.

How long could he hide the truth? And what would the Crabtrees do to him when they found out he was not Miss Rowena Fairchild? When he was, in fact, a man? In the stories of the Wild West, men were always getting shot or hung for cheating at cards. This was several magnitudes worse than that.

He eyed the driver, Wayne Crabtree. The man was sullen and kept spitting brown tobacco juice—a disgusting habit. Marcy Crabtree was quiet and listless. This didn't bode well for the Crabtree family. Except . . . Except there was also the other one.

Sheriff Trace Crabtree.

Now there was an unexpected plot twist. *Rowena's fiancé's brother?* The man had been as unlikely as pixie dust since the moment he'd walked up and challenged the Bowery Boys. He hadn't shown a spark of fear. He was cool and cordial on the surface, but you could sense an underbelly of deadly steel. Maybe the Bowery Boys hadn't known what to make of him, or perhaps they hadn't wanted to take on a lawman on a public street. Or maybe they just hadn't been sure if Rowena was worth it. But Trace Crabtree had led Robby away as easy as pie.

If Robby had conjured up an image in his mind of what the most enticing vision of a Wild West cowboy would look like, that man would be Trace Crabtree. He was big-boned and rangy. His shoulders went on for a mile and so did his legs in those black pants. His light brown hair hung thick to his shoulders, and his eyes were the golden brown of the desert. His skin was tanned and slightly wind-chapped, and he had a strong, stubbled jaw and long, thick sideburns. More than anything, that lazy, coiled-snake manner of his was enough to make Robby break out in a cold sweat.

Sheriff Crabtree had appreciated Rowena Fairchild too. Robby had seen the spark in his eyes. Of course he did. Robby looked damn good as a woman. But unfortunately, Rowena Fairchild did not exist. No, Robby had entirely different plumbing under his skirts. And even if Clovis Crabtree turned out to be as attractive as his brother, no amount of wishing in the world would change that or change the fact that Robby would be an imposter and a liar in their eyes.

There was only one thing for it. He had to get away as soon as possible. And until he did, he had to be convincing in the role of Miss Rowena Fairchild.

"Do you live near to Clovis?" Robby asked sweetly.

Marcy blinked away a dazed look, like she'd been miles away. "We all live at the ranch."

"All?"

"Pa-Pa, me and Wayne, our three kids, Roy and Emmie and their baby George, and Clovis."

"But not Trace?"

"No. Trace lives in town."

"Oh. Well that's a lot of family for one house." That was a lot of people Robby had to fool.

Marcy shrugged. "It's a big spread."

"What's Clovis like?"

Marcy bit her lip and looked at the back of her husband's head. As if feeling her gaze, Wayne turned to give Robby a hard look.

He was a big man—tall and thickset. He didn't much look like Trace, except maybe a bit in the nose and mouth. He'd barely said a word since they'd met. Now he looked Robby up and down. "Marcy, see if you can scrub off some of that dang paint, or Pa will be livid. He didn't pay no two hundred dollars for a lady who looks like a . . . Like a lady oughtn't look." He turned around again, shaking his head.

Robby swallowed a surge of anger. He might have grown up poor, but his family had manners.

"Yes, Wayne," Marcy said meekly. She took a handkerchief from her sleeve and spit on it. She gave Robby an apologetic smile and began to wipe at his cheek. "I'm sure things are different where you come from," she said quietly. "It'll be all right. But it's best if you fit in. We ain't used to city ways."

"I'll do it." Robby pushed Marcy's hand gently away.

He fetched a mirror and hanky from the trunk and set about trying to lighten the makeup without removing it entirely. It was one thing to look feminine in exaggerated rouge, lipstick, and eyeshadow, another to pass for a woman without props. For once he was grateful for his angelic countenance. And given how drab Marcy looked, a little rouge would go a long way in this family.

She sent him curious glances as he primped. He had a strange urge to put some lipstick on the poor little thing. She was probably not much older than he was, but she was so washed out. Worse was the way she scrambled to obey her husband. And that bruise on her jaw. No, Robby didn't like that one bit. He had to get away from these people.

As he finished and put the mirror away, nerves got the better of him again. Sweat trickled down the inside of his dress. He was hungry and exhausted, but all he could think about was an escape plan. He needed a means of travel and some idea of where he was going so he didn't end up wandering in the desert, vulnerable to coyotes, rattlesnakes, and bandits.

A day or two, Robby told himself. He had to be Miss Rowena Fairchild just a day or two more. Then he'd disappear for good.

Chapter Six

They passed through the town of Flat Bottom, which was even smaller than the Pennsylvania town where Robby grew up. It had a dusty main street with a dozen faded wooden storefronts. Robby watched the building with the *SHERIFF* sign, turning his head as they rode past. He saw no sign of Trace Crabtree, but he was probably still in Santa Fe.

"How big is Flat Bottom?" Robby asked Marcy, feigning girlish curiosity. "Is it big enough to . . . Oh, I don't know . . . have regular stagecoach service?"

"Not what you'd call 'regular'," Marcy hedged.

She glanced nervously at the back of her husband's head. As if sensing her gaze, Wayne turned to peer at Robby suspiciously. "You leavin' already?"

"No! I . . . No. Certainly not." Robby primly folded his hands in his lap. *Yes. Please, God, get me out of here.*

"The stagecoach to Santa Fe goes Saturdays," Marcy said helpfully. "But it don't come back till the next Saturday, if then, so most folks take their own rigs. The only other coach goes east to Silverton. That's on Wednesdays."

Wayne snorted. "*When* it goes. I wouldn't count on it puttin' ya out if you was on fire."

Robby narrowed his eyes. Well, that was a quaint saying. "I see. And what about the mercantile we passed? Does it carry ready-made clothing? Or fabric?" He asked this just to distract them from the stagecoach question. Not that he couldn't use an item or two, especially if he had to remain in this disguise for any length of time.

Wayne turned to give Robby a full-on stare. "Gal, you ain't been here two minutes, and you're already askin' about clothes? Ya gotta lot to learn. A *lot* to learn."

His tone was condescending, dismissive. Marcy looked away, as if suddenly interested in the landscape. Robby felt his cheeks burn. If he were himself, he'd give this hayseed an icy retort that would make him cold for a week. His bollocks would remain permanently frozen and his tongue would be stuck to the roof of his mouth.

But Robby couldn't do that. Because he *wasn't* Robby.

To his surprise, Rowena spoke up sweetly. "Never mind, dear brother. I can tell all I need to about the town's offerings from your habiliment and coiffure. Apparently, there isn't a barber shop but there *is* a taxidermist. I'll keep that in mind."

Rowena's vocabulary and her dulcet tones seemed to leave Wayne confused as to whether he'd been insulted or complimented. Looking puzzled, he turned around and focused on driving. Marcy's hand clenched in her skirt, her face still turned away. Robby hoped it was because she was fighting a laugh and not because she wanted to smack the mail-order bride.

After leaving the town, Robby expected to arrive at the ranch shortly. But the drive went on and on. Each mile alarmed Robby a little more. It would be a long walk on foot. He tried to memorize the landmarks at every turn. Fortunately, there were only a few.

It was another half hour and the sun was setting by the time the wagon rolled under a sign that said, *Crabtree & Sons*.

The ranch itself was nicer than Robby expected given the state of Wayne and Marcy's clothes. At least Rowena's letters hadn't lied about that. There were grazing cattle almost as far as the eye could see on the flat landscape, and acres of sturdy fencing along the road. They passed a large wooden barn in good repair. Next to it was a pen with a half-dozen of the biggest red pigs Robby had ever seen. The ranch house was made of boards weathered a natural gray. It was at least four times the size of an ordinary farm house with a long porch and what looked like later additions on both sides. There was a practical-looking kitchen garden fenced in tall chicken wire. But there weren't any homey touches—no flowers around the house, no rugs or curtains visible, not even chairs on the porch. The starkness made it look abandoned, though that clearly wasn't the case.

When they pulled up, two dark-haired boys around six and eight, came bursting through the screen door. They stared at Robby like he was a new type of insect. A few minutes later, a young woman with dark hair came out, wiping her hands on a towel. She had a nervous smile. Her eyes flickered over Robby, but she addressed Wayne.

"Pa-Pa says Miss Fairchild's to wait here till he comes out. He wasn't expectin' y'all so soon."

Wayne didn't bother to answer. He yelled at the two boys to unhitch the team, then he hopped down and went inside. Marcy made her way off the wagon, backing down carefully. So, Wayne couldn't be bothered to give his wife a hand. What a charmer.

Robby sat primly on the bench seat, hands folded in his lap. He felt like he was about to go onstage before a hostile audience. Rowena had to be very, very convincing for the next few hours. A small part of him was terrified. He was at the complete mercy of these people. He didn't even have a weapon. The most lethal things in the trunk were hairpins and his heavy volume of Shakespeare. He could perhaps bore them to death with a soliloquy.

Marcy came around the wagon and looked up at him. "You can get down, Miss Fairchild. Just stay here by the wagon. I'm sure Pa-Pa wants to greet ya proper."

She offered her hand. It was a kind gesture, and it made Robby feel a little less threatened. He smiled at her gratefully, took her hand, and climbed down in a ladylike fashion. He made sure his skirts weren't caught before he jumped down the last foot to the ground. He was overly aware of all the ways this could go wrong. Heaven forbid he trip and let out a manly *ooff* or lose his bonnet.

After the Bowery Boys had left the wagon train yesterday, he'd spent the rest of the day altering Rowena's pale green dress, lowering the hem, letting out seams in the shoulders and under the arms, and nipping it in at the waist. He'd sewn a few of her stockings into soft conical shapes that gave the impression of small breasts. But he could only do so much with limited time and resources. A close inspection of his gloves or boots would give him away. What he wouldn't give for the Burton's costume room right now.

He checked that his high lace collar was still there, smoothed his fingers around the edge of his bonnet to make sure the ends of his hair were tucked back, and wrapped his shawl more tightly around himself. The dress buttoned up the back now, but he was still worried his shape would give him away, his breasts fail to pass muster.

The other woman stood on the porch watching him with what looked like admiration. She was dark-haired and sallow-cheeked and wore a gray dress and apron that looked ancient.

"Good day." Robby nodded to her. "I'm Miss Rowena Fairchild."

The woman blushed. "Oh! Sorry for my poor manners. I'm Emmie Crabtree, Roy's wife. He's Clovis's brother."

"It's a pleasure to meet you. I'm sure we'll be the best of friends."

"Gosh, really? That's awful nice of you!" Emmie said breathlessly, as if Robby had been sincere.

Lord, Marcy and Emmie were green. But that was probably a blessing. They'd be less likely to see through his act than a woman of the world.

Neither Marcy nor Emmie made a move to speak again. Marcy watched the house anxiously while Emmie stared at Robby's clothes. Next to their drab dresses, Rowena's green silk stood out like a Monarch butterfly on a pile of dung.

"Have you been married to Roy long?" Robby asked brightly.

"Nearly three years." Emmie smiled but it didn't reach

her eyes. "We have a baby. Baby George? He's takin' a nap."

"Aw, the little rascal," Robby cooed.

There was another awkward silence. Good God, he just wanted to get this over with. If Mr. Crabtree intended to "greet her properly," he was sure taking his time about it.

Robby's gaze went to the barn. How was he going to get out of here? There were a few horses in the paddock, a white one and a dappled pony. Plus, there were the two chestnut horses the boys were now unhitching from the wagon in a listless way, probably worried they'd miss something if they took the horses to the barn.

Robby wasn't the best rider. His father was a practical man who thought any use for a horse other than to pull a plow or buggy was wasteful. But he could ride if he had to. The question was—where to? It was Monday. So, there wouldn't be a stagecoach for two days, and that was assuming Robby wasn't on fire. Or something like that.

Could he ride to Silverton by horse? What other towns were nearby? And if he did, would they come after him as a horse thief? He had a vision of himself hung on a tree with a sign that read *HORSE THIEF* around his neck. Or, given the local dialect, more likely *HOARSE THEEF*. That would make for a dramatic scene on stage, but it wasn't one he cared to act out in real life.

He was about to quiz Marcy further about the travel options in town when the door of the ranch house banged open. An old man shambled out, his legs as bowed as a wishbone. He was bald on top, wore black pants, shiny black boots, a leather vest dyed gray, and a white-ish shirt with a flouncy bow under his neck. It looked like his Sunday best. He stopped in the doorway and assessed

Robby with keen eyes, then he plastered on a friendly smile.

"Welcome! Welcome to Crabtree Ranch!" He came down the steps and took Robby's hand in his, kissing the back of it awkwardly, like it was something he'd never done before in his life. "I'm Clyde Crabtree, the head of this here operation."

Robby withdrew his hand as quickly as he could. He hadn't had a chance repair the split glove. Fortunately, the old man's attention was fixed on Robby's face.

"Let's take a look at ya." Pa Crabtree walked around him slowly, looking him over like a horse at auction. "Ya cold or somethin'?" he asked, poking Robby's back. He was obviously angling for Rowena to open her shawl.

"A bit." Robby cast his eyes down shyly and pulled the shawl tighter.

When he'd made the full circle, Pa Crabtree stopped in front of Robby. Robby had no idea what Clyde Crabtree's history was, or if he would be better able to spot the deception than his sons and daughters-in-law. His heart tripped in his chest as he lowered his eyes to the man's bowed legs and prayed for a touch of luck. *Please, God, just this once.* He was certainly overdue for some.

After a tense silence, Clyde Crabtree cackled and slapped his knee. "Yes sir, this here is a fine gal! You boys see? I told you it was worth that two hundred dollars! She ain't too fat and ain't too skinny. Looks healthy enough. And she's as pretty a gal as any in these parts. Nice, clear eyes. Look at me, gal."

Robby raised his eyes and gave Pa a level stare. He didn't know if he should be amused or horrified. Possibly both. Behind Pa Crabtree on the porch stood three men—

Wayne and two others. But before Robby could get a good look, Pa Crabtree took his jaw in two gnarled fingers and moved his head to one side, then the other. Robby had a feeling he was going to ask to inspect his teeth. Robby hoped he did, so he could bite him. But Pa thought better of it.

"Go on and say somethin'," Pa ordered, letting go.

Robby raised his chin and pursed his lips primly. "I have come so very far to meet you, sir. It's a pleasure to make your acquaintance. I compliment you on your beautiful and well-tended establishment."

Pa Crabtree's face split into a grin and he howled with laughter. He turned to look at his sons. "Listen to that. Told you she was high class!"

Robby took a steadying breath, in and out, in and out. He kept a smile plastered on his face.

"Come on in the house, gal," Pa said in a jovial manner. He waved his hand in the direction of the porch, then paused. "Gol dern it, I forgot. Rowena, them three on the porch are my boys. You met Wayne already. The middle one, that's Roy, and the dark one, that's Clovis. He'll be your husband."

He said it so matter-of-factly. *He'll be your husband.* But it made Robby's stomach clench in paroxysms of anxiety. What a nightmare. This was literally like something Robby would have dreamed—finding himself trapped and engaged to some uncouth giant, one that thought he was a woman and would be mighty put out on their wedding night.

Because that's what Clovis Crabtree looked like—an uncouth giant. The second brother, Roy, looked much like Wayne, with a beefy, thick-necked appearance and stringy, long brown hair. Clovis, however, had hair nearly black in color and way too much of it. It stuck up around his head like someone had plastered his face in the middle of a tumbleweed. He had a bushy beard that could hide a heron's nest, and the curly black stuff disappeared down inside his flannel shirt. His face was broad with a hawk-like nose, and it was red as a beet. He stood with a down-cast gaze, his beefy hands stuffed into the front pocket of his black work pants. He looked horribly self-conscious, like he'd borrowed limbs for the occasion and had no idea what to do with them.

Robby swallowed hard and did a brief curtsy. "How do you do, gentlemen."

This sent Pa into more fits of laughter. "Gol dern, but your fancy ways sure do tickle me. Not that they'll be a lick of use here on the ranch. Anyhow, come on in. Marcy! Emmie! What are you two doin' standin' around gawkin'? Is supper ready yet? Get movin'!"

The worst is over. Just a few more hours, Robby promised himself as he followed the Crabtrees into the house.

Chapter Seven

The room they gave Rowena was an unheated back porch that had a single narrow bed. Pa-Pa said, with a wink, that it was "only for one night" and that Rowena would find Clovis's bedroom "right comfortable" soon enough.

As if that was ever going to happen. Robby didn't mind the porch. It had a door to the backyard, and it was private, and that was all he cared about. A full moon lit the way as Robby snuck along the house's shadow, then made a run for it across a dirt patch to the barn.

He lit a lantern he'd brought from his room and moved quickly to the horse stalls. He petted the nose of a white mare who seemed friendly.

Could he really ride her to Flat Bottom by moonlight? Were there wolves or coyotes out there? He'd heard them at night on the wagon train, but they'd never approached the group. Might they attack a lone rider? And once he got to Flat Bottom, what would he do then? He hadn't even noticed a road that went in the opposite direction from

Santa Fe. And the road to Santa Fe itself was really not much more than a worn dirt rut.

Despite his doubts, Robby looked around for a saddle. He checked every space in the barn and was surprised not to find any tack at all, not even the reins or harnesses for the wagon. All he found was a door with a big padlock on it near the horse stalls.

Was this the tack room? Why would they lock it? It felt ominous, as if they were trying to hold him prisoner. It did nothing to ease his creeping sense of dread.

He jiggled the padlock. It was solid and heavy.

He was about to turn away when a hand closed over his mouth and a strong arm wrapped around him, grabbing him tight. A scream got stuck in his throat.

"Quiet!" drawled a man's voice in his ear. "It's me, Trace. I'm not gonna hurt you, Mr. Riverton."

TRACE WASN'T sure if he wanted to strangle the young man in his arms or tuck him under his wing and protect him. But he did know he needed answers. And, by God, he was going to get them.

Riverton was still in the woman's get-up, that green dress and bonnet. But there was nothing feminine about the tight muscles against his chest, or against his arm where it was pressed to Riverton's taut waist. He didn't fight. He just stood there, frozen.

"I'm just here to talk to ya. All right?" Trace whispered, annoyed at the way the huge brim of the bonnet got in his way.

Riverton nodded once, and Trace let him go.

He turned, slowly, raising his hands. Trace kept his hand near his gun and took his time studying Riverton's face by lantern light. He looked defiant—and fearful. And he was just as damned attractive as Trace remembered. Only now that Trace knew he was a man, that objective appraisal of handsomeness hit him in an entirely different way, caused a warm tightening in his gut. Not that it mattered a whit. Trace was fit to be tied.

"Well, Mr. Riverton. I've seen some sticky situations in my life, but this one takes the prize."

Riverton slumped back against the wall of a horse stall, instantly defeated. "Bollocks. I swear I didn't mean for this to happen. I was just trying to evade the Bowery Boys."

Trace's gaze flickered to the horses. "That may be. But you steal a horse from Pa, and even God won't be able to help ya."

Riverton covered his face with his hands. He slid down the wall until he was sitting on the stable floor. And Trace . . . Trace actually felt sorry for him. He was still irate, but sympathy was edging in too.

He squatted down a few feet from Riverton, elbows on his knees, and pulled out a smoke. He rolled it between his thumb and finger and lit it. He took a drag and offered it to Riverton, nudging his knee to get his attention.

Riverton looked at the smoke and shook his head. "It's bad for your voice, and . . . I'm an actor."

"Kind of figured that. What with the poster and all," Trace said dryly. "Robby Riverton. That even your real name?"

"Yes, it is my real name. But just call me Robby, if you please." Robby searched Trace's face, as though trying to judge how mad he was. His eyes were desperate, his face drawn tight in the lantern glow. Trace felt an urge to reassure him, but he hardened himself to the feeling.

"Here's the thing, Robby. I don't like trouble in my town, much less in the midst of my own damn family. It's too much work. And this here is a whole stinkin' mess of trouble. I'll give ya one chance to tell your side of the story. And I wouldn't lie, if I were you."

Robby nodded vigorously. He seemed eager to talk. He told Trace about witnessing a murder in New York City, and about how he'd thought he'd slipped the gang members until they caught up with the wagon train two days ago. He told Trace about Miss Fairchild, and how she'd left with a new beau in Dodge City. He'd put on her clothes in desperation.

"I planned to slip away in Santa Fe. But then the Bowery Boys caught me, and you came along, and then Wayne and Marcy. And now . . . here I am. No matter what I do, the hole just gets deeper." Robby's voice was a hiss. "Believe me, Sheriff, there's no one sorrier about this situation than me!"

Trace wanted to believe him, and he mostly did. But there were parts of it that didn't quite hang together. He thoughtfully smoked his cigarette down to a nub, then ground it out on the stable floor and put the remnant in his pocket.

"Well?" Robby asked, voice shaky. "Are you going to give me away or help me? Because if you're going to give me away, maybe you should just kill me now!"

Trace snorted. "Calm down there, Beauregard. I ain't gonna kill ya. I'm just orderin' things in my mind. Give me a minute."

Robby held his tongue while Trace thought about it a little more. Dang. It really was a shit stew. Looked like he could wave good-bye to his nice, quiet existence.

"Tell me what ya know about these Bowrey Boys," Trace said. "The ones that followed ya out here. There was an older one with cold eyes."

Robby folded his arms over his chest defensively. "I recognized him. He was one of the men in the alley that night. He was holding the victim while Mose . . . ." Robby's voice broke off and he swallowed.

So Cold-Eyes could be counted an accessory to murder, Trace figured. Which meant this was personal to him.

"And the other one? The blond one with the blue feather in his hat?"

Robby shook his head. "I never saw him until two days ago when they caught up to the wagon train. I don't know their names."

"It's just those two? Or are there more?"

"They're the only ones I've seen."

"Uh-huh." Trace thought some more. "What did Pa make of ya today?"

Robby grimaced. "No one seems suspicious, if that's what you mean. But Pa-Pa was pushing to have the wedding *tomorrow*. I told him I was sick, and I went to bed early. But I don't know how long I can hold him off. Can you take me back to town with you? I'll pay you for your trouble."

Trace scratched his neck. "I'm not sure that's the wisest course. I have a feelin' those, whaddya call 'em, Bowery Boys, will be coming to Flat Bottom lookin' for ya. And if they hear Miss Fairchild absconded, they'll smell a rat. If they don't suspect you're Riverton already, that'd do it."

Robby's brow furrowed, and he clenched his arms tightly over his chest. "Why would they come to Flat Bottom? I answered their questions. Or rather, Rowena did. Surely they'll go back along the trail, maybe to Fort Union."

Trace heaved an unhappy sigh. He wanted to light another cigarette. He wanted to reach out and comfort Robby. He did neither. "Look here, before I left Santa Fe, I did some checkin' up on that wagon train of yours. Learned a man was found with his throat slit behind the saloon. His name was Stoltz."

Robby flinched. "Oh no. No, no, no."

He slumped over, head to his knees, and Trace didn't curb the impulse to reach out and lay a steadying hand on his shoulder. For a moment, Robby just breathed in harsh pants, head hung low. He seemed overcome by fear or maybe rage.

If this reaction was a charade, it sure was a convincing one. Even for an actor.

After a bit, Trace pulled back his hand. "Ya knew Stoltz?"

"He owned the wagon I rode in. It's my fault he's dead." Robby's voice was wrecked.

"No, now, come on." Trace grasped Robby by the arms and stood, bringing them both to their feet. "Pull yourself together, son. I'm surely sorry for your loss. But it's not your fault they came after ya, not your fault there are bad men in the world."

Robby looked at him doubtfully, his eyes damp. "Do

you think they . . . Do you think they got him to confess before . . . ?"

Trace shook his head. "Stoltz was stiff and cold when I saw him, so he must have been dead when those men waylaid ya in the street. Seems to me they didn't know ya were Riverton then. But they sure are determined. If they went after Stoltz that hard, I figure there's a chance they're not done with Miss Fairchild either."

"Why won't they just *stop*?" Robby asked fiercely. "Why the hell would they chase me all this way? I don't understand it!"

Yeah, that was the part that didn't smell right to Trace either. He watched Robby's face. "You sure ya didn't skip a few details? Like maybe ya got somethin' that belongs to them? A pile of their money, maybe?"

"No!" Robby pulled away from Trace angrily. "I told you, I saw Mose McCann commit murder from across the alley. I never even got close to them! The only thing they want is the memory in my head." He tapped his temple pointedly.

"Well." Trace shrugged. "You'd best stay put for now. I'll see what I can find out. In a couple days, we'll reassess the situation."

"In a couple of *days*!"

Robby looked so stricken that Trace felt doubt. He didn't like leaving Robby at the ranch, fooling his family. He knew how much of a stubborn jackass his father could be. And Clovis . . . Probably the less time "Rowena" spent around Clovis the better.

God damn. Trace wondered what the heck Clovis made of his intended, anyway. The pair of them were as mismatched as bees and bears—in *either* of Robby's forms.

But the idea that Clovis might fall for his new bride-to-be was unsettling.

But there was an urge, deep down in Trace's bones, to protect Robby. Those Bowery Boys—the way they'd treated Miss Fairchild on the street, the way they'd slit Stoltz's throat . . . Robby didn't stand a chance against them. No. Trace might not trust Robby completely, but he didn't want to see him dead. And if protecting him meant causing his family a bit of inconvenience for a few days? Well, there were worse problems.

He wrapped his fingers around Robby's forearm without really meaning to. Worry softened his voice. "Look, I don't much care for the setup myself, but this is serious. So, tell me honestly. Do you think ya can fool Pa and the others a bit longer?"

Robby blinked at him. "Can't we just explain things to your Pa?"

Trace barked a laugh. "Hell, no. Wayne said Pa paid two hundred dollars to get Clovis a wife."

Robby snorted. "Yes, he mentioned that only a dozen times tonight."

"Well, if there's one thing that's guaranteed to make Pa feistier than a nest of riled-up hornets, it's wastin' money. If he finds out ya ain't Miss Fairchild, you'll be out on your fanny so fast, your head will spin."

Robby sighed and frowned. Then he sighed some more. His arm turned in Trace's grasp, and his fingers grabbed Trace's coat. It seemed unconscious, like Robby was depending on him. The small move brought a lump to Trace's chest.

"I guess I can keep this up for a few more days," Robby admitted. "As long as I can hold off the wedding. I get the feeling everyone's on their best behavior. I suppose we're in the wooing stage." He smiled wryly.

Trace nodded. "That makes sense. Pa will want to make sure his investment pans out. That's good."

Robby moved a little closer. His green eyes seemed to glow in the lantern light. "But couldn't you just hide me in town?"

"Look, I'm tryin' to save your hide. I need to check on some things, and I can't be watchin' over ya at the same time. My pa and brothers might not be fancy or sophisticated, but their orneriness is in our favor. If those men show up here makin' demands and wavin' guns, they'll be in a world of hurt."

Robby clenched his jaw. "What about . . . I noticed bruises on Marcy and Emmie."

Trace felt a flash of annoyance. Damn his crazy family, anyhow. "It ain't what you're thinkin'. I swear it ain't."

"Then what is it?" Robby insisted, meeting Trace's gaze stubbornly.

Trace sighed. "No one hits those gals, and no one's gonna hit *you*. Ya can take my word for it."

Robby's expression relented, and he nodded. "Very well. The show will go on."

"All right, then. Be polite and keep your head down. And whatever ya do, don't argue with Pa. Now—can ya do this? Tell me true."

"I can do it."

"And just stay away from Clovis," Trace insisted, a muscle in his jaw ticking. He felt something like jealousy. Which was ridiculous.

Robby smirked. "I don't think that's a problem. So far, he hasn't said a single word to me and Pa-Pa seems to want it that way. He said something about propriety, but he probably thinks the less I know about my betrothed the better. No offense to your brother."

Trace liked that Robby could joke a little, even in the midst of all this. He felt the corner of his own mouth tug up. "Good."

He realized Robby had moved closer still—or he himself had leaned in. It was far too close for two men to stand together, even if they were whispering.

His hand was on Robby's arm. Out of pure, wicked curiosity, he moved his thumb in a small caress to see what would happen. Robby's eyes widened in surprise. He licked his lips and leaned forward a tiny bit in silent invitation.

Trace's heart commenced to pounding. His blood flared so high, he felt like he was about to go into battle. Hell, maybe he was. He raised one hand to Robby's cheek and brushed the back of his fingers along the strong jawline. "I'll say this for ya; you've got a set of steel balls. How old are you, Robby?"

"Twenty-four." He touched his own cheek. "And to think I used to hate that I couldn't grow much of a beard." He was trying to joke, but his voice was unsteady. He leaned into Trace's hand a little.

Oh, yes. He was definitely a man of Trace's predilections. Which was not gonna simplify matters *at all.*

Trace stared, taking in Robby's long face and square jaw, those wide, pouty lips, and half-lidded eyes. He truly was the most beautiful man Trace had ever seen. Funny, he could still picture that poster the Bowery Boys had shown him. It helped him imagine Robby without the bonnet and all that nonsense.

"Ya make a pretty gal. But I sure would like to see ya the other way 'round."

"You would?" Robby's voice dropped to a breathy whisper. "Think you'd like me better that way?"

"I know I would." Trace's voice sounded like he'd swallowed rocks.

Desire sparked hot in Robby's eyes, and Trace's body answered. Lust sang loudly in his veins for the first time in a very long time. Not just mechanical need but true desire, an aching want for the man in front of him. At that moment, he'd have scaled a six-foot fence to get to mating, like a heat-crazed horse.

There was a *bang* outside as a gust of wind sent a loose shutter flying. Trace snapped out of his daze. What the hell was he doing? He pulled back abruptly. What if Pa or one of his brothers saw the light and walked out to the barn? How could he explain being caught sparking with Clovis's intended—who also happened to be a man? This was dangerous as dancing with a rattler. And twice as stupid.

"Much as I'd like to oblige us both," Trace growled, "we'd best keep our heads on straight."

Looking abashed, Robby stepped back too, putting more distance between them. "You're right. This is no time for . . . ."

He didn't bother to finish the sentence. They both knew exactly what they didn't have time for.

"You'd best get back in the house. Just remember, keep your head down and your mouth shut. I'll be back in two nights. Got it?"

"Yes. Thank you, Trace." Robby put on a brave smile. "Thank you for not killing me. Or throwing me out. And thank you for saving me from the Bowery Boys in Santa Fe." He shuddered, and his smile faded. "If they'd dragged me off the street . . . You probably saved my life today. You really did."

Trace nodded, but he didn't answer. He reminded himself that he could not get emotional about this. He had to check out Robby's story, for one thing. And he had to protect his town. And somehow, he had to protect his family from Robby and vice versa. And wasn't that a hell of a thing?

That right there was enough to worry about without letting his stupid heart go all soft for a perfect stranger.

Chapter Eight

Tuesday

The next morning, Robby rose early, while the dark was still thick outside. He shaved carefully, slicked back his hair, put on the lace collar and bonnet, and gilded his face with as much makeup as he dared. Afterward, he remained on the back porch, lying on the bed with a blanket over him. By lantern light he worked on altering another one of Rowena's gowns, this one a silvery gray silk.

Two days.

The sheriff—*Trace*—wanted Robby to stay put for two days while he tried to find out if the Bowery Boys were gone. Part of Robby was relieved. He'd been on the move for three months now, and the idea of stopping for a few days, stopping somewhere safe and protected, was a welcome respite. Even this cold little back porch felt like luxury after the wagon train. He needed the rest, not just his body, but his spirit. Also, he'd really had no idea how to make his escape from Flat Bottom. Maybe Trace would help him if he cooperated now.

On the other hand, this performance could end in disaster if Robby wasn't very, very careful and very, very good.

Can you do this? Tell me true.

Robby had said he could do it. He had to.

Tell me true.

The needle went in and out of the hem of the dress as those words echoed through Robby's head. He heard Trace's voice, low and gravelly and serious. Robby wasn't sure what to make of Sheriff Crabtree. Tempting as sin? *Yes.* Mutual attraction that threatened to burst into a forest fire? *And then some.*

Robby had met plenty of men with his tastes in New York, but he'd never met one like Trace, so rough and raw, with that lazy, drawling manner, and such an immutable sense of self-assurance. Robby had had no idea that was exactly the type he most favored. It was a little surprising.

But, as Trace had reminded him, this was neither the time nor place to indulge a purely physical longing. Too much was at stake. Trace had Robby's life in his hands. And he was a Crabtree. Desire was nothing compared to blood. What if Trace decided Robby was in the wrong? Or was somehow taking advantage of his family? Until he could get out of here, Robby had to be very careful to stay on Trace's good side.

Not long after sun-up, Marcy tapped gently on the door and peeked in. "Good mornin', Miss Fairchild. I hope you're feelin' better this mornin'?" Her expression was genuinely worried.

Robby clutched the blanket. "I'm sorry to say I'm still

under the weather. Please give my regrets to the others, but I think I'll rest up today."

Marcy bit her lips and looked ready to cry. "Please, Miss Fairchild. Please at least come to breakfast. Otherwise, I fear Pa-Pa will be . . ." She swallowed. ". . . very disappointed."

Robby was caught, and he knew it. He couldn't ask Marcy to do his dirty work for him, and Trace had warned him not to anger Pa-Pa. He wasn't going to get away with hiding out on the porch.

Robby gave her a sweet smile. "Very well, Marcy. I'll come to breakfast."

"Thank you." Marcy gave a relieved sigh. She wiped her nose with the back of her hand. "We're just sittin' down now, and we made a whole heap of food. Surely you must be hungry, what with skippin' supper last night."

Robby was, in fact, starved. His stomach reminded him of that fact with a very unladylike rumble. Marcy pretended not to hear it and left him alone.

After checking the pale green dress over one more time and making sure his bosom was in the right place, Robby left the porch. He found the Crabtrees at the breakfast table. Pa-Pa was dressed in the same clothes he'd worn the day before, the gray leather vest and the shirt with the fancy white bow at his throat. All the others looked similarly polished up. Apparently, this was a second attempt at the family meal Robby had dodged last night. And no one around the table looked happy about it.

Robby put on his most charming smile. "I'm so sorry to keep you all waiting," he said as he stood in the doorway.

Pa-Pa rose from his chair. "Good mornin', Miss

Fairchild." There was a hint of annoyance in his voice. "Now you come sit right here by me. Got a chair and a plate all ready for ya."

"Oh, how lovely!" Robby walked gracefully to the empty seat. The table was laden with food. None of the dishes matched—there was a mix of cracked china, wooden trenches, and tin plates. But there were pancakes and eggs, stacks of toast and gobs of butter. Robby's stomach hurt, it was so empty. Dear Lord, when was the last time he'd eaten a meal?

He waited politely by his chair, but Pa-Pa plopped back down and no one else appeared interested. So Robby tugged his own chair out gently and sat with exaggerated care. "Please accept my apologies for last night. But I was simply—"

His words were drowned out in a clatter as everyone around the table attacked the food. It was as though the act of Robby sitting down had been a gun fired at a race. Serving dishes were snatched up like they contained the last morsels of food on earth.

He watched in amazement as Wayne forked six pancakes in one jab and raked them on to his plate, breaking up the pancake beneath and sending hunks of it onto the plain white tablecloth. He shoved the platter at the oldest boy, Billy, who grabbed it and dragged nearly as many pancakes onto his plate, ignoring the exploding crumbs.

A younger boy spilled a glass of milk that went sloshing everywhere. Pieces of scrambled egg went flying as two kids fought over a serving bowl.

"Will you slow down, you idjits!" Pa-Pa bellowed.

Everyone froze and looked at him.

"Now what did we talk about yesterday?" Pa-Pa barked. "Do ya want Miss Fairchild to think we're a bunch of heathens? Christ on a crutch."

The gathered ensemble went back to loading their plates slowly. The clanking of silverware became tolerable.

Robby kept a smile plastered to his face. His gaze went to Clovis. His intended had been put as far away down the table as it was possible to be. He looked even hairier at the dinner table than he had on the porch the night before. He reminded Robby of a bear with his huge, rounded shoulders, massive hands, and that hirsute pelt. His gaze was cast down at his plate and he shoveled a huge bite of potatoes into his mouth.

"Would ya care for some eggs, Miss Fairchild?" Marcy asked with exaggerated politeness. She leaned over Robby's shoulder with a fresh bowl.

Pa-Pa nodded at Marcy approvingly and stuffed half a pancake into his mouth from the end of a jackknife.

Robby thanked her demurely and put some eggs on his plate. "This looks wonderful. My mother made eggs, bacon, and pancakes every Sunday."

There was an awkward silence around the table. The Crabtrees looked at one another.

"We don't have any bacon, I'm afraid," said Marcy nervously.

"Oh. I didn't mean—I don't need bacon. This is more than enough." Robby sought to change the subject. "Though I did notice you had a whole corral of red pigs near the barn. I've never seen pigs like that."

There were more dodgy looks all around.

"Them hogs ain't for eatin'," Wayne said flatly.

Robby blinked. "Oh. Yes, I see."

"Them's a special breed of hog all the way from El Paso del Norte," Pa-Pa said proudly.

"Ah. Well. What do you do with them?"

No one would meet Robby's eye.

"Never mind them red hogs," Pa-Pa said testily. "They ain't got nothin' to do with nothin'. Now, did ya get a gander at our beeves? The cattle is what makes this here ranch. Got over three hundred head!"

"My stars!" Robby exclaimed. "That is an awful lot, isn't it?"

Pa-Pa went on to explain the type of cattle they had—mostly longhorns, what months they drove the beeves to market, and a lot of other details about the ranch business as he ate his breakfast with his hunting knife and talked with his mouth full.

Robby had the feeling Pa-Pa was trying to convince Rowena of the family's wealth so that she'd want to marry-up as soon as possible. He listened politely and cooed in appreciation. There were lots of "You don't says" and "Well, I nevers!" Robby figured he might as well butter Pa-Pa up while he had the chance.

But he wondered: What were they hiding about those pigs?

Maybe they fed unwelcome visitors to them? Maybe the bones of past mail-order brides were buried in the muck of the pig pen.

He ate daintily, but everyone else was being so barbarous, he felt safe having a plate full of food. He felt much better for it.

The table manners in the house were truly, *truly* appalling. If a piece of food didn't pass inspection, or was dislodged from a plate or bowl, it was tossed over the shoulder and onto the floor. There were no napkins present, and fingers were wiped on the tablecloth or clothes. Gobs of butter ended up in strange places. Wayne had a habit of wiping his fingers on his shirt under the armpits, which made Robby want to gag. There were more belches than spoken words and frequent orders of "Marcy get more of this" or "Emmie, can't you see we need more of that." Marcy and Emmie never got a chance to sit down for a second. In fact, they didn't even have places at the table. It was as though they were servants.

Robby took it all in and said nothing.

He could see why no woman familiar with this family would willingly sign on. The *real* Rowena Fairchild, bless her lying little heart, would have been aghast and agog. Lively Rowena had dodged a bullet there, she and her little bank officer.

Honestly, Robby felt sorry for Marcy and Emmie. In the home he grew up in, his mother and sisters had done all the cooking and cleaning. But they'd sat for meals like everyone else. And no one made a big mess expecting them to clean it up. And this was with Pa-Pa's warning earlier for everyone to behave. Robby shuddered to think how they'd act if he wasn't there.

Wayne reached a long arm across the table for some butter that was in front of Robby. His shirt sleeve was pushed up and Robby noticed a large bruise on his forearm. Curious, his gaze went around the table and he saw bruises, some small and some not so small, on everyone except Missy and Baby George. And Clovis, because he was so hairy you could hardly see any skin at all.

Strange. Trace had likely been telling the truth about Marcy and Emmie's bruises then. But either this was the most accident-prone family in the world, or ranching was a much more physically onerous life than farming had been. Good thing Robby had no plans to stick around.

Pa-Pa finished eating. He gave off a long belch, wiped his jackknife on the tablecloth, folded it, and put it in his pocket. Then he pushed back from his seat and patted his belly. "You get enough to eat?" he asked Robby.

"Yes, Pa-Pa. The food was delicious. Thank you, Marcy and Emmie," Robby said pointedly.

Pa-Pa went on cheerfully, "Now me and the boys have some work to take care of this mornin'. But you, me, and Clovis will ride into town this afternoon and take care of this marriage business. Preacher knows to be expectin' us sometime this week."

Robby's stomach threatened to cast up the eggs he'd eaten. He glanced down the table at Clovis. He was done eating, his plate practically licked clean. He gazed straight ahead, picking his teeth with a bit of wood, but Robby got the feeling he was listening.

"I, uh, well, I've been thinkin' on that," Robby said in as calm a voice as he could muster. He turned a sad gaze on Pa-Pa, letting his lower lip tremble. "We didn't discuss the weddin' per se in our letters. Which is *entirely* my fault. But, you see, the Fairchild family has certain traditions, and seeing as a girl only weds once in her life, I hope you'll be so generous as to accommodate me."

Pa-Pa's nose crinkled like he'd smelled something bad. "What do ya mean? What kindy accom-y-date? You want a fancy dress? I already paid two hundred dollars for your trip out here!"

"Oh, no!" Robby insisted. "It's not about money at all.

I don't need anything fancy. Why, I'm just a simple girl at heart."

Pa-Pa looked relieved to hear it.

"But, you see," Robby went on, thinking fast. "It's always been a Fairchild tradition to get married on . . . on the Ides of August. Yes, that's right. You've heard of the Ides of March?"

Everyone around the table looked at Robby like he'd grown two heads. He plowed on. "Well, the Ides of March is March fifteenth, and it's considered very lucky, you see. But the Ides of August is August first, and it's the *most* propitious time of the entire year. Why, all Fairchild brides have been married on August first!"

Robby was pulling all this out of his behind. But it was only July sixteenth. Hopefully, please God, he'd be out of there long before August came around.

Pa-Pa glowered. "Gal, that's two weeks away!"

"I know! Just enough time for us to get to know one another. Why, I couldn't have planned it better."

Pa-Pa's face grew redder. "Now see here, this is a workin' ranch. And that means we gotta work. We need to get this weddin' business over with so's we can get back to it. We ain't got time for sittin' and chatttin' for two weeks."

"Oh, I wouldn't dream of keeping you from work," Robby said with a smile. "*Please*. Carry on as you normally would. And I'm happy to help out as well."

Pa-Pa slapped the table with his hand, making a loud *bang*. "No, now, I ain't gonna be strung along for no girlish whim. We're gettin' this done today and that's final!"

It wasn't lost on Robby that Marcy and Emmie both flinched. His own heart pounded in his chest, and his face grew hot. He sat silently, struggling to maintain his sweet Rowena act while both fear and, yes, *anger* rose up inside him. Being nice wasn't working with this old bully. Who did he think he was, trying to intimidate a young woman? Robby was sorely tempted to punch him in the face.

"I do believe the bride must give legal consent," Robby said stiffly.

Chapter Nine

Pa-Pa's jaw dropped open and he looked pole-axed. But before he could say anything, there was a sound from the end of the table.

"No."

The voice was quiet but firm. Robby turned his head and saw Clovis slowly get to his feet. He looked at Pa-Pa, his face a mottled red. "Iffen Miss Fairchild wants to be wed on those eye-dees, she should be. That's the least we can do, seein' as how she come all this way, Pa."

He stared at Pa-Pa. Pa-Pa stared back. It went on for several minutes, like a gunfight, only with glares instead of bullets. Robby could see Pa-Pa wanted to argue. But something held him back. Probably he was still trying to impress Miss Fairchild. And there was that lingering notion of legal consent.

Finally, Pa-Pa swallowed hard and his face relaxed. "Well, now, I was just tryin' to get things accomplished around here. Iffen it has to be August first, I guess that ain't the end of the world. But not one day later! And you all—" He pointed a finger around the table. "Ya need to be on your best behavior for two whole weeks. And no you-know-what!"

Robby blinked. That wasn't ominous at all. No what? Dancing naked in the living room? Cooking human body parts?

Smacking around the wives?

Without another glance at Robby, Pa-Pa left the table and everyone else scattered. Within seconds only Marcy, Emmie, Robby, and baby George were left. The baby sat in a beautiful homemade high chair with egg all over his face, chatting happily.

Robby stood and took in the room. The table and a two-foot perimeter around it looked like a war zone.

Marcy folded her hands on the back of a chair and gave Robby a curious look. "Clovis must like ya. I ain't never seen him go against Pa-Pa like that."

"Well, he ought to," Emmie spoke up, wiping George's face and hands. "He'll be a married man soon."

"Well, Roy's *been* married, and he don't do that. And Wayne hardly ever."

Emmie gave Marcy a warning look. She picked up George and bounced him on one hip. Robby had four younger siblings, so he'd held, bathed, and diapered his share of babies. But it had been a long time. George looked to be about a year old, and he was adorable, with fat cheeks, fine brown hair, and big brown eyes.

Robby imagined he looked a little like his Uncle Trace.

"You can rest up a spell if you like," Emmie told Robby. "We won't all sit down again till supper time. But when you're ready for lunch, let us know and we'll fix ya a plate."

It was a good excuse to go back to the porch and escape the unholy mess left by breakfast, and Robby knew he should take it. The less he was seen the better. But sitting around stewing didn't sound like fun. Plus, he'd feel strange lazing around when everyone else was working.

"I'll tell you a secret," Robby said in a conspiratorial whisper. "I can't cook to save my life, but I'm happy to wash dishes. Or I can help with the baby. What do you say, George?" Robby went to Emmie and chucked the baby's chin.

"Oh, that would be a big help," Emmie said sincerely. She dumped George into Robby's arms. His warm weight brought back memories, as did the sweet scent of his hair. George was a quiet, good-natured little soul. Robby was surprised how much he enjoyed holding an infant again. They chatted while Marcy and Emmie cleaned up. And he was almost sorry when George fell asleep and Emmie took him to put him down.

They were just finishing up the dishes when Clovis stepped into the kitchen, hat in his hands. He gazed studiously at the floor.

"Miss Fairchild, I thought—um, since you'll be on the porch longer than we figured, you'll be needin' a place to hang your clothes. I set somethin' up in there for ya." Without waiting for a response, Clovis ducked out.

Good Lord. You'd have thought he'd turn to stone if he so much as looked at Robby.

"Thank you?" Robby said to the empty space.

"Let's go see," Emmie said, her voice eager.

On the back porch they found a rustic-looking clothes rack. Two sturdy forked branches held a smooth wooden dowel between them. The bottoms of the branches were set into round discs sliced from a tree trunk, still wearing its bark. Pegs were set every few inches in the dowel. It was an interesting-looking piece. Robby suspected it might have fetched a fair price in New York.

"Well, that's thoughtful," he said with some surprise.

"Clovis is quiet, but he's a good man," Marcy said.

"Can we help you unpack?" Emmie eyed Robby's trunk with longing.

Robby hesitated. But it would seem rude if he insisted on unpacking alone. And he'd already thought up a cover story for the few male items in the trunk.

"All right," he said with a welcoming smile. *Dear Lord, let it be all right.*

Marcy and Emmie were enamored by the gowns in the trunk—three silks, a fine summer linen with braid trim, a heavy brocade, and a pink summer dress. They didn't seem to notice when Robby picked up his small leather case with his makeup and grooming supplies and casually placed it under the bed.

They hung the gowns and petticoats on the rod and folded camisoles, gloves, and unmentionables, including a lone corset which Robby refused to wear. They sighed over the fabric and colors like they were the clothes of a queen. And Rowena's clothes, while fine, were nothing like the sequined and lacy confections the rich ladies in New York wore.

"Is the ranch not doing very well?" Robby asked, as delicately as he could.

Marcy and Emmie looked at each other.

"The ranch gets along fine, don't worry your head about that," Marcy assured him.

"Yeah. Pa-Pa's real good about puttin' money away," Emmie agreed wistfully, still eyeing the dresses.

"Hmm. Maybe he puts too *much* away, then," Robby said. Or rather, Rowena said it. The character Robby was playing put a hand on her hip and cocked a haughty eyebrow. Rowena had very definite opinions on the subject of clothing. And of women too, apparently.

Emmie blushed and smoothed a hand down her faded brown dress. "Pa-Pa don't like to spend on gee-gaws and what he calls fripperies."

Marcy looked down self-consciously and folded her hand over a badly frayed cuff. She and Emmie had been wearing those same dresses since Robby arrived. Which meant, like Pa-Pa's gray vest and white shirt, they were probably the best things they owned, worn to show off for Miss Fairchild. And that was a tragedy right there.

"Well. Decent clothing is hardly a frippery," Robby said firmly.

"Please don't say nothin' to Pa-Pa," Marcy begged. "He would about kill us if he thought we'd given you a bad notion!"

"The two of you have not given me a bad notion," Robby promised sincerely. In fact, they were the best thing about Crabtree Ranch, in Robby's opinion.

"Anyway, I don't mind for myself," Emmie said. "But I do wish we had better things for the kids. It's hard on the ones that go to school. The other kids can be cruel."

"Still," Marcy reminded her. "We have good food on the table, and a solid roof over our head. And there's never a worry about money. We have it right good. And clothes ain't all *that* important."

Robby reminded himself he wouldn't be there long, and his primary task was not to rock the boat. But *Rowena* wasn't inclined to be meek. "I know! How about we go into town tomorrow, just the three of us? We can pick up some fabric at the store in Flat Bottom."

Emmie giggled. "I'm startin' to like you, sister-in-law."

But Marcy shook her head. "Oh, we ain't allowed into town alone. And the menfolk never have time to take us 'cept on Saturdays."

"I can drive a buggy," Robby said.

Marcy and Emmie shared a grimace.

Marcy sat down on the daybed and patted a spot. "There's somethin' you oughtta know."

Robby was sure it couldn't be anything good, but he sat. Emmie took a spot on the other side of him.

Marcy looked around as if to make sure no one was listening. "See, Pa-Pa's wife, the boys' mama? She ran away. She went to visit her family and just never came home."

"Oh, my."

"It must have been awful hard on Pa-Pa," Emmie said sadly. "What with four little boys. He ain't looked at another woman since."

"So, Pa-Pa, he's real touchy about us goin' off alone," Emmie said. "It's just best to wait till Saturday."

"Hmm." That explained the locked-up tack in the barn. "So, there wasn't a woman in this house for years, not until you married Wayne?"

Marcy nodded. "I tried to get them to learn some manners. My pa was just a farmer, but he was . . . well.

Better. But there was four of them and one of me, and Pa-Pa didn't like me criticizin'. So . . ."

Emmie nodded, a frown on her face. "Really, Rowena, it ain't worth it. They ain't got nice manners, but all in all, they're good men. Hard workers. Clovis too. You'll see."

She looked at the open trunk and stood. "Now let's finish unpackin'. George will be up soon." She took out a shirt from the bottom and held it up. "What's this?"

It was one of Robby's white shirts with large, stiff cuffs.

He felt his face heat. "Oh, I brought a few of my brother's things. I thought they might look nice on Clovis. But now I realize how silly that was."

Marcy and Emmie both looked at the shirt and burst out laughing. The idea of Clovis in the delicate shirt *was* pretty hilarious, so Robby laughed too. They laughed so hard, his side started to hurt. As soon as one would sober up, the other two would set them off again.

Finally, the laughter died down.

"Rowena, I do hope you'll stay," Marcy said with spontaneous affection.

"Me too," Emmie agreed earnestly.

Robby felt a pang of guilt. Marcy and Emmie had no idea Robby would escape the moment he could. And that felt awful. He swallowed a lump in his throat, and his gaze fell on the row of pretty dresses.

"Well, ladies. How are you with a needle and thread? Because I think this—" He took the peach silk and held it up to Emmie. "—and this—" He held the pink dress up to Marcy. "—would look lovely on you two. And I want you both looking your best at my wedding."

The squeals could probably be heard in Flat Bottom.

Chapter Ten

Trace started out for Santa Fe before daybreak. It was downright annoying to have to make the trip two days in a row. But after talking to Robby in the barn, there were things he needed to know. And he could only figure them out in Santa Fe.

He arrived by ten o'clock. He left his horse at the livery stables and went to the Palace of Governors on the plaza to see the sheriff. Sheriff Brooks was in his forties, with graying brown hair, skin bronzed by the sun, and a broken front tooth. Besides being Santa Fe's sheriff, he was a territorial marshal. Trace had met Brooks but had never had a reason to work with the man before.

"What can I do for you, Sheriff Craptree?" Brooks asked, after making Trace wait an hour in the lobby.

"That's *Crabtree*."

"My apologies." Brooks's toothy grin said he thought he was funny. Trace decided to ignore it.

"That man who was killed yesterday—Stoltz. I was

wonderin' if you had any idea who did it, or if anyone else's turned up dead?"

Brooks leaned back in his chair and studied Trace. "Why would you care about that?"

Trace shrugged. "I heard Stoltz came in on a wagon train on Tuesday. A lady who was travelin' on that same wagon train is stayin' with a family in Flat Bottom. Thought I'd best check up on it."

He kept his tone slow and disinterested. He took a cigarette from a pocket and rolled it between his fingers.

"What's the lady's name?"

"Miss Fairchild. She's from St. Louis." Trace figured even the Bowery Boys knew that much, so there was no point being coy.

Brooks grunted. "Why would the murder of Stoltz have anythin' to do with this Miss Fairchild? She didn't kill him, did she?"

Trace gave him a disgusted look and lit the cigarette. "Want one?"

Brooks shook his head, instead picking up a cigar from a box and lighting it. He seemed to think it over. "Yup. Something smells bad about that wagon train all right. Three of the other drivers unloaded and set back out again yesterday. Not even a full day in Santa Fe. Drivers don't do that."

"That so?"

"Maybe they were worried they'd get their throats cut like Stoltz. And maybe it has something to do with this."

Brooks searched through a stack of papers on his desk and held one out to Trace. It was a *WANTED* notice. It had a drawing of Robby and his name at the top.

Feeling sick, Trace took it and scanned it quickly. The

U.S. Marshal's office was looking for Robby Riverton, a New York actor. He was wanted as an eyewitness to a murder. If he was spotted, he was to be detained and guarded until a U.S. Marshal could pick him up.

The feeling of relief was strong and sweet. The poster verified Robby's story. And it also explained why the Bowery Boys were still after him. If the U.S. Marshals wanted Robby to testify, they had to want the murderer pretty damn bad. Or perhaps the man who was killed was an important dignitary or a member of the upper class. In any case, the Bowery Boys would want to get to Robby first to make sure he kept quiet. As quiet as the grave.

"Keep that, if ya want. I got more."

Trace folded it up and put it in a pocket. He looked up to find Brooks watching him closely. "You think this Riverton has somethin' to do with Stoltz's murder?"

Brooks pursed his lips. "Talked to one of the drivers who stayed in town. He said a couple of Easterners searched that wagon train lookin' for someone. Sure sounds like this man."

"Hmmm." Trace took a long drag on his cigarette and let the smoke out slowly.

Brooks flicked the ash off his cigar. "Had a wire that U.S. Marshals are on their way. Maybe a few weeks out? Maybe less. You have any idea where this Riverton is?"

"Nah." Trace blew a perfect smoke ring. "What about the Easterners who stopped the wagon train? You think they're still around?"

"Oh, I know they are," Brooks said easily. He stretched his arms behind his head, cigar clenched in his teeth.

"Can't you arrest them for killin' Stoltz?"

"No one saw them do it. Can't prove it. Can you prove it?"

Trace just gave him a look.

"Maybe it was them. Maybe it was someone else. Maybe Stoltz sat on the wrong bull, insulted a man, cheated at cards."

"Maybe."

Trace and Brooks smoked and watched each other.

Trace considered telling Brooks everything. But he'd heard rumors that Brooks was crooked. Something to do with a rich ranchero's son getting off on murder charges. Something else about wagon trains having to pay him off to avoid getting robbed by "bandits." Trace didn't put much credence in rumors. But he also couldn't be 100 percent certain they were wrong.

His imagination conjured up an image of Robby sitting in a Santa Fe jail cell, Brooks taking a wad of cash from the Bowery Boys, and then letting them in while he went out for a walk. The thought made him sick.

Trace ground out his cigarette in an ashtray. "Welp. Been good talkin' to ya." He turned and put his hand on the doorknob.

Brooks spoke up. "Maybe your Miss Fairchild is right to worry. I hear those two men from the East, they're hiring guns."

Trace paused. "How many guns?"

Brooks shrugged.

"Know where they're goin'?" Trace asked coolly.

"I suppose they're still after this Riverton fellow. Wherever he might be. Pretty sure he's not in Santa Fe. If I see they're headed up your way, I'll send a wire. Okay?"

Trace nodded. "'preciate it."

Trace opened the door.

"I expect the same, no? You hear anything about Riverton, you tell me. Understand, Crabtree?" Brooks's eyes were flinty.

Trace tipped his hat and left.

TRACE HAD a lunch of fresh corn tortillas, beans, and spicy beef at a little cubbyhole restaurant near the livery stables. The senoritas there served the best food in town, and it was cheap.

As he ate, he pondered his next move. He could try to track down some of the men who'd been on the wagon train, as Brooks had done. See what they'd told the Bowery Boys. But if he made too much of a fuss here in Santa Fe, word would get back to Brooks and maybe the Bowery Boys too. And that would just bring more attention to Flat Bottom and, thus, to Miss Rowena Fairchild.

Besides. If the Bowery Boys *did* question everyone they could find from that wagon train, sooner or later they'd hear one of two things: either that Miss Fairchild had not been on that wagon train after Dodge City, or that Riverton, aka Nick Smith, *had* been on it up till the end.

Either of those things would send the Bowery Boys charging after the "Miss Fairchild" they'd talked to in Santa Fe. And they wouldn't come alone.

And goddamn, but it chafed his hide. He'd gone back to Flat Bottom to get as far away from drama and danger as he could get. And it had just moseyed its way on into his town anyhow.

After lunch, Trace left Santa Fe. Once again, he didn't visit Rafael the barber.

Chapter Eleven

Wednesday

The following day, Trace had things to square away in town, and he got to the ranch just as the sun was setting. As he tied his horse Jasper up to the corral fence, he had an unusual moment of introspection.

It had been years since he'd been able to look around at the "Crabtree & Sons" ranch and not feel an urge to leave it, to get away as soon as he could. But those bad feelings had more to do with his pa than the ranch itself. Objectively, it was a fine-looking spread. The house, barn, and pig pen were in good condition. The yard and garden were clean. Neat fencing ran all along the road. Trace had spent enough of his boyhood cutting grass, pulling weeds, and sweeping the porch to appreciate the work that went into its maintenance. Pa always had been "land proud," and he had enough free labor to keep things neat and tidy.

But his pa's rigid control grated against Trace's independent streak like broken glass on broken glass—always had. He'd been only four years old when his ma had left. Growing up with Pa as the only parent had been rough. Trace left home before Marcy and Emmie came along. But the few months he'd spent at the ranch recently with his shot-up leg had driven him crazy. In some ways, the women improved the place—the meals were a hell of a lot better than anything Pa had ever fixed, and the house was clean. Plus, Trace was genuinely fond of his nieces and nephews—in small doses. But watching Pa boss the gals around, and his brothers letting him, had renewed Trace's disgust. He wanted nothing to do with the place.

Now Robby Riverton was in there. In that very house. That caused such a mess of conflicting urges it made Trace's head hurt.

He entered the house without knocking. Hearing voices, he went on through to the dining room. The family was eating supper. And there was Miss Rowena Fairchild sitting next to Pa, who was spruced up in his best gray vest and shirt with his hair slicked back and his face and hands clean.

The image was so strange, Trace's mind caught on it like a hangnail. He stood dumbly in the doorway. Robby stared at him with wide, alarmed eyes.

"Ya decided to come for supper, did ya?" Pa snorted. "It must be a blue moon out there tonight. Or hell's froze over." He jabbed a piece of steak with his jackknife and stuffed it in his mouth.

"Howdy, Trace. Let me set you a place." Marcy rushed to the cupboard.

"You don't need to go to any trouble," Trace replied,

not meaning it because he was hungry, and the steak smelled good.

Marcy squeezed him onto the end next to Clovis. Clovis shifted over with a grunt and looked at Trace warily.

"Hey, baby brother." Trace slapped Clovis on the shoulder.

"No big gunfights to break up in town tonight?" Clovis drawled.

"Shut up and pass the potatoes."

He ate, forcing himself not to look at Robby. But he couldn't help overhearing Pa tell an old cowboy yarn about a lost calf, laughing as he did so. "Rowena" looked charming as she listened raptly, smiled and cooed, and even gave the old man a bit of sass. Pa laughed like she was the funniest thing.

Stunned, Trace looked at Clovis with one eyebrow raised and Clovis looked back. He blushed pink and shrugged as if to say, "Don't ask me."

At least the charade seemed to be going well. That was good, though Pa'd be livid if he ever found out he'd been fooled.

After dinner, Trace asked to speak to Pa alone. He ignored Robby's panicky look as he and Pa left the dining room. He didn't speak until they were alone in Pa's study with the door firmly closed.

"What is it?" Pa asked. "I shoulda known you wouldn't come to supper without a damn good reason."

"We got trouble," Trace said.

Pa poured a shot of whiskey into a dirty glass that was always on his desk. "Well, say what you come here to say, boy."

Trace went to the window and looked out over the ranch. He told Pa how two men from a gang in New York were looking for a fugitive that had been on Miss Fairchild's wagon train and how at least one man had been killed so far. He described how he'd met Miss Fairchild in Santa Fe as the two men accosted her on the street.

"Well, what kindy wagon train is that?" Pa said bitterly. "I paid two hundred dollars for her fare and they let damned fugitives ride along? That ain't right!"

"They probably didn't know he was a fugitive, Pa," Trace replied, managing not to sound impatient.

"Well, what the hell has Rowena got to do with it?"

"She was in the wrong place at the wrong time," Trace said, which was more or less the truth. "But if the men are goin' after everyone on that wagon train to twist their arm, they might come after her."

"Well, they can't have her! I paid two hundred dollars for that gal. And from what I've seen, she's worth it. I reckon her and Clovis are gonna have a passel of long-faced, tall, and hairy children. But, by God, they'll have gumption!"

Trace wasn't sure if he wanted to laugh or cry over that statement. Pa was as crazy as ever.

"I just wanted to warn you. And I suppose it'd be wise to make some preparations."

"Aw, they won't come here," Pa said dismissively. "This place is way out from Santa Fe. Anyhow, this household is cattywampus enough as it is what with waitin' on the dang weddin'."

He took another sip of his whiskey, savoring it. Trace knew his father. Pa wasn't afraid of hard work—or rather, having others do hard work for him. But if he didn't think something was important, he could be stubborn about not wasting a moment's thought on it.

Trace leaned against the windowsill, crossing his arms. "I think they might. They probably think Miss Fairchild's fiancé is some slack-jawed hick. Probably think they can just waltz in here and take her iffen they decide to," he said with a low, disgusted grumble.

Pa choked on whiskey and coughed until his face was red. He stood and pounded on the desk. "Any goddamn Easterner lookin' for any goddamn fugitive dares come on *my* land, I will fill his behind so full of buckshot, he'll be workin' as a salt shaker!"

"I don't know, Pa." Trace rubbed the stubble on his chin. "I heard they're hirin' guns. They might be kindy tough."

"Tough? Tough?" Pa bellowed. "There ain't an Easterner who knows the meanin' of the word! I'd like to see them work with a herd of animals that weigh a ton each or sit in a saddle from sunup to sundown. No sir! I'd like to see them try to take Rowena! I got me four strong boys, and I'm still in my prime. Plus, you're the best gun I ever knew."

Trace felt a pang of warmth at Pa's praise. It was so rare. And goddamn but he hated that he could still want the old man's approval.

"We're of a like mind on the subject then," Trace agreed. "I reckon we should all brush up on our shootin'. And we can shore up a few spots along the lane."

"I guess," Pa said testily. "This sure is messin' with our routine. I'll be glad when they're done married. Did you know that gal is makin' us wait till *August first*? Somethin' about it bein' lucky. Bunch of hoo-haw if you ask me, but she got her way. Yes sir, that gal's got gumption."

Trace bit back a smile. So Robby had managed to push off the wedding. Pa's tone was downright admiring. He was going to be awfully disappointed at the end of this thing, when his mail-order bride disappeared. But right now, Trace could only think about saving Robby's skin.

TRACE WAS AT THE CORRAL, untying his horse, when Robby came out of the house. He strolled toward Trace casually and stopped ten feet away, pulling the shawl tightly around himself in the cool evening air. The biggest red pig, Killboar, came over to the fence and sniffed the air, curious about the stranger. Trace ignored his anxious snorting.

"You shouldn't be seen talkin' to me," Trace said with a glance at the house.

"What did you tell him?" Robby sounded upset.

Trace gave Robby a measured stare. "I didn't betray you, if that's what you mean. I wouldn't do that."

Robby's expression relaxed, and he blinked back some emotion. After a moment he took a deep breath. "Sorry. It's just all so . . ." He shrugged.

"Don't be apologizin'." Trace led Jasper back from the rail.

"Did something happen today?"

Trace got up onto his horse. "Meet me tonight by the privy once everyone's asleep. Don't let your guard slip, Robby. Be strong."

Trace rode away. He refused to look back, even though he wanted to. He also wanted to pull Robby Riverton up onto his horse and take him away, put him somewhere safe. But that was a foolish instinct, and Trace the soldier knew better than to listen to it. Slow and deliberate and strategic, that's how a man avoided making stupid mistakes in a war.

Though it occurred to him that he might be fighting a war on more than one front. And when it came to his softer feelings, he refused to lose.

Chapter Twelve

The privy was a smart place to meet, Robby realized. It was set some ways off from the house and close to a stand of trees. In the dark, it would be safe from prying eyes. And if he got caught going there, he had a ready-made excuse.

Trace was waiting for him on the back side of the privy, the side that faced the trees.

"Hello," Robby whispered, not knowing what else to say.

"Hey there," came Trace's deep drawl. He leaned one shoulder against the wooden privy wall. A flash of white in his fingers announced the presence of a cigarette, but it wasn't lit.

Robby was relieved to see him. At times the day had seemed interminable. And since supper, Robby could think of nothing beyond finding out what Trace had told Pa-Pa.

His feelings about Sheriff Trace Crabtree swung wildly, like a weather vane before a storm. Trace had seemed to be on Robby's side last night in the barn, and he'd felt so grateful at the time. But what if Trace changed his mind? All day, Robby had worried about how he'd acted in the barn, how close they'd stood, how he'd leaned into Trace's hand. It was stupid to have risked that. Yes, the sheriff seemed to share Robby's tastes, but he'd stepped away, hadn't he? Robby needed his help too much to risk angering or disgusting him.

But now, being this close to Trace again, seeing the calm, relaxed solidity of him, hearing the straight-forward bluntness in his voice, feeling the aura of care he exuded, Robby's fears seem foolish. The knots in his stomach eased. He could trust Trace. He really thought he could. And Trace was the one person who knew Robby as Robby. And just being *known* was a relief.

"Do you have news?" Robby asked.

"Yup. Now, I need ya to stay calm and listen. Can ya do that?"

Robby nodded. He crossed his arms over his chest and grasped his elbows tight.

Trace tilted back his hat and scratched his forehead with a thumb. Robby's eyes were adjusting to the dark and he thought Trace's expression was sympathetic. "Well, I went back to Santa Fe this mornin', and I learnt a few things. First of all, seems ya got yourself a *WANTED* poster."

"*What?*"

Trace shushed him and told Robby about the notice from the U.S. Marshals. They wanted him officially as an eyewitness! He also said the Bowery Boys were still in Santa Fe, still looking to question other members of the wagon train.

It was the worst news possible. If the Feds wanted Robby's testimony to finally nail Mose McCann, he and his Boys wouldn't rest, not until Robby was six feet under.

He sank against the wall of the privy, his breath coming hard. "Good God. This nightmare just won't *end*."

"It will," Trace said levelly. "It'll end. But I have a feelin' the hardest lumps are still to come."

Trace didn't say anything more, didn't offer any lofty promises. Robby was upset, and he was terrified, but he was also sick of feeling that way. He quietly pulled himself together, turning his back to Trace and squeezing his eyes shut.

It was all very well and good to *want* things. To want this to be over with. To want to be free to just live his damned life, to start over, to try again. He was only twenty-four, for God's sake. But it *wasn't* over with, and he had to face facts. After the initial anger and resentment faded, Robby felt strangely calm. Maybe this was what prisoners felt like going to their deaths.

He turned back to Trace. "Thank you for going all the way back to Santa Fe and learning what you could. I'm not sure what I should do next." He'd almost said *we*. He wanted to believe it was *we*. But that seemed presumptuous.

Trace laid a reassuring hand on Robby's shoulder. "We hold tight. I telegraphed the U.S. Marshal's office and told 'em to come here. Seems to me once you've told them everythin' you know, those Bowery Boys won't have any reason to keep after ya."

Robby thought about that. He supposed he was willing to talk. It certainly couldn't get him into any worse trouble than he was already in. And he supposed, too, he owed Stoltz that much. He shouldn't have died for nothing. "All right. How long will it take them to get here?"

"I dunno," Trace admitted. "A few weeks probably. Meanwhile, we keep ya safe here at the ranch. I figure it'll take at least four or five days before the Bowery Boys get organized and show up in Flat Bottom. Maybe a week. If they've only got a couple of guns with 'em, I might be able to arrest 'em in town. If not, Pa and my brothers will hold 'em off here."

"Is that why you talked to Pa-Pa?"

Trace nodded. "I told him there was some fuss about a fugitive on your wagon train, and a man had been murdered in Santa Fe over it. Told him it was possible the Easterners might come lookin' to question ya."

Robby squeezed his arms tighter, feeling the cold. "What did he say to that?"

Trace snorted. "About what you'd expect. That they'd step foot on his land over his dead body." Trace sounded grimly pleased. "I never thought I'd be glad my father is such a stubborn old cuss."

Robby could well imagine Pa-Pa saying exactly that. But still. The idea of gunmen attacking the ranch on his account didn't sit well at all. "If we have four or five days before the Bowery Boys come here, maybe I should just—"

There was the squeak of a door opening. Trace grabbed Robby's hand and pulled him into the trees. They stood in the shadows, Trace behind Robby, one arm around his waist as though he might try to escape. Robby hadn't the least intention of escaping. The warm muscle behind his back felt so damn good. He watched

Pa Crabtree walk with his bow-legged gait across the yard to the privy. He was wearing a long night shirt, a wool hat, gloves, and galoshes over bare legs. He stumbled, half asleep. He went into the privy and the door banged shut.

Robby tried to calm his racing heart. His pulse pounded along Trace's arm. Electricity radiated in time with the *thud, thud*. Dear God above. This attraction was officially insane. How could he feel even a speck of lust at one of the most dangerous and dodgy points of his life?

Unless that was *why* he felt it? He'd heard a close brush with death brought on the urge to copulate, as if the body was reminded of how imperative it was to reproduce, and soon. Of course, if *Robby's* body was thinking about offspring, it shouldn't have set its sights on Sheriff Trace Crabtree.

Something tugged under Robby's chin. It was Trace, untying his bonnet. The damn thing was perpetually in the way. How did women stand it? He felt cool air as it was tugged off his head and tossed on the ground. He raised a hand to rake his fingers through his hair, loosening the tamed locks. It felt so good to be free.

"Are ya doin' all right here at the ranch?" Trace asked in a voice that was so low, Robby wouldn't have heard it except Trace's mouth was against Robby's ear.

He replied just as softly. "So far. But I still think I should run while I can."

Trace pulled him closer, so that Robby's back was pressed tight against Trace's chest. His palm spread out along Robby's ribs, making his skin dance with awareness. His words were firm despite the whisper. "Ya can't go south, and the way north is dangerous. Besides, ya ran all the way from New York and didn't outrun your troubles. Don't run, Robby."

His words were so sure, so certain. Robby needed to trust someone, needed to not feel alone. He turned, grasping Trace's waist under his open canvas coat and resting his forehead on Trace's chin. He was acutely aware of the texture of Trace's wool vest beneath his fingers and the smooth, thick leather of his gun belt where one pinky rested, of the warm sweat-smell of man and the faint whiff of horse. Those things had never been his favorite smells, but right now they were more than merely good, the scent was life itself, like the smell of the woods and the night air.

Trace's hands covered Robby's. Probably he was nervous with Robby so close to his guns. But that was all right. Robby didn't blame him in the least. All he wanted was to be allowed to stand here for a moment. To not think—just for a moment.

Behind him, Robby heard the privy door bang as Pa-Pa exited. Trace held still until there was the fainter sound of Pa-Pa going back into the house.

Trace relaxed. "He's gone."

Robby sighed and stepped back. "It's going to be hell sitting here waiting. With no idea what's going on, or when they'll come."

"I'll be keepin' an eye on ya. Is there a time of day ya can get away? Take a walk?"

Robby thought about it. "Afternoons. The men and older boys work outside and the little ones nap. Marcy and Emmie are usually occupied."

"All right. There's a trail behind the barn that goes to

the river. Walk south on the riverbank maybe ten minutes, and you'll find an old cabin. Meet me there tomorrow."

Robby nodded, relieved he wouldn't have to wait too long for another update. "Tomorrow."

"And if ya ever need to get out of that house, just go to the cabin. All right?"

Robby nodded again. He wasn't sure what else to say and, honestly, he didn't want to say anything. He wanted to stand there like this, feeling Trace's warmth and strong confidence. He made everything seem so much more manageable, turned monsters into annoyances. He seemed to think Robby could do this, that they'd be fine. And maybe he was right.

Then he realized that Trace was all but holding him. They were only inches apart and Trace looked down at Robby's hands, which he still grasped in his own. It should be awkward, but it didn't feel that way. And Robby wasn't stupid enough to push away the only good thing he'd felt in ages.

"Why are you doing this for me?" Robby asked at last. The intimacy of Trace's closeness in the dark was doing strange things to his head.

Trace met his gaze, his eyes troubled. "I'm helpin' you because it's the right thing to do. I don't want to see ya dead. And, in case it's not obvious . . ." He huffed out a resentful sigh. "I kind of like ya."

Robby laughed. "You don't have to sound so put out about it."

"Well, I am. I am put out about it. It's the goddamnedest, most inconvenient thing."

Robby couldn't argue with that. But he felt a surge of

happiness that Trace had admitted it. It made him feel reckless. Without over-thinking it, he leaned in for a kiss.

Trace stopped him, releasing Robby's hands to grasp both upper arms. "*Don't*. You know it's foolish."

Robby felt a flash of irritation. "What I *know* is that I'm scared out of my fucking mind. And I know that I might not be alive next week. So I'm not interested in nursemaid morality."

Trace glowered at him for a long moment before responding. "Fine. *One* kiss. But we can't be doin' this."

It was the worst logic ever, but Robby wasn't about to point that out. The arms that were holding Robby away now pulled him in. And, despite Trace's words, his lips were the ones that sought out Robby's. And they were hungry.

Robby's eyes slammed shut as the banked fire inside him shot up in delicious licks of flame. He pressed tighter, wanting all the contact he could get. Trace's body molded to his, and Robby gave back the aggressive desire, passion bright on his tongue, need thick in his veins as he sucked on Trace's tongue.

Trace made a sound in his throat and cupped Robby's ass. The hard jut of his flesh against Robby's hip made him want to lie down right there in the dirt.

Then Trace turned away, stepped back, and shook his head. *No more.*

Robby clenched his suddenly empty fingers. He huffed. "I sure hope those marshals hurry up."

"Me too," Trace said, his voice like sandpaper. "Go on back now."

He picked up the bonnet and held it up. Robby took it and stumbled toward the house.

Chapter Thirteen

Thursday

Robby woke up the next morning and sat straight up in bed. Something burned low in his belly.

Anger. It was anger.

Enough was enough. He was tired of being worried and afraid and hoping that if he laid low enough, or ran fast enough, or smiled winningly enough, his problems would vanish. Being weak and fearful fit him about as well as Rowena's dress the first time he'd tried it on. Robby Riverton wasn't a cowering man. He was a handsome, charming, green-eyed devil that could hold the audience in the palm of his hand—so sayeth *The Weekly Sun*.

It was time to reclaim *that* Robby Riverton.

He'd made all of New York City believe he was Miss Annabelle Smith playing Ophelia. He could damn well fool the Crabtree family. It was time to stop worrying about being discovered and take charge of the situation—

in this house, with the Bowery Boys, and with that tempt-ing-as-sin, big-gunned sheriff too.

It was time for some *tiger-footed rage.*

And that, ladies and gentlemen, was how this play would go on.

He got up and got dressed, his movements sure and delib-erate. In the mirror as he shaved and then put on his makeup, his back was ramrod straight, and his eyes were flinty steel.

Pa-Pa Crabtree was about to meet his match.

WHEN ROBBY APPEARED in the kitchen, Marcy and Emmie were cooking and Marcy's five-year-old, Missy, was solemnly putting plates on the table.

"Mornin', Miss Fairchild," Missy said.

"Good morning, sweet girl!" Robby kissed the little dumpling on the head. "Marcy, where might I find napkins?"

Marcy, who was stirring a huge pan of scrambled eggs at the woodstove, wrinkled her nose in confusion. "Napkins?"

"Yes, *napkins.*"

"Uh, I think there's some in the sideboard," Emmie said. "Back behind that big soup dish."

"Oh, yes," said Marcy. "Those things belonged to . . ." Her eyes darted toward the door. ". . . to Wayne's mama."

Robby marched to the old sideboard in the dining room. It was a massive piece with various drawers and cupboards. In the bottom cupboard, he found a stash of fancy dishes he'd never seen. There were candlesticks and a huge china soup tureen, serving dishes, a big silver ladle, and other items more at home on a society table than at the Crabtree ranch.

He found a stack of old linen napkins crammed in the back. Robby pulled them out and took them to the kitchen. "There's no time to iron these, but we can make do for this meal," he announced. "Missy, set a place for your mama and Emmie too."

"Oh, we don't normally—" Emmie began.

"You'll sit at the table like members of the family," Robby said, with a hint of steel in his tone. "How about Emmie on the end here. We can just move baby George's chair like so."

Marcy and Emmie regarded Robby as if he were crazy, but they didn't say a word as he organized the table to his liking.

Wayne, Roy, and Clovis came in from doing chores and sat down heavily at their seats. Wayne ordered Marcy to get the kids to the table so's they could eat, and she went and rounded them up. Pa-Pa was the last to enter. He'd given up on wearing the gray leather vest and white shirt with a bow, and he now wore a flannel work shirt that had seen better days and a pair of old brown pants. But everything was clean, and his hair was slicked back. He still smelled of a cheap men's cologne, which he put on surely for Rowena's sake.

"Now!" Robby said, looking over the table. "Is everything on? Salt and pepper? Bread? Let's make sure we have everything, so no one has to get up ten times."

Marcy put a large wooden bowl of scrambled eggs on the table and Emmie a bowl of gravy to go with the biscuits. After a moment's hesitation, they took their seats and Robby sat next to Pa-Pa. Marcy and Emmie got some strange looks, but no one said a word.

Wayne picked his napkin up off his plate, looked at it with a frown, and tossed it over his shoulder to the floor. Robby watched as Roy, Clovis, and the kids around the table followed his lead. Pa-Pa stuffed his napkin in an empty glass.

Robby's blood surged, and his cheeks got hot. He slowly stood, a brittle smile on his face. "I see I need to demonstrate the use of the *napkin*." Robby picked his up, flicked it open with a snap of his wrist, and smoothed it over the lap of his dress. "You place a napkin in your lap. During the meal, you wipe your fingers on it. This keeps the jam and butter and grease and *drool* in one place. Instead of all over the tablecloth and your clothes and—" He leveled a stony look at Wayne. "—under your armpits. This minor alteration on your part means much less work for Marcy and Emmie and less stained clothing."

They all stared at Rowena like she was speaking a foreign language.

"So pick them up. Go on." Rowena's tone was cheerful.

Pa-Pa took his napkin from the empty glass and stared at it. "Where the heck did ya get these? I—"

Robby could see the moment when Pa-Pa remembered. He swallowed hard, blinked rapidly, and put the napkin in his lap with shaking fingers. "Well?" He glared around the table. "You heard the gal! Got wax in your ears?"

With some reluctance, everyone picked up the napkins.

Robby sat back down and fluffed the napkin in his lap. "Please pass the eggs," he said to Missy, who was to his right. The little girl hurried to obey.

"Thing is, Rowena, we ain't much for airs and graces," Pa-Pa said, looking at Robby with a wary expression.

"That's the marvelous thing about life. You can always *learn.*" Robby scooped eggs onto his plate.

There was a strangled sound that might have been laughter from Clovis's end of the table. The dishes were grabbed and fought over as usual. Food landed on the tablecloth and on the floor. And *that*, Robby decided, was a battle for another day. But the napkins stayed in laps and Marcy and Emmie ate with the family. And that gave Robby a small sense of accomplishment and control that he desperately needed.

The meal had nearly ended when he spoke up again. "After the breakfast dishes, Marcy, Emmie, and I will take the rig into town. Pa-Pa, we'll need money to buy fabric for new outfits for the kids. And for Marcy and Emmie too."

The table went silent. All movement ceased. Billy had a fork half-raised to his open mouth and his eyes shifted from Robby to Pa-Pa and back again with a look of eager anticipation. Wayne's lips had all but disappeared his mouth was pressed so tight.

"We don't have time to take you gals to town today," Pa-Pa said in a firm voice. "Maybe Saturday."

"You don't need to take us. I can drive the rig. Missy, please pass the strawberry jam."

Missy's chubby little hand planted the bowl in Robby's palm, and she smiled big.

"Thank you kindly, sweet pea," Robby cooed.

Missy squirmed in delight.

Pa-Pa put down his jackknife very, very carefully. Robby could tell he was struggling to control his temper.

Robby waited patiently, painting jam on his toast with broad swipes. His hands were perfectly calm and steady, but a reckless fire burned in his chest.

"Now listen, the gals don't go into town by themselves. It ain't safe. You hafta wait till one of us can take ya."

"It's perfectly safe. And it must be today. We need to make new outfits for the wedding, and we've only got a few weeks to do it. As it stands, the children don't have a scrap of decent clothing to their name, or Marcy and Emmie either."

A tremor of fear went around the table. Wayne's face went red and Roy glared at Robby. Clovis put his head in his hands. Even the children shrunk in their seats. Marcy and Emmie looked horrified, staring at Robby with wide eyes.

"Now . . . that's not exactly true," Marcy put in hesitantly.

"Yes, Marcy. Sad to say, it is true," Robby countered in a no-nonsense tone. "However, it's fine. We can fix it."

In his peripheral vision, Robby could tell Pa-Pa's face was red, so red it looked like his head was set to explode. But Robby did not care a whit. He was itching for a fight—of any kind, with anyone. And if Pa-Pa was going to be that one, God rest his soul.

He turned to look at the man. Robby's chin lifted. *Go on and hit me, if that's what you do.*

Pa-Pa's eyes narrowed, and a flicker of confusion crossed his face. He looked at Robby for a long moment, his tongue poking at his cheek. Then he looked away, took a bite of toast, and chewed thoughtfully.

"Our ways are foreign to ya, gal," he said at last, with

only a slight tremor of anger in his voice. "So I'm gonna give ya some slack. But let me tell you somethin' about the Crabtrees. We don't take to throwin' money around on fancy folderol and what-have-you's. I didn't build this here fine ranch by having loose pockets. Any gal with a lick of sense would appreciate security over vanity, and I'll be disappointed if I learn that ain't you, Rowena. Besides which, the kids ain't goin' to no weddin'. It's you, me, and Clovis what's gonna be there. Nobody needs new clothes."

Robby smiled sadly and touched his arm. "Of course, I want the whole family there, Pa-Pa. Especially since my own beloved family will be absent. I'm all alone in the world here in Flat Bottom. But I'm so glad you mentioned family."

"I didn't—"

"My father built up a successful farm from nothing—"

"I thought he was a lawyer." Pa-Pa looked confused.

Robby continued, on a roll now. He let Rowena have full steam and she was charming, ruthless, and glorious. "My sainted father built up a successful farm while *also* making sure those who were dependent upon him—his wife, his children, and my grandparents—" She looked at Pa-Pa pointedly. "—had decent clothing and other basic necessities like hair ribbons, coats that were warm, and shoes that didn't pinch or let in the rain and snow. Not fancy things, laws no! But *necessary* things."

Pa-Pa's gaze dropped to Missy's shoes, which were on the rail of her chair. The little girl wore boy's shoes that had gaping holes in the side.

"My beloved father always said to me, 'Rowena,' he said, 'I don't care how much land a man has, or how much gold. A man is not a success in this world if he doesn't take care of his family!'"

Pa-Pa's face went the color of blueberry pie. His eyelid twitched.

Robby forced a sympathetic smile. "Now, I know men just don't care about these things. Why, I'll bet you can drive a herd of cattle in circles for days and diagnose a dozen diseases, but not know the difference between a bolt of serge and one of calico. Which is why Marcy and Emmie and I will take care of everything, don't you worry." She patted Pa-Pa's hand.

Marcy spoke up, timidly. "I think . . . What Pa-Pa always says is that . . . children outgrow things so darn fast. It's not worth spending money for things that don't last."

She was trying to play peacemaker. Bless her heart.

Robby took a sip of coffee and summoned up his most carefree manner. "Well, there's nothing I admire more than a frugal man, and they can write that on my tombstone! But I'll tell you my mother's philosophy. You would have liked her, Pa-Pa. Everyone thought she was a tremendous beauty." He gave Pa-Pa a dazzling smile. "My mother believed in sturdy, practical fabric made into sturdy, practical clothes that looked nice and fit comfortably. Why, a body must be able to breathe and move around! It's just *exactly* like a horse with a good saddle. And when one child outgrew a thing, it was passed on to the next child. Most evenings she had something on her lap that she was mending."

Marcy nodded eagerly at the word "mending." She glanced between Robby and Pa-Pa anxiously.

"*However*, there comes a time when a piece of clothing

crosses the line between being a useful article to being a downright embarrassment that gives a bad impression to other folks."

"I never cared a fig about what other folks think!" Pa-Pa said, but his voice was a little wobbly and he sounded more defensive than angry now.

"You are so right, Pa-Pa!" Robby agreed. "A man's pride should come from his own conscience. I couldn't agree more. On the other hand, as an important businessman in this town, I'm sure you know the value of keeping up appearances. Why, it's just like fencing. Have you ever ridden by a farm with fences that are falling down? And the whole place is goin' to weed? Now, would you do business with a place like that, or would you think that farmer is on the verge of losing everything? Or that, if he's too lazy to keep up his own place, he's not a man you can trust to work hard?"

Pa-Pa stared at him, his eyes wide.

"The fences on *this* ranch are all in excellent repair, and that speaks highly of you, Pa-Pa," Robby chatted on. "It tells people that you're a man who protects and maintains what's his."

Robby delicately ate some toast. There was dead silence around the table. Wayne stared at his plate and Roy exchanged an unreadable look with Clovis. Marcy and Emmie watched Robby with faces still anxious, but there was hope there too. Marcy nodded at her in agreement, just once.

Robby gave her a smile. "And! Sooner or later Billy and Paul and Missy, and all these fine grandbabies of yours, they'll be of an age to marry too. You know how time flies. And it *will* matter what people think of this family when they're looking for wives and husbands in Flat Bottom."

More silence. The clock in the hall ticked. Baby George started fussing and Emmie gave him another scoop of eggs on his tray to hush him up.

Robby finished his toast and wiped his mouth daintily with a napkin.

Pa-Pa was still silent, but his face was less blueberry pie now than strawberry cream. His eyes were distant and thoughtful. He didn't answer, but he did reach out to pick up his cup and take a big drink of coffee. His hand only trembled a little.

"Perhaps, Pa-Pa, you'd like to come to town with us this morning," Rowena offered sweetly. "I'd be happy to show you some fabric bolts that are sturdier than the dickens and not expensive at all. Why, I bet we could make new clothes for every soul at this table for less than twenty dollars."

"I'd rather jump onto a pitchfork," Pa-Pa said in a flat voice.

Robby laughed gayly. "Men! It must be in your blood to hate shopping. All right. I surely wouldn't want to torture you."

Pa-Pa cleared his throat. "Wayne, you take the gals."

Wayne blinked at him, his jaw hanging open. "You're gonna . . . You mean . . . Well, I can't, Pa. You know me and Roy are goin' to the horse auction today. We gotta leave right after breakfast."

Pa-Pa grit his teeth and looked down the table. "Clovis?"

Clovis looked at Robby and Pa-Pa, his eyes twinkling.

"I'd sure like to take 'em, Pa. But did ya forget that you, me, and Billy are bringin' in the south herd today?"

Pa-Pa frowned. He was working up to a hard no, so Robby had to think of something. He opened the drawstring purse at his waist and brought out a locket on a chain, handling it carefully. "That reminds me, Pa-Pa. I was wondering if you could hold on to this for safe keeping? It was my grandmother's and it's solid gold. It's my most prized possession in the world, and I'm always so afraid I'll lose it. I'd be grateful if you take care of it until the wedding."

Robby gave Pa-Pa a tremulous smile and pressed the treasure into his palm. His eyes met Pa-Pa's. *I'll be back.*

Pa-Pa licked his lips and tucked the locket into his shirt pocket. "Wayne, you hitch up that rig before you go."

Chapter Fourteen

Marcy and Emmie could not stop talking about it the entire drive into town.

"Lord, you about gave me a heart attack this morning, Rowena!" Marcy exclaimed, fanning herself. "I have never seen anyone go up against Pa-Pa like that. I'd like to have up and expired."

"And he gave in!" Emmie gasped. "He gave us twenty whole dollars. I can hardly believe it!"

Robby smiled to himself. Both Marcy and Emmie were as chatty as schoolgirls this morning. Both of them wore the best things they owned for the trip to town—the tan calico on Marcy and a faded green cotton dress on Emmie. There hadn't been time to modify Rowena's dresses for them, but Robby had added a big blue brooch and lace collar to Marcy's dress and a soft dappled knit shawl over Emmie's. They'd taken more time with their hair, too, worn back in buns with loose tendrils around the face. And Robby had even applied a hint of rouge on their cheeks and lips before they'd left the house.

They were so different than the resigned, mousy women he'd met upon his arrival. It was amazing what a little honest rebellion could do. Robby's heart sang to see it.

It also helped that Robby had bribed Billy into baby-sitting with the promise of store-bought candy.

"Of course he gave in." Robby flicked the reins to get the two horses to pull the rig faster. "Because he's wrong, and, deep down, he knows it. He's just never had anyone challenge him on it before."

"Well, you won't get around him quite so easy once you're wed up with Clovis, but it sure was a sight to see all the same," said Marcy with satisfaction.

"Twenty whole dollars," Emmie mused, shaking her head. "I can just see all the kids cleaned up and dressed in something *sturdy* and *practical*, like you said, Rowena. The sturdier the better when it comes to the boys. Last time I was at the general store, they had some of that new dungaree cloth."

"Dungaree pants for the boys," Marcy said happily. "And I wonder if we could make a dress for Missy from it too. Or do you think it's too stiff, Rowena?"

"It depends on what kind they carry. When we get to the store, we can take a look."

In truth, Robby wasn't adept at regular clothes. Putting together garb for Egyptian pharaohs, medieval kings, and French tarts had been fun, but he had no idea how to make children's clothes, nor any interest in learning. Still, any project that would take his mind off the Bowery Boys would be welcome.

But as they drew close to town, anxiety gripped Robby. He didn't think the Bowery Boys would be in Flat

Bottom—not by what Trace had said last night. But he still felt exposed riding out in the open, and his fear rose up without warning. The prickly heat of it cramped his stomach and his breathing became heavy. He pushed it down and lifted his chin. He would *not* be afraid anymore, not of shadows. He couldn't live that way.

But the town looked somnolent as they approached. There was no sign of any movement at all. By the time they drew up at the general store, Robby's fear had subsided. The Bowery Boys weren't here. He was sure of it. Still, his hands shook as he laid down the reins.

Beside him on the bench seat, Marcy and Emmie stiffened their backs and held their heads up high. They both descended from the wagon with exaggerated propriety.

From a house with a *Rooms for Let* sign in the window, an older lady came out and stared. So did a man at the livery stables, eyeballing them while wiping his hands on a cloth. Trace burst out of the sheriff's office at a near gallop. He slid to a stop on the porch, wearing an alarmed expression.

Robby ignored them all. He climbed down and tied up the horses to the rail while Marcy and Emmie waited outside the store.

"Go on inside. I'll be there in a minute," he told them.

With a nod, they went in.

"What the hell are ya doin'?" Trace hissed low, coming up behind Robby.

"Shopping," Robby replied with an arched brow. As if it were perfectly normal. As if he hadn't just been scared witless himself a minute ago.

"Ya should be at the ranch!" Trace's face was stony, but

there was a manic look in his eye, like he wanted to hit something.

"You said it'd be four or five days before you-know-who showed up. I needed to get a break while I had the chance, and I needed to do something for Marcy and Emmie. So here we are. Don't worry. I won't miss our appointment this afternoon at the cabin."

With a saucy wink, Robby turned and went into the store.

They took their time looking over the mercantile's bolts of fabric. It was a basic selection, but not as bad as it might have been. While they browsed, a dozen women decided they really needed something at the mercantile right then. Emmie and Marcy introduced Rowena to lady after lady until there was a small crowd gathered around the bolts of fabric on the back table.

"You're looking well," Mrs. Jones told Marcy, dissecting her and Emmie with her gaze. "And, my, isn't that a lovely shawl. I've never seen anything that soft-looking."

Marcy and Emmie exchanged a look. "Well, it really belongs—" Marcy began.

"The yarn is called mohair," Robby cut in smoothly. "That dappled cream is divine on Emmie. And doesn't Marcy look well in that collar? It brings out her lovely brown hair."

Emmie blushed and fingered the heavy dungaree cloth she'd been examining.

"You must be that mail-order bride who's marryin' up with Clovis," Mrs. Jones said, eyeing Robby dubiously. One of the other ladies gasped, and Mrs. Jones grimaced. "Sorry. I'm a plain-speakin' woman, but that didn't come out the best. What I mean is, I hear Clovis is gettin' married to a gal he courted through the post. Is that right?"

In Robby's head, Rowena took offense to the way Mrs. Jones said "mail-order bride." He tilted his nose up. "I am engaged to marry Mr. Clovis Crabtree, yes."

"Well, I'm sure we wish you every happiness." Mrs. Jones sounded doubtful.

A great deal of chatter commenced among the ladies. They apparently found the marriage as shocking and unlikely as Robby did himself. But a petite blonde in a modest blue skirt and white shirtwaist frowned worriedly at Robby from near the bolts of blue calico.

Robby leaned over to whisper in Marcy's ear. "Who's that?"

Marcy followed her gaze. "That's Miss Stubbens, the schoolmarm. Clovis had an awful hankerin' for her, but she refused to let him come callin'."

Marcy gave Miss Stubbens a glower, obviously defensive on Clovis's behalf. But Robby was intrigued.

They picked up a few pastel shades in sturdy cotton, then Robby left Marcy and Emmie discussing buttons while he worked his way over to Miss Stubbens. She was studying rolls of eyelet lace, two red spots of color high on her cheeks.

"I hear you're the schoolteacher. I'm Miss Fairchild."

The petite blonde gave a curtsy. "How do you do? I'm Miss Stubbens."

"Charmed, I'm sure. Marcy and Emmie mentioned you."

Miss Stubbens winced and looked away. "There was

never anything between Clovis and me. You don't need to worry on that account."

Robby looked at Miss Stubbens curiously. She and big, bearish Clovis would be an odd match in nearly every way, yet something about her gentle demeanor rang a bell. Clovis had a gentleness to him too. And Robby, feeling guilty that Rowena would leave Clovis at the altar, wanted to lay some seeds if he could.

"I haven't known Clovis long," he said slowly. "But I can tell he's a decent man. He works long hours on the ranch, has a real talent for woodworking, and he's spoken up for me to his family when it was important. He's ever so big and strong. Why, I doubt there's a finer fellow in all of Flat Bottom."

That wasn't a huge stretch given the size of Flat Bottom. And Robby wasn't counting Trace.

Miss Stubbens wrung the lace between her fingers, not meeting Robby's gaze. "It sounds like you'll be very happy, then."

That wasn't the response he wanted, drat it. It was frustrating not to be able to say what he meant. But Rowena would hardly push her betrothed onto another woman.

"Do you . . . feel quite safe there?" Miss Stubbens asked. She gave Marcy and Emmie a pointed look then looked back at Robby, her spine stiffening with determination. Miss Stubbens was trying to warn Rowena.

Ah. Now it made sense—the way these ladies acted, stiff and formal with something like pity in their faces, Marcy and Emmie's delight in being talked to. They must normally get a cold shoulder. Maybe their clothes were part of it, and their meek ways, but the bruises were part of it too. Trace told Robby the gals were not smacked around, and Robby believed him. The men and boys had bruises too. And Pa-Pa had been very angry with Rowena that morning, but he hadn't come close to raising his hand.

If he had, Robby would have punched him right in the kisser.

"It isn't like that," Robby said quietly. At least, he was pretty sure it wasn't.

Miss Stubbens studied his face as if trying to judge whether to believe him or not. The fact that she seemed so invested in the answer made Robby think she cared for Clovis at least a little.

Mrs. Jones nudged Robby hard from the other side. She was holding out a card of robin's-egg-blue lace. "Now, what do you think of this color, Miss Fairchild? This blue is all well and good, but I saw the most divine gown on a gal in Santa Fe once. I won't forget it as long as I live! She looked just like a peacock. The gown had midnight blue and emerald green stripes and this exquisite midnight-blue lace. It was richer than a navy but not quite a purple. Have you ever seen lace that color back in St. Louis?"

"Why, yes I have," Robby said in Rowena's peaches-and-cream voice. "There's a shop that sells every color of lace you could possibly imagine. They have lace that looks like real gold, shiny and all. And emeralds and sapphires and the most gorgeous black lace from Spain. Ruby reds . . . Pinks that would shame a rose. It's delightful."

The shop Robby was thinking of was in New York city. But no one here would ever know that. The ladies looked amazed and envious.

"I suppose now that we have someone from St. Louis

in our own little community," Mrs. Jones said leadingly. "You'll be able to get things like that sent to you from home. Whatever you desire."

"I suppose I could," Robby said thoughtfully. "As long as I cared to make the effort." She gave Mrs. Jones a challenging look, eyebrow cocked. "Now, darling sister Marcy, we simply must get some of this gray broadcloth for you. You have such an air of dignity, and this would suit you to a T."

They picked out yards of blue dungaree material and a heavy blue poplin for the kids, some bits of white lace for Missy's dress and all the accessories. When the shop-keeper rang them up, it came to nineteen dollars and ninety cents, so Robby tossed in some penny candy for everyone back at the ranch.

He also got a chance to speak to the mercantile's owner for a moment in private. He said the Silverton coach had been running surprisingly regular of late, why practically every single Wednesday. You could set your watch by it.

Chapter Fifteen

After Robby went into the store, Trace hurried a few doors down to City Hall. He went straight up to Floyd, a thin, middle-aged man with spectacles and wispy brown hair.

"Have there been any wires for me?"

"Why no, Sheriff. Not a thing since you checked last night."

"Ya sure?"

Floyd nodded his head solemnly. "Nothin's come in today at all."

"All right, all right."

"You want to send somethin'?" Floyd asked.

But Trace was already heading out the door. He went across the street to the saloon which had a second-story window that faced south. He jogged up the stairs and to the end of the long hall. He opened the window and stuck his head out.

The land around Flat Bottom, as the name implied, was pretty damn flat. The road to Santa Fe was visible for a good mile. And even after it turned at a clump of rocks and vanished from sight, you could tell if riders were approaching from plumes of dust in the air.

But the sky was clear and blue today, so clear the horizon went on forever. There was not a disturbance in the atmosphere anywhere to be seen. Trace listened. There were no sounds either.

Reassured that the Bowery Boys were not about to bust into town, Trace loped downstairs again. He tilted his hat at the bartender, Stan, and at a couple of men drinking at the bar. He waved away their offer of a whiskey and left the saloon.

He moseyed on over to the general store and leaned against the Crabtree wagon in a lackadaisical way, as if his heart weren't pounding clear out of his chest. The two chestnut horses, Bella and Buster, nickered at him, so he pet their noses for a spell.

Glancing inside the store's windows, he saw a clutch of ladies around the fabric table—Marcy and Emmie and Robby among them.

"Huh," he said out loud.

He'd been a Crabtree his whole life, so he was used to getting a lukewarm reception in town, even after he'd become sheriff. The townspeople were polite, but not overly friendly. He knew what they thought of his family, and especially his pa.

Now he watched "Rowena" hold court, chatting happily and holding up bolts of fabric to various ladies around the table. Trace figured the storekeeper was about to have one hell of a good day. A pang of warm and gooey feeling struck Trace in the belly. Damn Robby Riverton, anyhow. He was like a litter of puppies—loads of rambunctious trouble and just as appealing. And he'd no doubt leave just as much of a stinking mess behind too.

When the gals paid for their purchases and headed for the front door, Trace slunk off like a coward. He didn't trust himself not to yell at Robby or otherwise give himself away. So he watched from the chair on the sheriff's office porch as the gals loaded up a lot of bags, unhitched the horses, and set off again.

Marcy and Emmie waved to him, both smiling to beat the band. Trace wiggled his fingers back stupidly, confused as hell.

It wasn't until they were practically out of sight that Trace figured out the source of his confusion: They'd come into town without any of the menfolk. Robby had been driving the wagon.

Now how the hell had he pulled *that* off?

ONCE THEY WERE GONE, Trace knew in his gut what he had to do. He went into the sheriff's office and up a narrow set of stairs in the back that led to the room above.

He looked around regretfully. The room was plain enough. A wooden half-wall separated a space for his bed in the back. There was a woodstove and a sink with real running water. There were a few chairs, a small table, and a braided rug that Mrs. Jones had given him.

The first time he'd laid eyes on this place it had looked like heaven, because it meant he could move away from the ranch. Away from Pa, away from the endless chores, away from Marcy and Emmie looking harried all the time, away from the constant reminder that he'd never be like his brothers, would never have a wife and family. He loved his nieces and nephews, but they could be exhausting.

He wasn't like them, and he never would be.

He looked around the space with a sad feeling, as if he had to sell his favorite horse. With a sigh, he stoked the embers in the woodstove, added a dry log, and left the little door open. The place began to fill with smoke.

He coughed and waved it away from his face. A bit more. Just enough to make it unbearable for a few days. Hell.

Chapter Sixteen

Trace paced at the hunter's cabin, hands on his hips. Anxiety gripped him down low, even though he knew Robby had gotten home safely from town. He knew because he'd seen Marcy on the porch beating a rug when he'd ridden by the ranch.

Trace fumed. He was going to give Robby one hell of a talking-to. The one morning he didn't sit on the Crabtree ranch like a hen on an egg, and Robby pulls a stunt like that. Trace had been busy trying to get some plans in order. He should be able to count on Robby to sit tight for a single goddamn day.

He paced some more, then decided, in disgust, that he ought to do something useful while he waited. The tiny cabin had been built by Ansel Maynor years ago as a fishing retreat, but more likely to get way from Mrs. Maynor, who scolded that man to within an inch of his life. Ansel had passed away when Trace was a boy, and it looked like no one had used the place lately. There was an old broom in one corner, its bristles half gnawed away by mice, but Trace quickly swept the worst piles of dust and animal droppings out the door and beat some life into the old straw mattress and faded quilt set in a wooden bed frame. Other than a rickety table and two chairs, that was all that was in the cabin.

Land's sake, why was he even bothering with this? You'd think the queen was coming.

Back outside, Trace scanned the river bank and saw what he'd hoped to see at last—Robby walking toward him. Trace's mouth went dry and he got an awful swimmy sort of ache in his belly. Yet Robby strolled along, dawdling along the thick grass at the river's edge as if he wasn't in any particular hurry to see Trace. Despite the dress and bonnet, Robby's movements were sure and undeniably masculine. He wasn't even pretending now.

By the time he got close, Trace was ready to strangle him. He grabbed Robby's arm and pulled him into the old cabin.

"What are ya *doin'*?" Trace demanded.

Robby untied his bonnet, his face determined. "At the moment? Getting out of these clothes. God, I need one hour without skirts wrapping around my knees every time I move—and this blasted bonnet! I swear it was designed by Satan himself. I will be in heaven the day I can set fire to the cursed thing."

The bonnet was cast onto the table along with his lace collar and gloves. Robby reached behind himself and started undoing the buttons on his dress.

"What if someone followed ya?"

Robby rolled his eyes. "They didn't. This would go quicker if you helped."

Trace wanted to argue, but he could see a desperation

in Robby. And then Trace figured that if he had to wear women's clothing all the time, he'd probably just go out and stand in front of the Bowery Boys and beg to be shot. Besides, it was unlikely anyone else would come along. So he undid the buttons at Robby's back.

Robby stepped out of the dress. He wore long johns on the bottom and a thin muslin camisole on the top. "Oh, thank God!" Robby scrubbed his hands through his hair, which sent the smooth dark locks into a riot of curls and pokey bits. He rubbed his hands down his body with a shiver of distaste, like a young boy checking for leeches after a swim. "I have to be me again before I lose my mind."

Trace was mesmerized by this new "me," but he made himself go to the window and look out. There was no sign of anyone up or down the river's banks. This was an isolated spot, but he was still uneasy. "Sure no one followed ya?"

"Will you stop worrying? Wayne and Roy went to a horse auction, and Clovis and Pa-Pa and the two boys went to round up some beeves. None of them are expected back until dark. Marcy and Emmie are so excited about the new fabric and laying out patterns that they wouldn't notice if a buffalo herd ran through the yard."

Trace grunted. He finally turned and let himself really look at Robby. The undergarment he wore up top was a woman's, but its thin straps and see-through fabric looked erotic over Robby's broad shoulders and slim chest. His dark nipples were visible under the muslin. From the waist down, he had on a pair of men's white long johns. Those were far from alluring, but what they clung to was—slim hips, muscled thighs, and a serious bulge.

Trace's mouth went dry and his heart began a sickly rhythm like maybe he'd just up and pass out.

He was being ridiculous. He made himself focus on his anger. "I can't believe ya rode into town this morning, easy as pie! I about grabbed ya and locked you in my jail cell."

"Maybe that's what you should do," Robby said seriously.

Trace swiped a hand through his hair, frustrated. "I don't have enough manpower to protect ya in town. I said four or five days before the Bowery Boys show, but I don't *know* that for sure. Ya could have been— Christ, Robby."

Robby looked a little guilty. "Nothing happened. It worked out fine."

"Well, don't do it again! Don't. Leave. The Crabtree ranch. Again." Trace said it with every ounce of conviction he could muster. Hell, he'd tie Robby to a tree if he had to.

Robby's guilty look turned coy. "Why, Sheriff, I didn't know you cared so much," he said in Rowena's sexiest purr.

"This isn't a joke, Robby. Promise me!"

Trace wasn't going to let Robby charm his way out of this. The idea of coming across that wagon stopped on the road, Robby with his throat cut, and maybe Marcy and Emmie too . . . It was too hellacious to contemplate. He'd seen enough horrors. That might just tip him over into insanity.

Robby's face grew solemn. "I promise. Honest, I do."

Trace let out a relieved breath. "Fine. All right, then. Christ on a crutch."

Robby leaned against the wall watching him, his eyes

bright. He didn't try to argue or defend himself, which Trace liked. He seemed stronger today, more determined, cockier. Trace sort of liked that too.

After Trace had calmed down, he asked, "How's it going at the ranch anyhow? No one acts like they suspect anythin'?"

"They don't suspect. It's going all right, Trace."

Robby's voice was calm, and it helped settle Trace a bit more. With a sigh, he took his tin of cigarettes from a pocket. He almost offered Robby one until he remembered—Robby didn't smoke.

Robby rested back against the log wall. He had on those city boots with the long johns, which should have looked ridiculous but somehow looked damned titillating, or probably that was just Trace's addled brain. It was a bit cool in the cabin after the heat of the summer afternoon outside, and Robby folded his arms across his mostly-exposed chest. Trace resisted the urge to go and warm him up.

"Do you have any news about the Bowery Boys?" Robby asked.

"No. But I paid a boy to keep lookout up on Eagle Rock. He'll be able to see them comin' from a good two miles out of Flat Bottom. And I've got a friend in Santa Fe who's keeping his ear to the ground. He'll wire me if he hears anythin'."

Rafael the barber was well-connected in Santa Fe, so Trace hoped he could get the gist of what the Bowery Boys were doing without getting himself in trouble. He'd promised to send a wire when they rode out.

"And when they come? What then?" Robby frowned at Trace worriedly.

"I'll handle it. Don't worry."

Robby watched him, chewing his lip. He didn't have to say it—*what if you can't?*

Trace wasn't afraid. He might be a lazy man, but he'd never been a fearful one. He trusted his guns. And his brothers and Pa. They'd be all right. As long as the Bowery Boys didn't show up with an army.

Robby pushed himself off the wall, kicked off his boots, and pulled the camisole over his head.

"Hey now," Trace warned. He'd told himself he wasn't going to do this.

But Robby ignored him, pushing his long johns off to reveal a dark nest of hair and a long, soft cock. He headed out the door buck naked.

Trace followed, because of course he did. He watched Robby wade into the river, as eager as a child. He let out a big *whoop* and splashed water to the heavens. He ducked under and came up gasping and laughing, his dark hair streaming. He raised his face to the sun, smiling.

With a stab of pain, Trace understood. Robby's new defiant attitude, his recklessness . . . Trace had seen more than a few battles in his army years, and he'd watched a lot of young men chase life *hard* the night before—laugh too loud, drink too much, wrestle and carry on—right up until the morning when they were cut down.

It hurt so badly for a moment, it stole his breath. This is what he'd run from, why he never wanted to care about anything again, or be close to any kind of action *whatsoever.*

He let it hurt for a moment, the aching pain throbbing bright as a knife wound then fading out. When it was done, he peeled off his clothes and went for a goddamn swim.

Chapter Seventeen

The river had looked so crystal clean and welcoming on Robby's walk. He was anxious to get in it. The icy cold shocked his body but there was only a moment's breathlessness before the slick felt wonderful against his naked skin. It was like a baptism. When he submerged and rose up again, he was 100 percent Robby Riverton and no one else. Dear God, he needed that.

The river's surface was mostly calm here, dotted and dimpled with the current. It had enough force to drag against his skin, but not enough to knock him off his feet. He swam, broad, overhand strokes, first with the current, then against it. All the while he was aware of Trace watching him, treading water up to his shoulders. His expression was melancholy.

He looked so good though, with those bare shoulders, his stubble-roughed jaw, and his sandy hair darkened and slicked back. Robby was no saint and his willpower was in short supply. Suddenly he couldn't swim toward Trace fast enough.

He stopped an arm's length away. His feet found pebbled ground. He dug in his toes—smooth-hard rocks, the squish of mud. Every sensation was heightened today, every feeling magnified, echoing around in his chest, in his soul.

He didn't *want* to feel fatalistic. But the resignation that had taken root inside him made every breath feel important, something to be appreciated and savored, something that might never come again.

He watched Trace, memorizing the sight of him standing in that river. The water lapped at Robby's shoulders. His legs were going numb. His genitals felt floaty and shy in the cold. His toes got slimed in the riverbed.

"So. *Do* you like me without the dress?" Robby asked, smiling in invitation.

"You're about the best-lookin' man I ever saw," Trace said seriously, his eyes still sad. "Hell yes, I like ya like this. I'd also like ya done up in nice trousers, and a vest, and a shirt pressed so crisp it'd cut, like they do in the laundry in Santa Fe. I *will* see you like that someday, Robby, and take ya out to a nice dinner. Or I'll be damned."

The words were meant to reassure him. But Robby didn't want promises right now. He craved oblivion in the form of rough hands and a hard cock.

"We have time. This afternoon, I mean," Robby said firmly.

But Trace didn't attempt to argue. When Robby pressed forward, closing the gap between them, Trace opened his arms and pulled Robby in. He crushed Robby to his chest like he was extracting the essence from an herb, one arm a band across Robby's back, and the other gently cupping one cheek of Robby's ass. His kiss was hot and wet and filthy. And, *thank God*, this was going to happen.

The kiss went on and on, as hot as the water was cold. It was dizzying and desperate. In the same way he'd been aware of the muck between his toes a moment ago, Robby now was hyperaware of the silky hair of Trace's chest smashed up against his nipples, of the smoky, intoxicating flavor of Trace's kiss, of the strong thighs like iron under his, and the growing heft of Trace's cock as it came to attention.

Robby's own cock gave it a good try. But it was damned frigid in the river.

He pushed back. "Cabin," he ordered. Then he waded to the shore.

TRACE FOLLOWED Robby out of the river, his cock heavy and swaying awkwardly as he walked. He paused in the cabin's doorway. Robby was spread out on the narrow bed, one leg bent, one arm behind his head, and a hand on his thigh by his cock. It grew as Trace looked at it, lengthening and shifting to point straight as an arrow up his belly.

Trace had a fleeting wish for a real bed, or at least a fresh blanket. But then he was too busy looking at what he *did* have to give the cabin's shortcomings another thought. Robby sure was a sight to see like this, without the makeup or the dress, naked and wet. A week ago,

Trace wouldn't have thought a man like Robby was his type. His flat stomach, narrow hips, and long, slender limbs were boyish. But his shoulders were broad for his waist, and the muscle in his chest and biceps were full and tight. There were only a few dark hairs around his nipples, but a prominent line went down his belly and grew thick between his legs. His cock was long and ripe. There was no doubt Robby Riverton was a full-blown man. And a gorgeous one, by any standards.

In the army, Trace had met an eighteen-year-old recruit from Texas. Private Davies had been a stunning young man with black hair and blue eyes and a fair countenance. Cheeks like cream, lips like rose petals. Trace had felt a certain fondness for him, but he'd never thought to seduce the boy. He was too innocent, too good, and he talked about a gal back home with stars in his eyes.

Trace had never had anyone like Private Davies as a lover.

But Robby's beauty and youth were like that—and it captivated him. Better yet, Robby wasn't innocent at all. The way he was looking at Trace made it clear he knew all about the way things could be between two men, and he liked it. He was gutsy and strong. Smarter than he had any right to be. And there was that pull between them that came from out of the blue, but was mighty powerful all the same.

If Trace wasn't careful, he could end up building castles in the air over Robby Riverton, become as neutered as a love-struck steer. He refused to let that happen. But a dalliance on a quiet afternoon before things got ugly? He wouldn't deny Robby that. Or himself.

"You gonna just stand there and look?" Robby asked. He trailed his fingers slowly up his cock.

"All in good time," Trace drawled, proud that his voice sounded calm. As if he weren't sporting a prick as stiff as an iron bar.

Robby shifted up onto one elbow and let his fingers continue their seduction. "I haven't got all day. *Lawman*."

The throb of lust caused by those words reminded Trace that looking was all well and good, but touching was better. In a heartbeat, he was kneeling on the bed, half sprawled over Robby.

Robby looked up at him, eyes burning. "Damn, you're handsome. Thank God you have no interest in the stage."

Trace chuckled. "Forget the sweet talk and kiss me."

Kiss me? Why had he said that? He'd meant *fuck me*. Or *let's get on with the sex*. But then, kissing Robby was a singular pleasure. He kissed in such a delicious, filthy way. It stoked the embers inside Trace into a full-blown forest fire and made every part of him pull tighter, ache deeper.

This time, though, kissing wasn't enough, not with Robby naked and wet. His hands roamed, enjoying the firm-slippery feel of damp skin. He ran his hand up the inside of the thigh Robby had hiked up. His thighs were firm but the skin there was baby-soft despite the light covering of hair. The mix of textures fascinated him. From the round, firm flesh of Robby's behind, over the moist canyon of him, and the spongy-prickly texture of his sac, to the hot bar of his shaft, then back again. Trace's palm and fingers learned the textures like braille. And again. Again.

Robby's hips rose, seeking his touch. His hands clutched Trace's back as though all he could do was hold on. It drove Trace mad with lust. This handsome young man shouldn't be here, shouldn't be in Flat Bottom at all, yet here he was. And at the moment, Trace could only feel like the luckiest son of a bitch that ever lived.

Robby opened the floodgates on everything Trace Crabtree had ever found arousing. He wanted him in a purely base and carnal way. And yet the need dug down deeper than that too, like roots in the earth.

Robby groaned. "That feels good. But if you don't get down to business, I think I'll die."

He tugged again, moving his leg up and over Trace's back and pushing down with his heel. Trace gave in, laying heavily on top of him and grinding against his hip. A sweet shock of pleasure sang through his entire body.

Robby clutched Trace's ass to grind them together hard. He broke off the kiss and arched with frustration. "Want you," he begged. "Come on, Trace. Take me hard."

Trace froze even as his cock pulsed hopefully against Robby's. He wanted nothing more than to flip Robby over and pound into him. But . . . "I don't have any slick. Don't wanna hurt ya." His voice sounded like glass over gravel.

"I have some. Let me up."

Trace rolled onto his side, not happy at the interruption. He was high on lust, inflamed, and he didn't want to cool down.

But the view of Robby bending over his dress to fish in a pocket, and then running back to the bed with his erection red and leaking, was one Trace couldn't regret. It was like his eyes reminded his brain of why he wanted this so bad in the first place.

Robby put something in Trace's hand. It was a piece of half-melted butter wrapped in a linen napkin. A bubble of happiness climbed up Trace's throat and erupted as a laugh. "Oh, I see. Ya always intended to have your wicked way with me."

"It's helpful to have a vision. Now stop talking."

Robby leaned over and kissed Trace again hard, then he climbed onto the mattress on his hands and knees, looked over his shoulder.

Trace stopped talking.

The river water had left Robby clean and tasting slightly of iron and earth. Trace opened him with his fingers, taking advantage of this new angle to map out new textures of flesh and bone. He tasted the light fur on the backs of Robby's thighs, sucked the firmness of his round behind, licked the warm, soft sac that hung low between his legs, all while he slicked and pushed with the butter.

The butter tasted lovely on Robby's skin.

"*For God's sake,* Trace. Before I die!" Robby panted impatiently. He reached back with his hand to tug on Trace's arm.

So Trace draped himself over Robby's back. The head of his cock found that slick entrance, and he pushed.

God. Dear God above. He was tight and hot, slick and perfect.

Trace gripped Robby's shoulders and gritted his teeth. He let Robby lead, let him push and pull, squeeze around Trace's sensitive cockhead. It was difficult, but he held himself back until at last his balls were against Robby's, and Robby relaxed and surrendered beneath him like a hot mountain pool.

Then Trace grabbed Robby's hips and *took him hard,* pounding and circling and grinding in place and starting all over again. The moans and gasps Robby made sank into his ears, his brain, the tension tightening in his belly until he couldn't take much more.

He let go of one of Robby's hips to reach under him. Robby's hand was already there. He squeezed Robby's fist tighter and moved it fast, pounding into Robby in the same rhythm. In seconds, Robby cried out and seized up, nearly forcing Trace from his body with the strength of his contractions. But Trace held deep, deep, deep, as spasms of pleasure wracked through him and stars spun away before his eyes.

SOMETIME LATER, Trace panted against Robby's forehead. Robby's chin nudged his shoulder blade. He had an urge to feel Robby's heartbeat, so he covered Robby's chest with his palm. Rapid. *Bum-bum*. Strong and fast as a rabbit's.

What was this strange urge he had to touch this man? The awareness of Robby's skin, bones, and muscle. Craving things like *textures* and finding hair arousing. Liking *heartbeats* for Christ's sake. It was downright peculiar. Trace had never found such pleasure in the minute details of someone's body. He'd never imagined the blood rushing beneath their skin.

He probably only felt that way because of Robby's precarious situation, because he was aware of how vulnerable Robby was. Trace worried about Robby when they weren't together, and when they were together, he couldn't keep his hands to himself, no matter how strictly he told himself he would.

Or maybe Robby had bewitched him.

He considered the idea seriously for a moment. After all, who knew what Easterners got up to? But then he realized Robby had enough to worry about being a successful New York actor, a fugitive from gangsters, wanted by U.S. Marshals, and impersonating a mail-order bride. No matter how productive the man was, adding "witch" to his list of accomplishments was highly unlikely.

The thought made Trace chuckle out loud.

"What's so funny?" Trace felt Robby's smile against his chest.

"Just wonderin' when this fire in my belly for you is gonna let up, is all."

Robby sighed and rubbed his forehead against the hair on Trace's chest. "Not for a good while, I hope. I've never had anyone touch me the way you do."

Trace froze, unable to read the meaning in Robby's tone. He supposed his touches gave too much away, exposed his eagerness. Well, Lord, of course they did. Men didn't treat each other tenderly like this, didn't hold each other like this.

He sat up and pulled away.

"*No.*" Robby propped himself up on one elbow. "I'm not complaining. I've never felt so good in my life."

Trace was somewhat mollified, but he still felt the need to put distance between them. He got up and put on his pants, hung his gun belt over a post of the bed, just in case he needed it. He lit a cigarette and sat on the end of the bed, his back against the wall. Robby shuffled around until his head was in Trace's lap, his body splayed on the mattress like a rag doll. He seemed content to let everything hang out in plain sight.

Trace avoided looking at Robby's softening cock. It caused a low feeling of discomfort in his balls when his body tried to respond and couldn't. He also resisted the urge to card his fingers through Robby's unruly curls, and another urge to make Robby get dressed and hurry back to the ranch out of fear he'd be missed.

What a stupid situation. Trace was acting like a nursemaid.

He cleared his throat. "Ya should probably get back. What if they come lookin' for ya?"

Trace wished he could stop time, change the way things were. But the deck was stacked against them.

Chapter Eighteen

It seemed to Robby that Trace was always trying to get rid of him. He knew it was out of worry, but Robby didn't care. It felt wonderful to be in his own skin, and he was going to linger as long as he possibly could.

"I told you, the men aren't expected back until suppertime, and I told Marcy and Emmie not to expect me back before then either."

Trace took a long drag and held it. He didn't reply, but he made no move to leave.

"Besides," Robby said. "I'm not putting that dress back on until I have to."

"Is that something ya did in New York? Dress up like a woman?" Trace asked. He sounded merely curious.

"No. Well. I did have one big role as a female. Ophelia in fact. And may I say, I was brilliant." He grinned, and Trace smiled back. "But no, it's not my milieu."

Trace relaxed finally, slouching loose-boned against the

wall. He started to play with Robby's hair, which was lovely.

"There was a house I went to once in San Antonio where men dressed up as women. They sang and danced," Trace said.

Robby knew of a tavern liked that in New York. The show was amusing, and the performers were talented. Robby knew how hard it was to pull off a female convincingly. But that had never been his ambition.

"I want to play all the great male roles. Hamlet. Macbeth. Faust. There's an actor in New York named Charles Fechter. He's so commanding on stage, and what a magnificent voice! That's the career I'd love to have." Robby sighed. "Then again, Rowena is quite something."

Trace raised an eyebrow. "Ya talk like she's a separate person."

Robby shrugged. "All the characters I play are real to me. They have to be real in my head for them to be convincing. Rowena is especially vibrant."

Trace rubbed his thumb along Robby's jaw. "Ya must be quite a sight, up there on stage. I'd love to see ya in a real performance someday."

The idea of Trace being in the front row at the Burton Theater made Robby smile. Lord, he would love that. He'd love to show Trace what he could really do.

"Have you ever thought about acting, yourself?" Robby asked.

Trace snorted. "Hardly. Can't see me singin' and dancin'."

"There are other ways to be on stage. Dramatic acting. Plays."

"Can't imagine that either."

Robby nuzzled into Trace's bare stomach contentedly. There was a line of fuzzy brown hair that went from his navel to below his trouser line that was utterly mesmerizing. "It's just as well you have no ambition for it. If you were on stage, no one would notice me."

Trace looked down, his face serious. "There ain't a person alive who could cast *you* into shadow, Robby Riverton. I can't imagine you're ever in a room where ya ain't the most fascinatin' thing in it. I can't keep my eyes off ya. Guess that's what they call charisma. No wonder you were a star in New York."

Robby got a lump in his throat. It had been a long time since he'd felt acknowledged like that. "You say the sweetest things."

Trace made a disgusted face. "There ain't a sweet bone in my body. I'm just statin' facts."

"What about you? Have you always wanted to be a sheriff?"

Trace huffed. "Nah. I left home at seventeen—against Pa's wishes, of course—and joined the army. I only came back after I got wounded. I was shot in the thigh. The sheriff job is convenient is all."

Trace rubbed at his right thigh through the cotton. Robby remembered feeling a scar there, though he'd been too distracted at the time to examine it. And he'd noticed Trace had a slight limp.

"Does it still bother you?"

"Not much."

Robby took a heavy breath and took over rubbing Trace's thigh. "I was fifteen when I left home. There were eight of us, and I was number three." He laughed. "I think the first night I ever spent without being woken by a crying baby was in New York. And I could live without ever having to muck out another cow stall."

"Did they treat ya bad? Your family?"

"No. My parents were good people. There were just too many bodies, too much noise, too many rules. I wanted adventure."

Robby swung to sitting, the telling making him antsy. "Guess I wanted to see what I could do on my own. It's hard to be noticed in a family with that many kids. I knew I wanted to be an actor, so I went to New York City. Worked backstage until I got my break."

Robby felt a sense of pain at the memory. Those early years had been hard. Very hard. Many times, Robby had gone hungry. He'd spent a few nights in alleys with only newspapers for warmth, and many others sleeping on the floor in the theater or in a compassionate actor's rented rooms. And then he'd risen to such heights. Now here he was again, nearly broke and without a job. It was frightening if he let himself think about it.

"Looks like ya found more adventure than you'd bargained for just lately," Trace said dryly.

"Guess I did."

"Was the wagon train truly awful?"

Robby tilted his head, considering it. "Surprisingly, no. I never wanted to come west. But when I was on that wagon train, it was like . . ." He laid back down again, his cheek resting on Trace's thigh and his hand wrapping around Trace's waistband, just to have something to hang on to. "It was like I remembered that thirst for adventure I'd had as a kid. I'd gotten so caught up in my career I couldn't see anything else. You forget there's an entire huge world out there that doesn't care a fig about who's playing what on the New York stage."

Trace grunted. "Well. Can't say as *I* ever gave it much thought."

Robby laughed. "Honestly, I think I could fall in love with the West. There's something addicting about the open spaces."

"Got in your blood, did it?" Trace said with a smile.

Robby thought it was more than the West that had gotten into his blood. He traced the fur on Trace's muscled belly. Damn, he loved that. He wanted to memorize it. He wished he could draw a picture.

"Maybe it's not so awful if I can't go back to New York. Assuming I can stay alive and shake the Bowery Boys for good, I'd like to go to San Francisco."

"I had that notion once," Trace admitted.

"Really? You should come with me." Robby said it lightly. It was too soon to try to stake a claim, and he honestly wasn't trying to. But the idea of traveling with Trace was appealing.

Trace stiffened. "Kind of lost my yen to travel. When I left Flat Bottom, I wanted to see new places. Thought I was gonna be a famous gunfighter, only for Uncle Sam. I saw enough out there to know it ain't paradise."

There was something in his voice that spoke of dark times. Robby frowned, but he didn't probe.

"Anyhow, the quiet life suits me fine."

"And then I show up."

Trace smiled. "Yup. Then you show up. Trouble in a wide-brimmed bonnet."

Robby smiled too, but he felt stupid now for inviting Trace to go along with him. Why on earth would he? They barely knew each other. Robby changed the subject. "I still want to act. Hopefully I can get roles in San Francisco. I never wanted to do anything else."

"Never? How'd ya come up with the idea of actin' if ya grew up on a farm?" Trace stubbed out his cigarette on the wall and dropped the butt. He put both arms around Robby's shoulders.

Robby loved that Trace wanted to talk, that he seemed to find pleasure in learning about each other and not just in having sex. He snuggled deeper into Trace's lap. "Winter nights are long and cold in Pennsylvania. My mother entertained us kids by reading and acting out stories. We'd take turns playing various roles, half the time with dishcloths on our head." Robby smiled at the memory. "It was my favorite thing in the world. My older brothers got to an age where they refused to take part, but I never outgrew it. I only ever wanted more."

"I can't imagine growing up in a family like that," Trace said with a hint of envy. "Your ma sounds real nice."

"She was. Is. They came to see me perform a couple of times in New York. She was so proud." Robby felt a pang of longing for his family. It'd been years since he'd taken the time to go visit.

"When ya were a kid, what sort of things did you act out? Bible scenes?"

"No. We had a big old book of plays. Shakespeare and a few other things. My favorite was *Midsummer Night's Dream*. My brothers made fun of me because that was always my choice when it was my turn to pick. I loved playing Nick Bottom. I never did get to do that role on a real stage."

Trace grunted.

"And Romeo and Juliet too."

"Say somethin' for me." Trace asked so sweetly, and with such anticipation, that Robby obliged him.

He gave a huge sigh. "These violent delights have violent ends. And in their triumph die, like fire and powder which, as they kiss, consume."

Trace squeezed Robby's biceps. "Christ on a crutch. Your voice is like music. Like . . . like, I dunno, bells. And that sounds about like you and me. Fire and powder."

"Except there's nothin' keeping us apart." Robby suddenly felt unable to catch his breath.

"Except that we're both men," Trace said flatly.

That hurt. It shouldn't. It couldn't be truer or more obvious. But the way Trace said it, so final, with a hint of bitterness, it did.

Trace gave Robby's shoulders another squeeze. "Now come on, Robby. I need to get back to town to see if there's been any news from Santa Fe. And ya need to get back to the ranch where it's safe."

Yes. Robby's momentary reprieve was over. It was time to become Rowena again.

"Can we meet back here tomorrow afternoon?"

"Sure. But if ya have any trouble gettin' away, don't come. I'll figure it out."

"Believe me. When I want something, I can usually make it happen."

Trace gave a bemused shake of the head. "Now, that I can believe."

Chapter Nineteen

That night at supper, they'd all just gotten seated—Marcy and Emmie too—when Trace walked in. Robby was surprised. Trace hadn't mentioned he'd be at the ranch again so soon.

"Two nights in a row?" Clovis huffed in disbelief. "To what do we owe this miracle of nature?"

"What's the matter, ya need money or somethin'?" Roy asked.

Wayne said, "Bet there's some woman in town he's tryin' to avoid. Did old Mrs. Jones decide she needed a new husband?"

All the brothers laughed as if that was hilarious.

Trace shrugged. "Get used to it. I just moved some things into the bunkroom in the barn."

"Ya what, now?" Clovis looked astonished.

"Why would you do that?" asked Wayne.

"The stove got left open and it got all smoky," Trace said with a shrug.

"Ya moved out 'cause of *smoke*? Ya practically crawled

out of here draggin' one leg behind ya not a year ago!"
Roy sneered.

"I thought you were allergic to ranch work," Wayne
teased.

Trace's brothers gave him such a hard time that Robby
got a good idea of the distance Trace had put between
himself and his family. Only now he was moving back.
Robby kept his focus on his plate, pretending he had no
stake in this game. But honestly, it would be a relief to
have Trace nearby.

Then again, it meant Trace was taking the threat of
the Bowery Boys damned seriously. And that made
Robby's fear resurface in his belly like the fin of
a shark.

Pa-Pa, seated to Robby's left, looked down the table at
Trace with a knowing set to his face. He didn't seem
surprised in the least. "Will you boys stop chafin' your
brother's hide. Trace knows what he's doin'. Maybe he's
seen some cattle rustlers in the area. Maybe he thinks
they'll be comin' our way."

"Cattle rustlers?" Roy said in a disbelieving tone.
"Where have there been cattle rustlers?"

"Around," Trace said dryly.

"If cattle rustlers are comin', I'll shoot 'em dead!" Billy
put in, his "dead" sounding like "day-ed", which made
Robby smile despite himself.

"Hush, boy," Pa-Pa scolded. "Now y'all settle down. I
don't want Rowena to get the idea that any son of mine is
not welcome in my house. Rowena, guess ya already met
that scoundrel over there, but that's my third boy, Trace.
He was in the army and now he's the sheriff of Flat
Bottom."

Pa-Pa said this with pride, like he was introducing a celebrity.

Trace looked down the table and nodded. "Miss Fairchild. Yes, we met in Santa Fe."

Robby appreciated the cue because he wasn't sure what Trace had told his father. "I remember. It's a pleasure to renew your acquaintance."

Pa-Pa cackled. "Ya see how fancy she talks?" he told Trace. "I paid two hundred dollars to get 'er out here, and you can see what kindy class she is."

Robby gave Trace a wide-eyed look.

Pa-Pa turned to Robby. "Now ya might be wonderin' how it is that my third son is single and yet you're set to marry my fourth son, Clovis."

Clovis wiped his beard in a frustrated gesture, looking not at all pleased.

"Well, ya see, Trace there don't wanna get married. Not ever. No way, no how. Ain't that right, Trace?"

"That's right, Pa," Trace drawled.

"But he's not *entirely* a waste. He sure is a fine marksman. He was one of them sharpshooters in the army."

"Was he, now?" Robby said with genuine interest.

That shifted Robby's view of Trace a bit. He'd said he'd been in the army, but the word *sharpshooter* brought up a vision of Trace on horseback in uniform, aiming a rifle as he galloped along. It was not an unappealing vision.

"Maybe it's in the blood," Pa-Pa mused. "I swear, there's all kindy talent in the Crabtree family."

"Yes, I've noticed that," Robby said.

"Clovis, for instance, he's a good little woodworker."

"He is. He made a rack for my clothes. I've never seen

one so cleverly built. And Emmie said he made that high chair when Billy was born."

Down the table, Clovis relaxed. He even looked at Robby and offered a shy smile.

Robby saw through Pa-Pa. He was warning Rowena off Trace, and for good reason. He was obviously the "good-looking one," and poor Clovis couldn't compete in that arena. If Robby *were* Rowena Fairchild, Trace might well steal her heart. Hell, if Rowena were here, she'd probably throw herself at Trace with arms and legs spread akimbo.

Which was ironic when Robby really thought about it.

THAT EVENING, Trace had unpacked a few sets of clothes, his comb, shaving kit, and other items from his saddlebags, and was just sitting down on the cot in the bunkroom to take off his boots when there was a sharp rap on the door. It opened and Clovis walked in.

He stood there looking at Trace without saying anything, so Trace continued to remove his boots. He stretched his grateful toes and settled back on the cot, his back to the wall. "What?"

Clovis grunted and closed the door. He leaned against the wall. "What the hell are ya doin' back here, really?"

"Maybe I just missed your sorry face."

Clovis snorted. "Right. Hope it ain't 'cause there's a pretty gal in the house."

"What?" Trace scoffed. "Hell no." But his voice sounded false to his own ears.

Fortunately, Clovis didn't pick up on it. He took out a

bit of wood and picked at his teeth. "What do you make of her? Miss Fairchild?"

"What should I make of her?"

"She sure is somethin'." Clovis scratched at his scalp, though how he could even find it through all that hair was a mystery. "Ya should have seen it this mornin'. She told Pa-Pa she was drivin' the gals into town, and to give her twenty dollars to buy fabric to make everyone new clothes, and he *done* it."

Trace gasped so hard he choked on spit and commenced to coughing for several moments. He'd known about the shopping trip. But *twenty dollars*? That was a downright fortune.

Clovis nodded at him solemnly. "I know it. It's like hell froze over, but I seen it myself. Rowena said the kids hadn't a decent scrap to their names, and started talkin' about fences and what her ma always said. We expected Pa to lay into her, but he just backed down."

"Christ on a crutch. I've never seen Pa back down on anythin'."

"Me either."

"Plus, he let 'em go *alone*," Trace said. "I saw 'em in town." He'd been so upset, he'd forgotten to ask Robby about how he'd pulled it off.

"I know it. Rowena said they couldn't wait till Saturday, and how they had to make dresses for the wedding and, sure enough, she got her way."

Trace knew why Pa-Pa would never let the gals go to town alone. And he'd figured that paranoia ran deep. The thought of his mother still hurt. It stung in a peculiar way, a sort of bewildered way, as if every part of Trace had grown up, but that specific feeling was still four years old and just didn't understand. Trace didn't even remember much about his mother. It was more like he remembered the idea of her. Knowing that she had loved him so little she could just walk away—to this day he had a hard time believing it. As an adult, he knew better than anyone how being around Pa could drive a person to madness. He himself had run off as soon as he could. But that old pain was still there.

"What do you make of it all?" Clovis asked.

"I think Rowena has a lot of sand."

"Sand? What the hell does that mean?"

It was a word Trace had heard Robby use. "Gumption. Grit. Balls."

Clovis grinned. "She sure does. Wanna know somethin'? She scares me a little."

Trace snorted a laugh. Truth be told, Robby scared him too, but probably for entirely different reasons.

Then the fact hit him anew that "Rowena" was supposed to marry Clovis. Marry. *Clovis*. And all humor faded. He'd lain with Robby just that afternoon, had taken him in every way a man can take another man. And he wanted more, still craved Robby with a fever.

He felt like a heel. He knew Clovis's tastes, knew he wouldn't want Robby the way he really was, wouldn't want a man. He'd been female-struck from a young age. But it still felt like the deception was a sure-enough rotten thing to do.

"Do ya like her?" Trace asked, needing to know.

Clovis didn't answer for a moment, his entire face pursed in a frown. "I dunno. She's beautiful. And smart. But I can't see that she fits me. She ain't nothin' like Miss Stubbens."

Clovis didn't know the half of it.

"Once the weddin's over, I reckon I'll warm up to it. But . . ."

"But what?" Trace pushed.

Clovis frowned some more. "Aw, nothin'. Just don't wanna always feel I ain't good enough for my own wife. She's a bit fancy. Can't really see her bein' happy here."

Trace wanted to tell Clovis he was good enough for any gal. And he wanted to reassure him his bride would be lucky to have him. If this were any normal woman, Trace would buck up his baby brother. But this was Robby they were talking about, and that wedding was never going to happen.

"I think that's smart," Trace said carefully. "Not to get too attached just yet. She might not stay."

Clovis looked at him sharply. "What makes ya say that?"

"No reason. I'm just agreein' with ya, idjit. Smart to wait until all the chips are on the table."

"Somethin's goin' on. What is it?"

Trace just looked at him.

"You movin' back here is weird. Hell, I couldn't drag ya to the ranch with a lasso these past months. Ya said ya had to be in town of an evenin''."

"Stan's keepin' an eye out for me in town. Like Pa said—"

"Don't give me that bull about cattle rustlers. Tell me the truth, Trace."

Trace wanted to. He was lying about enough things to Clovis. Besides, his brothers should know what was coming. So Trace told Clovis about the fugitive on Rowena's wagon train, the Bowery Boys, Stoltz's slit throat, and about how they might come looking to question Rowena.

"I need to be close. And we need to get ready in case that trouble comes. Thought we should do some target shootin'. Maybe tomorrow after chores."

Clovis, surprisingly, was excited. "Well, hot damn! I always envied you goin' off to the army and havin' all that fun." He grinned. "Now it looks like a fight's gonna come to us, right here on this ranch. How lucky can a fella get?"

Chapter Twenty

Friday

Robby was helping Marcy and Emmie clean up after breakfast when he heard gunshots outside. Terror struck his heart and he raced to the window. He expected to see the Bowery Boys on horseback riding up the lane, just as he'd seen them coming up to the wagon train. But there was no one on the lane or the distant road.

He heard another shot and peered around. Standing in an open area next to the pigpen were Wayne, Roy, Trace, Clovis, and Pa-Pa. They were shooting at peach and bean cans arranged on four barrels.

A surge of relief rushed through Robby. The shooting *wasn't* the Bowery Boys. But as he watched the men aim and fire, it occurred to him that this wasn't a usual thing they did on a Friday morning.

Trace was preparing for a possible fight. Robby tore off his apron.

"Where ya goin', Rowena?" Marcy asked.

Robby pointed at the window and left the house.

Outside, he marched toward the men. He saw Trace step up to the firing line, which was a toed trench in the dirt. The cans were arranged in a pyramid shape with four cans in the bottom row. Trace stood with his hands open and hanging by his side. In an instant, he had both guns out of their holsters and *bang, bang, bang*—the heavy cans went flying. It looked like he'd hit one that had destroyed the pyramid and two more as they blew through the air.

"Oh, my stars!" Robby, in full Rowena mode, put a hand to his breast.

Pa-Pa cackled. "Ya see that, Rowena? Ain't that somethin'? Told ya Trace could shoot."

Trace slipped his guns back into his holsters and tipped his hat. "Miss Fairchild." There was a sparkle in his eye. The devil liked showing off. He probably knew what it did to Robby, who was never more thankful for voluminous skirts. Marcy and Emmie had begged Rowena to help with the sewing, so he hadn't had a chance to get back to the cabin since Wednesday. And his body missed Trace's like they'd been together forever instead of just one time.

Clovis stepped up with a rifle, put it to his big shoulder, drew a sight down the barrel, and aimed at another pyramid of cans. He took one shot, *bam*. He got the bottom middle can, which caused the stack above to slowly topple over.

"Now there, ya see? Clovis ain't so bad himself," said Pa-Pa.

Clovis blushed bright red, but he glanced at Rowena, obviously pleased with himself.

Robby gave him a smile. "That's very impressive, Clovis."

There was an exasperated huff from Trace's direction.

"I hope you gentlemen don't mind if I try my hand," Robby said.

"What?" Wayne gaped at her.

"Well you see, my father taught me to shoot. But it's been quite a few years. I'd like to see if I still can."

The truth was, Robby also needed to practice. If the Crabtrees were going to defend him in a shootout with the Bowery Boys, he'd be damned if he wasn't front and center shooting too. And stuff Rowena.

Marcy and Emmie walked up to the group. Emmie's arms were folded over her chest, as if she was not sure of her welcome, and Marcy looked curious.

"Well, now," Pa-Pa said. "I've always been of a mind that gals should be protected. No gal of ours needs to risk her neck while we're around. That just ain't right."

"And Marcy and Emmie too," Robby said cheerfully. "If they want to. We should all be able to shoot a gun."

"Now, Rowena, what the heck did I just say?" Pa-Pa said testily.

Robby ignored him. He went to Trace and held out his hand. Trace's eyes widened in horror. Robby could see the thought cross his face—not *my* gun! It almost made Robby laugh. But he just stood there, staring Trace down, hand out.

"I need to be able to defend myself," he said quietly.

Trace narrowed his eyes in warning, but he took one of his guns from its holster and laid the butt in Robby's palm.

"Thank you," Robby said with a sugary smile.

Roy and Wayne burst out laughing, but Pa-Pa didn't think it was funny. "Trace, what're ya doin? That's your *gun!*"

"It's a very fashionable sport, Pa-Pa," Robby said breezily, walking to the line. "Why, they have a ladies' day at the shooting range in St. Louis."

"They *do*?" Pa-Pa gaped.

Robby had no idea if they did or not. But he knew Jenny Daley went to the shooting range in New York and said a lady ought to be able to defend herself. She was known for keeping a little Deringer in her garter belt.

Robby aimed, arm straight out, trying to focus. His first shot didn't hit any of the cans. He tried again and missed. Now he felt like a fool.

Trace walked over. "You're holdin' it too hard. This here gun likes a light touch. Lemma show ya." He stood behind Robby, put his arm parallel to his, and wrapped his fingers around Robby's hand. "Loosen up your grip."

Robby relaxed his hand. This reminded him of another time Trace had wrapped his hand around Robby's fist and moved it. He swallowed hard.

"That's right. Confident, but not tense. Now squeeze."

Robby was a terrible, terrible person, because Trace saying "squeeze" made him stir down below. He gritted his teeth and put his attention where it belonged—on the gun. He squeezed the trigger.

The middle can in the pyramid shot straight back. The rest of the cans didn't even stir.

Roy let out whoops of laughter.

Wayne said, "By God, bet even you couldn't get that shot, Trace!"

"It was pure luck," Robby admitted with a smile. "But your instruction did help. Thank you."

"I'll set it up for you again, Rowena." Clovis lumbered over to retrieve the can.

Robby tried a few more shots and managed to hit the pyramid, though he never repeated that particular shot. He stood back and waved to Marcy and Emmie. "You ladies want to try?"

Pa-Pa came up and grabbed the gun from Robby. "No, now, that's enough. Them gals don't wanna learn to shoot. This ain't St. Louis."

"The gals do that other thing we thought they wouldn't like," Clovis put in mysteriously.

"That's true, Pa. And that's a lot more, er, rough than taking a few pot shots," Wayne admitted grudgingly.

Robby wondered what the hell they were talking about.

"I always thought we oughta be more security-minded," Trace put in. "Livin' out here, there's the chance of an Indian war party or cattle thieves or even army deserters. You know that. And then there's this other trouble. It's serious business, Pa."

"No, now, you hush up. I don't want the gals worryin' about that," Pa ordered. He gave Trace a dead-man's stare, rolling his tongue around in his mouth.

Trace pressed his lips tight. Robby knew they were talking about the Bowery Boys and the possibility they might come shooting.

A shiver went down Robby's spine. This discussion, and the target practice, was making it all too real. There were times when he forgot about the Bowery Boys. But, like a lurking wolf pack, they were still out there in the dark. The idea that they'd come for him *here* made him feel sick. It was one thing to be grateful that Trace and his brothers would protect him. That was a nice fantasy. But would they? *Could* they? What if they were killed trying?

Marcy stepped forward with a determined expression. "Trace is right, Pa-Pa. You men are sometimes gone all day with the herd. And we womenfolk have the children to protect. We ought to at least be able to aim and fire a gun."

Pa-Pa gave a frustrated grunt. "I can see everyone is set against me. Well, hell, if you gals want to shoot at some god-blame peach cans, I suppose there ain't no harm in it. But if we *do* have any trouble, the womenfolk will be hidin' in the house, and that's all there is to it!"

"Agreed," Trace said with a nod.

"Now can *I* shoot or are we gonna yammer all the live long day?" Pa-Pa complained.

He grabbed the rifle from Clovis, aimed it at the closest pyramid, and blasted the hell out of it.

Robby wondered if he'd pictured Rowena's face on that stack as he fired.

Chapter Twenty-One

That afternoon, Trace went off to town, so Robby worked in the garden. He craved time alone with Trace, craved the reassurance of his solid weight. And he needed the relief of shedding Rowena for a while. But it was hard for both of them to get away. And Marcy and Emmie were still busy with sewing, so other chores, like the garden, needed doing.

The July heat had killed off the more delicate peas and lettuce. But the tomatoes were going gangbusters and so were the weeds. Growing up, Robby's family had a large vegetable garden. His mother and sisters had mostly tended it, but he knew enough to tell a weed from a vegetable and when plants needed watering or were done for the season. At least while he worked, he was alone and could be Robby in his own head.

He'd worked for well over an hour when a shadow fell across him. He looked up hoping to see Trace. But it was Clovis standing at the garden gate. When Robby met his eyes, Clovis dropped his gaze to the ground.

"Hey there, Miss Fairchild. Ya all right? It's a hot afternoon."

Robby wiped his face with his elbow, feeling sweaty, then mentally kicked himself. He hoped he hadn't smeared his makeup.

"I am a bit thirsty." He stood up and swayed. The blood had settled in his haunches.

Clovis was there in a tick and he took Robby's elbow. "Here, lemma help ya."

"Thanks, Clovis."

Clovis steered Robby out of the garden and over to the pump. He worked the pump handle vigorously, causing a stream of cold, fresh water to spill out. Robby cupped his hands in the flow, took a drink, then dabbed some on his face. He patted it dry carefully with his apron, hoping there was still a trace of color left.

Clovis stood there, his eyes now raised to the blue sky as if looking for rain. Lord, the poor man was a mess.

"Wanna sit on the porch for a spell?" Robby offered. Because the porch was right there, its nearest corner in the shade cast by the house, and because Clovis could use a spot of kindness.

"Sure! That'd be nice," Clovis said eagerly.

They settled on the wooden boards, Robby closest to the house and Clovis a careful two feet away.

"My, it's warm today," Robby murmured, bringing Rowena to the fore. He fanned himself with his apron.

"Ya don't have to work in the garden, ya know." Clovis looked Robby in the eyes but swallowed nervously. "It don't seem like the kindy thing you'd like."

"Oh? And what kind of thing do you suppose I'd like?"

Clovis stroked his beard, his expression unsure. "I

dunno. Piana, maybe? Ya seem kindy refined."

Aw. That was sweet. Rowena thought so anyway. "Well, Clovis. I guess we all do what we must."

"Do ya play piana? 'Cause I could save up and get ya one if ya want."

"No, I don't play piano, though I've been known to sing a bar or two."

"Oh. Guess ya don't need anythin' special for that." Clovis hesitated, then spoke in a rush. "I had feellns for a gal once. Liked her so much my hands sweat every time I saw her. But she didn't want nothin' to do with me. I don't want that to happen again."

Damn. Robby got an ache in his chest. Poor Clovis. "Well. You're a nice man, Clovis. And that counts for a lot. But it's not everything."

He blinked, his brow troubled. "What else do ya want?"

If his tone hadn't been so honestly bewildered, Robby might have laughed. But he supposed he could take a few minutes to make some woman down the line a lot less irritated.

"Well, it's the way your brothers treat Marcy and Emmie. Wives are not slaves. Taking care of the house and garden, teaching the kids, putting up food for the winter, all those things that Marcy and Emmie do, those are just as important as your work with the cattle."

Clovis's face reddened, but he nodded slowly. "Every-thin's been so much better since Marcy come. Before her, the house was so awful bad, I could hardly stand to be in it. And we ate beans and burnt potatoes every meal. I do 'preciate what the gals do."

"So they should be treated with respect, like you men

treat each other."

Clovis got a devilish grin. "If ya knew how me and Wayne and Roy can fight, ya wouldn't say that."

"But you don't throw trash on the floor and expect your brothers to pick up after you and order them to fetch you this and that like you don't have legs," Robby said, undeterred.

Clovis's smile vanished. "No. I guess we do got bad manners. Trace always says so. But I don't rightly know how else to be."

Clovis sounded embarrassed and discouraged. Robby sighed. It was true that he could hardly expect fine manners when Clovis had never seen any. Well, any other than what Rowena had brought to the table. But most of the time Clovis was too shy to watch her.

Robby honestly didn't care about Clovis's manners. But if he hoped to win Miss Stubbens someday, he needed help.

Robby gathered up some leaves and rocks and sticks and arranged them on the porch between them. "This is our supper table." Robby shifted to face Clovis.

"That's just sticks and stuff."

"We're *pretending*. Now. These are potatoes," Robby pointed to a small pile of rocks. "And if you want the potatoes, what do you say?"

Clovis blinked in confusion. "Gimme them potatas?"

Robby laughed. "How about 'Pass the potatoes, please.'"

"Please pass them potatas," Clovis said obligingly. There was a twinkle of humor in his eyes.

Robby handed him a rock with a smile. "Here you go, my dear. Now say 'thank you.'"

"Thank ya kindly, ma'am."

Robby smiled. "Excellent! See, you know already. Why, you gave me flutters."

"I don't have to eat this rock, do I?" Clovis teased.

"No. I believe in penance, but that would be taking it a bit far."

They smiled at each other. It struck Robby that Clovis was not as unattractive as he had first appeared. His smile was nice, if a bit yellow. And there might be a decent face under all that hair.

"Tell me about this gal you liked. Miss Stubbens, is it?"

Clovis's face fell. "Yeah. But that don't matter now."

"She's pretty. I met her when we went into town."

Clovis looked down at the dirt. He tossed his rock "potato" from hand to hand. "I asked to court her. But she said 'no.' I reckon I shouldn't tell ya that. 'Cause ya might decide ya don't want me either."

He shrugged, like it was no big deal. But Robby could hear the raw hurt in his voice.

Ugh. Robby wished he could make this whole situation go away or resolve it neatly and tie it up with a little bow. But that wasn't possible. Rowena would be yet another woman who'd left him high and dry. Or horny and frustrated.

"If Miss Stubbens knew you the way I do, she'd be happy to have you court her."

Clovis looked at Robby sharply. "Do ya mean it?"

"When I saw her in town, I got the feeling she felt more for you than she let on."

"But . . . I'm marryin' you," Clovis said with a frown.

Robby swallowed a sigh. "I know. Let's just sit here for

a spell and you can practice courting me. Just be yourself, Clovis. Tell me something about what you want in life. Your hopes and dreams. And ask about mine. A woman likes to know you care what she thinks."

In truth Robby had never given any thought to what a woman wanted from a man. But Rowena had definite feelings on the subject.

Clovis turned red and twisted the rock in his meaty fingers. Haltingly, he began to speak. He wanted so little in life. A good woman to hold him, love him in the dark. Children. For the ranch to go on and on. For healthy beeves and a good crop from the garden.

Robby hoped he got all the things he wanted.

That night at dinner, Clovis said "please" and "thank you" for every dish, his face red. Trace looked at Clovis like he'd gotten heat stroke and Wayne and Roy made fun of him. They teased him by putting on high voices and simpering.

It was *obnoxious*.

Robby glared at them, chewing his steak slowly. He was building up to say something when Pa-Pa slammed his fist down on the table, causing all the plates and utensils—and people—to jump.

"Gol dang it! Can't you see Clovis is tryin' to impress this gal? You boys leave him be! Or better yet, learn a manner or two your own damn selves."

Roy and Wayne shut up and went back to their dinner. But Pa-Pa gave Robby a glower. "This ain't St. Louis. Just so's we're clear."

"Yes, Pa-Pa," Robby said meekly.

But he noticed Pa-Pa put down his jackknife and picked up his fork.

Chapter Twenty-Two

Sunday

O n Sunday afternoon, Trace waited for Robby by the cabin. He smoked too many cigarettes and wore a path in the grass with his pacing. His usual lassitude had deserted him. He was wound tighter than a watch. Robby appeared, hurrying in his direction, and Trace was disgusted with himself for the swoops of anticipation he felt at the sight of the man.

He had to get ahold of himself. This was plumb foolishness. He'd seen "Rowena" at breakfast that morning and again when they'd had another target practice. Yet here Trace was, feeling like he'd expire if he couldn't see that face—without the blasted bonnet. Hear that voice—Robby's *real* voice, which was surprisingly deep and melodic.

If he couldn't touch that skin.

It was a sexual fever, that was all. But it was damned

stupid timing for it. He forced himself to put on a poker face and greet Robby with a simple, "Hey."

"Hey," Robby answered, stopping a few feet away. He seemed to likewise compose himself. "I need to get out of this dress right this minute. And that isn't an attempt at seduction."

"All right."

Trace held open the cabin door and Robby slipped past him. Trace had brought a nicer blanket and a water skin in case they got thirsty. That seemed silly now, but Robby paid them no mind as he tossed aside the bonnet and collar and struggled to unbutton the back of his gray silk dress. "Lord, this thing! Help me, Trace."

Trace slipped buttons through fabric, his fingers clumsy in their eagerness. When Robby's creamy back was exposed, he couldn't keep from stroking it, from planting a sucking kiss on Robby's shoulder.

Robby made a strangled sound in his throat and wriggled the rest of the way out of the gown. He turned and wrapped his arms around Trace's neck, kissed him as if his life depended on it. He tasted faintly of tomatoes from lunch, and his tongue was hot and greedy. It made Trace's knees weak.

When he pulled his lips away to taste Robby's neck, Robby groaned. "God, I've wanted you. Seeing you at the dining table is like torture. And you were deliberately provoking me at target practice."

Trace smiled against Robby's ear. "Maybe I was."

Robby provoked him too, with a heated look now and then, or fingers trailed along the table or his arm. Not to be able to talk to Robby, touch him, or even *look* at him for long lest he arouse suspicion—that was the worst kind of frustration. It just made Trace crave him more, in a gut-groan kind of way, like another man might crave a drink of gin.

Robby pulled back to remove the rest of his clothing—camisole, boots, long johns. And there he was. A beautiful young man. Beautiful and coiled tight with vibrant life and purpose. Trace was struck again at how out of place Robby was, how twisted and nonsensical the paths of fate must have been to bring this elevated creature to lowly Crabtree Ranch.

Trace cupped Robby's face in his hands and stared at him for a long moment before kissing him gently. But Robby didn't want gentle. He sucked at Trace's mouth like he could eat Trace alive and tugged at Trace's clothes.

In seconds he was naked, and all of Robby's smooth skin pressed against all of Trace's. Pale olive expanses and dark hair at Robby's crotch and legs met Trace's flesh, pale where the sun didn't shine. The hair on Trace's chest rubbed Robby's brown nipples. Robby was shorter, but his long legs put his cock at a level with Trace's. Their rigid members lined up side-by-side, thrusting against flat stomachs, the spongy heads rubbing up and down steel shafts. Sweet pleasure rippled out at each push and pull while Robby and Trace stared into each other's eyes. The sensation was so arousing, Trace could have stayed like that for ages. But Robby pushed him back.

"Lay down. I want to taste you," he said. He looked tousled and dazed with lust, his lips redder now than they'd ever been as Rowena.

"Yeah. Yeah, all right." Nothing sounded more temping than exploring Robby's cock with his hands and mouth, up close.

"If you do me first, I can probably come off again when I do you," Robby suggested, flopping down to sit on the mattress and spreading his legs wide.

The sight socked Trace in the gut. He'd never get over how Robby could be so refined one minute and as bawdy as a strumpet the next. He fell to his knees, but he stayed back for a moment, drinking it in. His nostrils flared to catch the muskier scent between Robby's legs. The dark hair at Robby's crotch was shocking against his paler skin. His cock rose stiff and long and pink with a fat head fully emerged from his foreskin. His bollocks were large and distinct, hanging low between those slender thighs. Everything about the sight of him, smell of him, went straight to Trace's basest yearnings.

His mouth watered.

"The way you look at me, I could almost peak from your gaze alone," Robby said shakily.

"Don't. Not before I get to taste ya."

Trace took his time, kissing Robby's thighs and pulling his tender balls into his mouth one at a time to test their spongy weight, tugging on them with gentle suction. He moved one of Robby's legs over his shoulder, so he could give a nibble to the slight curve of his ass. The floor was tough on Trace's knees, but it was easy to push away the discomfort with Robby spread out for him like this. At first, he ignored Robby's increasingly desperate moans and the way he sank his fingers into Trace's hair and tried to tug him where he wanted him most. But finally, he licked his way up Robby's cock and took him in deep.

Robby's spine arched, his head thrown back, and he shouted Trace's name. The dewy moisture at his head tasted like the memory of a faraway sea as it coated the top of Trace's mouth and hit the back of his throat. He had to swallow away the desire to gag. It had been awhile since he'd done this, had a man in his mouth this way. He closed his eyes, finding the rhythm, drawing on Robby as he pulled out, slackening to allow him back in.

Trace wrapped his arms under Robby's thighs, cupped his hips. He could measure the effect he was having by the way those thighs began to twitch and then tremble on his biceps. Robby was loud in his pleasure, moaning and cursing, gasping Trace's name. The sound of sex in that rich voice made Trace feel every sensation Robby felt, until he was sure he would explode himself, untouched.

Then Robby grasped his head with both hands and raised stuttering hips. Bitter-sweet flooded Trace's mouth. He groaned around Robby's cock and held him tight, not letting him withdraw. He wanted to give him every bit of pleasure. He didn't let Robby go until he started to soften on his tongue.

He looked up to see a red flush on Robby's chest, throat, and cheeks, and a sheen of bliss in those green eyes. "Lord, I . . . That was the best thing I've ever felt in my life."

Trace grinned, feeling very cocksure of himself. "Yeah? It compares all right with those New York men?"

Robby managed a slight glare. "I didn't spend my days rolling around in bed, you know. But the few lovers I had, yes, you put them to shame. Now get up here and lay down. I'm going to start slowly because my heart is nearly done for. But I promise, I will give it my all."

He was true to his word. Trace was already so close that he welcomed the tease, even pushing Robby off a few times. But once Robby started milking him in earnest with that large, wide mouth, it didn't take long for the intense delight to overflow and shatter. And Robby's own hand, working between his legs, gave him a second peak moments later, just as he'd predicted. It was enough to make Trace want to do it all over again.

They slumped on the bed together. Trace was too relaxed to move until Robby pushed and prodded him to fully lay down. Robby reclined next to him, under Trace's arm, his head resting on Trace's sweaty chest. Trace felt his heart gallop against Robby's cheek. He might have dozed for a moment. When he woke again, Robby was tracing light patterns on his ribs, and the light through the window had turned golden.

The moment felt like a heavy thing, a step out of time, one that couldn't last and was all the more precious for it. He raised a hand to cup Robby's head and nuzzled his thick, dark hair. He smelled of pomade and of sex and of excitement—of things beyond the reach of Trace's plain, ordinary life. He felt a stab of longing and pushed it away sternly.

He wasn't going to pine over things he had no right to have. He was going to be with Robby right now and help him through the mess he'd gotten himself into. See him safely off to build a new, glamorous life somewhere else. And that was all.

Chapter Twenty-Three

obby traced nonsense patterns on Trace's taut ribs, feeling the peaks and valleys of flesh and bone. He felt at peace for the first time in days, and he refused to think about putting Rowena's dress back on and returning to the ranch.

The sex was great, but this sense of peace and the soft, warm feeling soothed his tired soul.

"How did you do it?" Trace asked.

"Huh? Do what?"

"Well . . ." Trace trailed lazy fingertips up Robby's back. "Today at breakfast I felt like I was in a different family. Marcy and Emmie sittin' at the table, Clovis saying please and thank you, *napkins*, for God's sake, and nobody threw crap all over the floor. How'd ya pull that one off?"

He sounded amused and Robby smiled against his chest. "I made it a game with the kids. Whoever had the least crumbs around their seat got a nickel. I ended up giving away three nickels. Worth it."

Trace grunted. "How'd you get Roy and Wayne to play along?"

Robby looked up and waggled his eyebrows. "I might have suggested that Marcy and Emmie could offer a more suitable reward if they won."

Trace barked a laugh. "Christ on a crutch. You're somethin'. Ya know that?"

"Rowena is on a mission." Robby settled back down again happily. "It keeps my mind occupied, I suppose."

"I thought you'd want nothin' to do with us after one meal in that house." There was tension in Trace's voice.

"You're embarrassed by your family," Robby said.

Trace snorted. "Wouldn't you be?"

Robby thought about it. "I didn't grow up with a silver spoon in my mouth. My family was humble." Though not, Robby thought, anything as wild as the Crabtrees. "Anyway, I like Marcy and Emmie. Clovis. The kids. Even Pa-Pa."

"Pa? He's the most pig-headed son of a gun that ever lived. He's always gotta have things his way, and he won't listen to a soul, no matter how wrong he is."

Robby considered that. "There was a stage manager at the Burton. He'd fight you tooth and nail about anything you suggested to his face. So you had to go around about it. For example, if you stood there looking at a big castle wall they'd built, glowing with admiration, like this"— Robby put on a look of childlike wonder—"and mused to yourself like so: 'Oh that wall is stunning! I can almost picture a real castle, as if there was an archway just there with morning light spilling through.' Why—" He snapped his fingers. "—the next day there'd be an archway with lanterns strategically placed behind it. You could bet money on it."

"Dear Lord. No wonder you've got poor Pa wrapped around your little finger."

"He's not that bad. He just hates to be criticized or told what to do. But if you give him a logical argument and let it go, he comes around."

Trace squeezed Robby gently around the waist. "Guess I ain't all that much better myself. I was such a rube when I first left home. Had a commander take a shine to me, General Armstrong. He'd invite a few of us to dine with he and his wife once a week. Everythin' was just like a picture book in his home. I learned a lot. I even got to speakin' better around them, not saying 'ain't' and whatnot. But bein' back home, it became a habit again."

"I understand. My brain is obsessed with picking up accents and mimicking them." Robby switched voices, impersonating Pa-Pa. "Why, iffen I was to hang out around Flat Bottom for long, gol dern it, I'd be sayin' *ain't* till the cows come home."

Trace's eyes widened, and he laughed. "Oh, Lord. That's funny. But please don't talk like Pa, or I may never touch ya again."

Robby grinned. "Sorry."

Trace smoked for a while and Robby lay there smiling. But then he had to ask, "Why didn't you do something when you came home? About Marcy and Emmie?"

Trace sighed. "I tried. I told Pa if he treated the gals that-a-way, they'd up and leave one day, like Ma did. He got so angry he nearly punched me. We never talked about it again."

Trace's mother. That was such a sad story. "What did happen to her? Your ma?"

Trace was quiet for a moment. "She went to visit *her* mother in Texas, and she never came back."

"I thought she ran away?"

"That's the way Pa likes to tell it. But Wayne says he remembers she got a letter that her ma was sick. She told Wayne she'd be back soon, but she never came home."

Trace's voice was flat, as if it were ancient history. But Robby had a feeling the damage done to Pa-Pa and those little boys had been deep and long lasting.

"What if she meant to come home?" he asked. "What if something happened to her?"

"I dunno, Robby. I can't fault anyone for wantin' to get away from Pa. Guess we'll never know for sure. I wish she'd at least sent us a letter. Somethin'."

"You don't think . . . . I mean . . . . I still don't get why your family is so prone to bruises," Robby hedged.

Trace froze up for a moment, then took another drag on his cigarette. "I told ya no one hits those gals. And no one hit my mother either. I'm sure of that, at least."

Robby shrugged. The few times he'd hinted around about it to Marcy and Emmie, they hadn't had a clue what he was getting at. But there was a closed-off edge to Trace's voice that said he didn't want to talk about it. Which of course made Robby more curious. There was something there, something no one was admitting to. He just didn't have a clue what it was.

Trace sat up and gave Robby a once-over, as if checking to see if he was still there, still okay. "I had a wire from the U.S. Marshals. They should be here by middle of August."

"But that's still three weeks away. And I'm supposed to marry Clovis on August first!"

"That weddin' ain't ever gonna happen," Trace said with calm conviction. "We'll figure somethin' out. The main thing is to keep you safe till they get here. After you talk to them, I reckon you can get on with your life."

Trace smoked his cigarette while Robby lay on the bed, arms over his head, thinking. Not touching felt like a wasted opportunity, though, so his feet found their way into Trace's naked lap. Trace held them with one hand while he smoked with the other.

Robby thought about what a strange period in his life this had been. Someday, he'd look back on it and laugh. If he was still alive, anyway. As crazy, and sometimes frightening, as it had been, he couldn't regret it. He'd experienced the West by wagon train, saw Santa Fe, and met Trace Crabtree.

Robby had a feeling that even when he was old and gray, these moments with Trace would be the highlights of his romantic life. And it wasn't just because Trace was handsome as the devil. He could be so gentle and protective. He acted lazy at times, but when push came to shove, he'd been there for Robby every time, from saving him, a stranger, from the Bowery Boys on the streets of Santa Fe, to moving back in at the ranch to watch over him. He was so confident and steely, intimidating even gangsters. But there was a thread of needful vulnerability in him. He touched Robby like he was a precious thing, looked at him like he was made of gold.

Yes, Robby could love Trace Crabtree. Maybe he already did.

"I've been doing a lot of thinking," Robby said.

"About what?"

"About what I want in life."

"Now, that's a dangerous thing."

"What is?"

"Wantin' things in life." Trace's tone was playful, but Robby thought he meant it.

Robby studied him. "Why, Trace Crabtree, you old cynic. This is the age when you should be dreaming those dreams and making them come true."

Trace gave him a wry look. "I'll bear that in mind. So, what are your dreams?"

"Oh, you know. Become a huge star in San Francisco. And . . ."

"And?"

Robby shrugged as if it didn't matter. "A family. I've realized my career isn't everything. I want someone to come home to. Maybe poor Clovis is rubbing off on me."

Trace's expression grew tight. "You want a wife?"

Robby gaped. "*No.* I want someone I can love completely, body and soul. Do you want women that way?"

"No," Trace admitted, looking at the floor. "Just men."

"Me too."

"Ya want to . . . to live with a man?" Trace's voice was tense, doubtful.

Robby shrugged. "Why not? There were men who did it in New York. One of the most famous actors in town lived with another 'bachelor'. Everyone knew they were lovers, but no one really cared."

"That may be in the theater, but it sure ain't the case in real life," Trace said with iron in his voice.

Another test of Trace's feelings on the subject and

another sound rejection. And, oh, but the stab of pain Robby felt was hot and fierce. "You'll stay in Flat Bottom, then, and marry a woman someday?"

But he thought: *Don't you know I could love you? Doesn't that matter at all?*

"No," Trace said. Then, more hesitantly. "Haven't really thought about it, Robby."

Robby doubted that. What man didn't think about it? But he didn't press, and he didn't miss the way Trace's hands grasped the arch of his foot more tightly and with a touch of desperation.

Trace was right. It hurt to want things.

"For God's sake, Robby Riverton, you have enough trouble!" Rowena's voice scolded in his head. *"How about you get clear of the Bowery Boys once and for all before you waste time mooning over romance? For all you know, you'll be dead in a week and none of this will matter."*

Rowena was right, confound her.

Chapter Twenty-Four

obby walked back from the cabin in a bit of a daze. His body felt relaxed and sated, but his mind tumbled with worries. The Bowery Boys. The U.S. Marshals. Disappointing Clovis. Trace's flat insistence that there was no possibility of them having a future, ever.

That sure ain't the way in real life.

Robby needed to put the hurt those words caused from his mind. This thing with Trace was a dalliance, that was all. God knew he was beholden enough to the man without acting like a spoiled child over what he couldn't have. But then, it was in Robby's nature to cling stubbornly to his dreams beyond all rhyme or reason. That trait had gotten him on the New York stage.

He was so caught up in his thoughts he didn't register the sounds at first. The path to the river was behind the Crabtree's barn, so Robby had to pass it to get to the house. But as he drew close to the large, brown plank building, he heard voices. Men's shouts, kids' excited jabbering. A loud laugh. And squealing. Lots and lots of piggy squealing.

Robby stopped in his tracks and listened. What the hell was going on? It was probably around four in the afternoon. The sun was low but not yet close to sundown. It was Sunday, the one day the Crabtrees seemed to take off work, so what were they—

There was a loud scream and a crash. Robby held up his skirts and raced around the side of the barn. He stared at what was going on at the paddock, unable to get the picture to make sense.

He saw Emmie, in a mud-covered old dress, standing just inside the corral fence watching something avidly and clapping.

Missy and Paul were outside the fence but had stuck their heads through to watch.

Baby George was crawling in the grass, contentedly playing by himself.

Wayne, Roy, Marcy, Emmie, Billy, and Clovis were in the middle of the corral, running around and they were . . .

Were . . .

Were?

Robby walked slowly toward the corral, blinking.

Squee-squee-squee. "Ha ha ha!" "Watch out, don't—" "You almost had 'em. Go that-a-way!" *Squee!*

They were . . . playing with the pigs. Robby watched, stunned, as Roy dove and the huge patriarch pig, Killboar, slipped out of his grasp. Killboar was covered with mud, as was everything in the corral. He gave a triumphant glare over his shoulder at Roy just as Wayne and Marcy tackled him from two different sides. Killboar squealed and flung himself around with powerful lunges, but Wayne and Marcy hung on.

"Hold 'em! Hold 'em!" Wayne shouted.

And Marcy was laughing *so hard*.

Robby, still not trusting his eyes, walked slowly toward the fence. Billy, likewise mud-covered, spotted him and waved, grinning.

Another pig must have stepped on Wayne's leg as he was being drug around by Killboar, because he let go. Then Killboar dragged a screaming-laughing Marcy a few feet and banged her into a fence post. When she let go, Killboar pranced away, nose in the air like he was the English king.

Robby rushed the rest of the way to the fence and knelt. "Marcy, are you all right?"

She smiled. "Oh, yeah, I'm—" She realized it was Rowena and she froze. A horrified look came over her face.

"Gol dern it! I told y'all not to wrassle before the weddin'! I told ya and told ya! Now you've gone and ruined everythin'!"

Robby turned to see Pa-Pa striding angrily toward them from his horse.

An hour later, they sat around the dining table drinking coffee. The ones who had been in on the fun in the corral had washed up and put on different clothes. Pa-Pa was tight-lipped and red-faced and Clovis . . . Clovis sat at the end like usual, elbows on the table, his big, shaggy head in his hands despairingly.

Trace had wandered back from the cabin too, arriving after all the fuss, and he sat beside Clovis, a spot of red high on each cheek proclaiming his embarrassment. He couldn't meet Robby's gaze.

"Y'all couldn't wait just a *few more days*," Pa-Pa said, disgusted. He shook his head and gave Wayne a wounded look. Wayne looked shamefaced.

"Sorry Pa. The gals said Rowena took long walks, so we figured . . ."

Robby sipped his coffee, pinky raised, and waited. Watching the family dynamics was like sitting ringside at a boxing match. Or perhaps "wrestling match" would be more apt.

"Listen here, Rowena," Pa-Pa began with an exasperated sigh.

"Um-hmm. Yes?" Robby turned to face him, eyebrows raised. *Do go on.*

"Now, I'm sure it's a heck of a lot different in St. Louis. Why, ya must have all kindy amusements," Pa-Pa put on a reasonable, lecturing tone. "But here on the ranch there just ain't a lot of . . . of . . ."

"Um-hmmm?" Rowena made an encouraging sound.

"Well, ya know. *Amusements* and such like. So's, we just . . . pig wrassle." Pa-Pa cleared his throat, his expression painfully awkward. "There ain't no harm in it! And it helps folks work the restless out of their systems. So . . ." He held out his hands and shrugged. "I know it's hardly a dignified, er, amusement—"

Pa-Pa needed some new vocabulary.

"But, well, I'm hopin' ya can find your way to see past it and marry up with Clovis anyhow. Ya have my word that no one in town knows about this, so no one will look down on ya for it."

"And you don't have to do it, Rowena," Marcy said,

looking like she wanted to cry. "Honestly, you don't. And I'm—I'm sorry. Emmie and me, we won't do it anymore either, if it makes you think ill of us."

The table fell silent. Everyone looked on pins and needles waiting for Rowena's decision.

Huh.

"So," Robby summed up slowly. "You wrestle pigs. As a family. And that's why everyone has bruises. And this is the big family secret."

Everyone looked at each other. Wayne gave a tight nod. Clovis let out a big, despondent sigh, head still in his hands.

Robby got a brief image of a revised mail-order bride advertisement. *WANTED: A gal with a fondness for hirsute men. Must love pigs!* He bit back a laugh.

It *was* funny. Pigs! Oh God! The memory of seeing Kill-boar dragging Wayne through the mud . . . . Everyone covered head to toe in mud and God knew what else . . . . Robby's mother would be absolutely *horrified.*

But then Robby realized that everyone, even Wayne and Roy, seemed truly worried that Rowena would cancel the wedding. Because they wanted her to stay. *Her,* not just "the mail-order bride." Rowena. He got a lump in his throat.

And then he thought: The pigs are an easy way out of this mess.

He could claim to be outraged. Ask Trace to drive him to Mrs. Jones's boarding house. Be done with this whole charade before he got even more entangled. Then he'd never have to tell them the truth.

But looking at Clovis's dejected, hopeless posture, and the shame in the ladies' faces, Robby just couldn't do that.

Robby—*Rowena*—shrugged. "Well. It's a little eccentric, I'll grant you. But anything that makes Marcy and Emmie laugh like that is all right in my book. However, I do demand a bribe."

"A what?" Pa-Pa asked.

Robby sipped his coffee. "Not now, because I'm starving. But after dinner, I'm giving you a haircut, Clovis Crabtree. That's my price for silence."

The brothers started whooping it up, poking fun at Clovis. Marcy and Emmie ran around the table to hug Rowena.

Pa-Pa said, "I knew ya had sense, gal. Knew it the minute I saw ya."

And from behind her, a hand landed on Robby's shoulder and squeezed. Robby knew that touch, even without turning his head, and he knew the message in it.

Thank you.

Chapter Twenty-Five

After dinner, the dishes went remarkably fast with even Billy and Paul chipping in, racing around the kitchen like little dynamos. It seemed everyone was looking forward to witnessing Clovis's torture as soon as possible.

When the last dish was put away, Robby set up a chair near the sink, laid out scissors, a comb, and pomade, and went to look for Clovis. He wasn't anywhere in the house or visible in the yard. But as Robby started toward the barn, he saw a flash of black hair behind the hen house, so he turned on his heel and went over there.

He snuck up quietly, stifling a giggle. With a yank, Robby looked behind the hen house and caught Clovis flattened against it, hiding.

"I was, um, watchin' for coyotes," he said, abashed.

"Is that right?" Robby cooed. "Well, even a coyote deserves a chicken dinner once in a while."

He grabbed Clovis's wrist and pulled him toward the house. Clovis could easily have yanked away, but he didn't. He came along meek as a lamb as Robby crossed the yard and marched up the porch steps. God, part of Robby had been dying to take shears to that mess of hair since he'd first seen it. It was so unkempt it was like a disturbance in the natural order.

He put both hands on Clovis's shoulders and pushed him down in the chair by the sink. Clovis's gaze darted around the room like a cornered rat. "Guess I could use a trim, but maybe we should wait till closer to the weddin'."

Robby patted his shoulder. "I'm of a mind to do it right now, so we might as well get it over with. Lean back."

He pushed on Clovis's shoulders, but the man didn't move, just looked up at him pleadingly.

"I promise it won't hurt," Robby said solemnly.

Clovis just rolled his eyes and groaned.

This was another trick Robby had learned in the theater. Sometimes actors arrived for a performance in the most appalling condition, and it was necessary to clean them up before you could even think about makeup and styling. So Robby knew the sort of bright, business-like attitude that best suited grooming other human beings. And he also knew that, no matter how much a man complained, they secretly liked having Robby's strong fingers massaging their scalp. Robby himself loved having a shampoo at the barber shop.

He had Clovis tilt his head back over the sink, and he soaked Clovis's hair with a pitcher of warm water. Robby still had a bottle of good shampoo left in his travel bag, saved for when he reached a town where he could do auditions. He decided to use some of that precious allotment on Clovis, soaping his head and scrunching around with his long fingers. The shampoo smelled of lemon and herbs, and Robby took his time working it in.

Clovis had plenty of height, and plenty of muscles, and plenty of hair—more than any single man should be blessed with. But, Lord, it was filthy. Robby could feel the dirt and oil caked in it. He rinsed and soaped again until the clean, coarse texture emerged under his fingers.

Clovis, on his part, relaxed further and further into the chair until he was practically a man puddle. His frown smoothed out and soon he was wearing a blissful half-smile, his eyes closed.

"I'd marry ya just for this," Clovis muttered.

The room had filled up with Crabtrees there to watch the spectacle. Trace leaned against the doorway to the hall, his expression unreadable. But the others stood close by and observed like it was a science exhibition. At first, Robby had to ignore the elbow pokes and snickers of the men. But as he worked Clovis's scalp, the room fell silent until you could hear the squeak of his fingers in the soap.

He gave Clovis's hair a final rinse and nudged him to sit up so he could towel-dry his hair. Clovis blinked, as if coming out of sleep, and sighed a huge sigh.

"See? That wasn't so bad," Robby said.

Clovis shook his head but didn't say a word.

Robby put a little oil on Clovis's hair to loosen the tangles and worked a comb through it, then trimmed it up considerably with the shears, cutting off inches of length and thinning it out so it wasn't so bushy. He used the simple method his mother had used and that he used on his own hair. When he was done, he scrunched up the drying ends with his fingers so they sprang to life.

Clovis stayed relaxed through it all, his shoulders

slumped, staring at nothing with half-lidded eyes and a pleasantly dazed expression, like an old dog having its belly rubbed.

Robby stood back and tilted his head. It didn't look too bad, if he did say so himself. But now the big bushy beard was even worse by comparison.

"Billy, go fetch me some shaving soap and a razor, please," Robby said.

Clovis gave a huff and shot Robby a wary look, but he didn't argue. Billy, his eyes wide as though he were witnessing some secret and arcane rite of adulthood, ran off like a shot. He returned moments later with a shaving razor, brush, and tin of soap.

"Those're mine!" Pa-Pa said, sounding disgruntled.

"Thank you for letting us use them," Robby replied sweetly. He was on too much of a tear to be distracted. He poured some boiling water from the teakettle onto a towel, added a bit of cool water, and wrapped Clovis's big, bushy jaw and neck before he commenced to shaving.

It was a bit like trying to cut down an ancient-growth forest, but Robby persevered. There was something satisfying about each inch of skin revealed. At the back of his neck, Clovis had a pelt that disappeared into his shirt, so Robby folded down Clovis's collar and shaved down to his shoulders.

He stepped back and surveyed his handiwork.

The whole room gasped.

Lord. Clovis looked a little like a newly shorn sheep. The skin on the lower part of his face was pale and soft next to the sun-darkened tone on his forehead and nose. Even so, the change was fantastic. He had a broad jaw, rounded with baby fat, and an honest-to-God cleft in his chin. Without all the fur, his shoulders looked broader and less rounded, and his brown eyes, with their long lashes, stood out like signposts.

Robby turned to look at the rest of the Crabtrees, wanting to get their opinion. His eyes went to Trace first. Trace's expression gave away nothing, but there was a spark of warmth in his eyes. Marcy had her hand over her mouth in awe, Emmie's eyebrows had practically disappeared up into her hairline, and the men stared at Clovis like they had no idea who he was.

Clovis stood up slowly and rubbed his hand over his jaw. "Heck, that feels kindy peculiar." He caught sight of the others and blinked. "What are y'all staring at, idjits?"

"Clovis, ya look wonderful!" Marcy said breathlessly.

Emmie nodded eagerly. "Why ya look so young and . . . and . . ."

The word "presentable" came to Robby's mind. But that wasn't exactly flattering.

"He looks handsome as a prince," Robby declared, wiping his hands on a towel. "Now then, I'll just clean this up."

Wayne stepped forward. "Would ya . . . That is, since ya already have the stuff out anyways . . . ."

"Me too." Roy scratched at his head. "I'm overdue."

"Well, I'm next," Pa-Pa snapped. "Cause I'm the boss. And 'cause I said so."

Robby laughed.

"Ro—Miss Fairchild, you don't have to do all that. This ain't a barber shop," Trace drawled, though Robby was pretty sure he wanted a shampoo too, if the frustrated tone in his voice was any indication.

"In for a penny . . . ." Robby said, waving Pa-Pa to the chair.

Trace was the last to sit down at the sink. By that time, Robby had decided that barbering was not a profession he cared to ever pursue. Clovis had been an intriguing challenge, like searching for treasure in a swamp. But Pa-Pa had been routine and by the time Roy was done, the task had become downright tedious. But Robby didn't really mind. He figured he owed the Crabtrees a hell of a lot more than a few shampoos and shaves.

But Trace . . . *This* one Robby was looking forward to.

TRACE SAT down at the sink with a huff. He knew it was foolish to be jealous of his brothers. But the sight of Robby-Rowena leaning over them and washing their hair had grated on his last nerve. It looked so intimate. He resented them for getting Robby's touches, as perfunctory as they were.

Funny, he'd never once been jealous of Rafael, the barber in Santa Fe. But then, he'd never gone weak in the knees over Rafael either. Or felt warm and happy to just hold him.

He was tense over such thoughts, his mind dissatisfied and restless. But when Robby poured warm water over his scalp, gently working it in, he looked up into those half-lidded green eyes and relaxed.

The life in those eyes never ceased to amaze him. The calm intelligence in them. The . . . kindness?

Yes, Robby was kind. He didn't have to be so nice to Trace's family. He didn't have to be sweet to Marcy and

Emmie. Trace had just about teared up this afternoon when Robby had dismissed the pig-wrassling.

If it makes Marcy and Emmie smile . . .

That damned stupid pig-wrassling. Trace had enjoyed it in his youth, but had come to find it a flat-out humiliation after he'd traveled the West. Why, he couldn't imagine what General Armstrong's wife would make of it. But Robby had taken it in stride.

Also, Robby didn't have to cut their goddamn hair. Didn't have to take care with Clovis. Trace wasn't sure how he felt about that. He didn't want Clovis falling in love with Rowena and he couldn't imagine Clovis wouldn't. How could anyone not?

The other family members had wandered away by now, finally bored, so they were alone in the kitchen. Trace grabbed Robby's wrist as he went to put down the pitcher. He held it and looked up into Robby's eyes. They gazed at each other for a long moment. Trace tilted up his head far enough to look around the room and make sure they were still alone. Then he gave Robby's wrist a brief kiss and released it.

"Risky, Sheriff," Robby said softly. He began working the shampoo into Trace's hair.

Trace grunted but fell silent, closing his eyes and giving in to the scent of lemons and the sensation of Robby's hands.

Lord, it was good. Robby soaped his hair slowly, turning the massage sensual, grazing over his scalp teasingly with his nails and rubbing his temples in circles with his thumbs. He wiped Trace's eyebrows with the soap, slowly, which was a strangely erotic gesture. Trace could imagine those slippery thumbs elsewhere.

He opened his eyes to give Robby a warning look. "Hope you didn't do that to my brothers." His voice sounded gravelly.

Robby just smiled. "Only for you, love. Only for you."

Love. Trace tried not to take that seriously. It was just Rowena's way of talking all dramatic-like.

Robby next massaged the soap around Trace's ear with his thumb. It felt like a tongue.

"Stop that," Trace snapped. "Or I won't be able to walk through the house when you're done without causin' a scandal."

"Now that you mention it, this skirt only hides so many sins," Robby agreed quietly.

Which made Trace glance at those skirts. They were eye-level and perhaps a bit fuller than usual. His throat went dry imagining what was under there.

Goddamn, why did Robby stir him so easily?

"You'll be the death of me," Trace said.

Robby didn't answer. He took his time with Trace's shampoo, then made him sit up and trimmed his hair.

Trace sighed as the scissors went *snip, snip.* From outside, he heard the kids calling and laughing. And for a heartbeat he felt a shift in time, as if this were years from now and Robby was cutting his hair, and they were in their own kitchen, kids that belonged to them out there playing. A stab of joy mixed with pain shot through him. That would never be.

"There. You look very handsome," Robby said, putting down the scissors and brushing off Trace's shoulders.

There was a hint of wistfulness in his voice. Maybe he'd had thoughts along those lines as well. Trace looked up.

"Come to the bunkhouse in the barn tonight," he begged in a whisper.

Robby glanced around. They were still alone.

"Yes, all right," Robby said, even though they both knew he shouldn't.

But Trace would be waiting for him. Hell, he'd be counting the minutes.

Chapter Twenty-Six

Tuesday

S ince he'd moved back to the ranch, Trace had been in the habit of riding into town every morning after breakfast. He'd check in with Stan at the saloon and see if there'd been any rowdy hijinks he needed to know about. Next, he'd check with Pete at the mercantile. And finally, he'd check in at the wire office. Normally, after seeing the wire of the day, Trace would sit on the porch at the sheriff's office so's folks could stop by and chat with him, see that there was still a sheriff in town.

He'd gotten impatient not hearing news, so he'd wired Rafael asking for a daily update and promising to pay next time he was in town. Rafael had obliged him. For the past week, his wires had been things like, *BB seen riding west this morning. Came back at sunset.* Or, *BB in saloon all day. Talking to hired guns.* Or, *No movement.*

Through Rafael, Trace had learned that the Bowery

Boys had settled on hiring the Durby Gang, gunslingers and cutthroats led by Dick Durby. Trace had heard they were sometimes hired out for "security," but more often robbed stagecoaches and wagons themselves. Then, two days ago there'd been a more ominous missive: *Two men found dead on the SF Trail. Throats cut. Rumored the BB done it.* Trace hadn't told Robby. He didn't want to frighten him any more than he already was.

That news wasn't exactly unexpected, but it was still bad news. Trace guessed the Bowery Boys were still tracking down people who'd been on Robby's wagon train, even people who'd fled Santa Fe. One of them was bound to talk. And when the Bowery Boys put two and two together, they'd be out for "Rowena's" blood.

On Tuesday morning he got the wire he'd been dreading. It read: *BB and Durby Gang heading to Flat Bottom tomorrow. Be careful.*

Trace stared down at the wire, feeling numb and cold.

"Everythin' all right?" Floyd asked, peering at Trace curiously.

"Yup."

"You sure? Is that the wire you been waitin' on?"

"Yup."

"Say . . . Is there gonna be trouble here tomorrow? I got my missus and kids to think of."

Trace looked at Floyd's worried face. He couldn't blame the man. "Just stay inside tomorrow, lock your doors. If trouble comes, it should just ride on through."

Floyd swallowed. "Yes, Sheriff. Do you . . . Ya gonna need an extra gun?"

Trace was touched. He doubted poor Floyd could hit the side of a barn. "No, Floyd. But thanks for the offer."

Trace left the wire office and went to the saloon. Stan was an older man, about Pa's age. He'd moved to Flat Bottom to buy the saloon when Trace had been away in the army. Trace didn't know a lot about the man except that he looked like he'd seen trouble a time or two and he didn't take shit from anyone. He was the main reason Trace felt comfortable leaving Flat Bottom in the evenings.

Trace sat down at a barstool but held up a hand when Stan went to pour him a shot. "No thanks. We need to talk."

Stan put down the bottle and nodded. He leaned on the counter.

"Remember I said I was expectin' some bad elements to come to town? Well, they're comin' tomorrow."

Stan's face darkened. "How many?"

"I'm guessin' six or seven, but I can't be sure till we see 'em."

"Whaddya want me to do?"

"They should be headin' for my pa's ranch. Hopefully, they'd just ride on through. Or they may stop and ask directions. Make sure you're around and you're the one they ask. Just point them right to us so's they move on. Or, if they want a drink or food, go ahead and serve them fast and see them on their way."

Stan grunted. "What about you?"

"We'll be ready for them at the ranch. But do me a favor. Carson Meeps is keepin' a lookout for them at Eagle Rock. He's to ride hell-bent for leather to the ranch to let me know they're comin' when he sees them. So, if ya can slow 'em a few minutes, that'll buy us some time. Don't do it, though, if they look like they'll shoot ya down for it."

"I got it," Stan said with a nod. "Delay 'em if possible, but don't risk any trouble in town."

"That's right."

"What about y'all at the ranch? Want me and Pete and Joe to follow up behind 'em? We can back ya up."

Trace had thought about that, about trying to gather a bigger force. But he believed he and his brothers and Pa could take care of it. Besides, there were other considerations.

"No. I want you three to protect the town. Again, I don't think there's anythin' they want here. But if a few of them come back from the ranch het up and ornery, it'll be up to you to make sure nobody gets hurt."

"Got it." Stan straightened up.

Trace shook his hand and went off to find Carson Meeps.

When there was nothing more Trace could do in town, he decided the thing he needed the most was one more quiet afternoon with Robby.

Chapter Twenty-Seven

On Tuesday afternoon, Robby got corralled by Marcy and Emmie into working on a dress for Missy. The time slipped by, and when Marcy mentioned starting supper, Robby realized he'd missed the window to go meet Trace by the river. At supper, Robby offered him an apologetic smile. But the look Trace returned was burning.

"You gals are gonna stay in the house tomorrow," Pa-Pa announced. "Breakfast needs to be early, then we gotta hunker down."

"What for?" Marcy asked, more curious than alarmed.

"Yeah, Pa-Pa. What for?" Billy asked.

"Can I help?" asked Paul.

"No, now, you kids will be in the house with the gals, and I don't want any guff about it! That means you, Billy. And you too, Pauly. I see one hair on your head, and you'll get a tannin'. You hear?"

"Yes, Pa-Pa," both boys grumbled.

Robby heard the words, but they sounded funny. His

blood had run cold, his limbs felt weak, and everything sounded muffled. Was this it? He looked down the table at Trace.

Trace looked back, his face grim. He nodded once.

Oh God. Robby was going to be sick.

"Everythin's fine," Trace said to the table, maybe responding to the panic on Robby's face. "Me and the boys have it all under control. But yes, we're expectin' some unpleasant visitors tomorrow mornin'. So y'all need to stay in the house."

"Excuse me." Robby stood abruptly, swayed. He left the table, unable to eat or even sit still. He paced in his room on the back porch. Marcy checked on him, but Robby resisted the urge to tell her anything. It was a long three hours before the household went to bed and he could finally seek out Trace.

He found Trace in his bunkroom. When Robby slipped in the door, Trace stood up from the cot and grabbed him, holding him tight. He felt so good, his vitality and strength. For a moment, Robby allowed himself the grace to just close his eyes and drink it in.

"I missed ya today at the cabin," Trace said, his voice gravelly the way it usually sounded after sex.

"Sorry. I didn't know . . ." *Didn't know it might be our last time.* He swallowed. "Are they really coming tomorrow morning? You're sure?"

Trace stepped back and nodded. "Yeah. I got a wire. They're comin', all right."

Tomorrow. Robby had thought he had at least another week at the ranch before the looming deadline of the wedding forced him to act. Now suddenly, time was up.

"Did they hire guns?"

Trace nodded again. "A bunch called the Durby Gang. Nasty lot, but there's only four or five of them I think."

Only four or five. The bottom fell out of Robby's stomach. He knew this day might come. But part of him had foolishly hoped the Bowery Boys would forget about Rowena, maybe follow the wagon train's path back East, looking for him in every small stop along the way.

"Oh God." Robby sat down heavily on the cot. "I'm sorry I'm so weak, but I'm terrified."

"Don't apologize, Robby. I know it's frightenin', but I won't let anythin' happen to ya." He sounded very determined.

Robby looked up at Trace, blinked. "I don't suppose there's any way they just want to ask Rowena some more questions?"

Trace shook his head. "We have to assume they know Miss Fairchild *is* Robby Riverton. They won't leave here without ya."

"I'm going to get you all killed," Robby said with quiet certainty.

"No, we've got the buildings. We've got advantage," Trace said. "There's not much cover on the lane. A few trees is all."

"Marcy and Emmie and the kids—"

Trace started pacing in the small space. "Pa and I reinforced the wall up at the hayloft with some chicken wire and boards. I'll be up there. And we put some bags of grain out behind the hen house to make a blockade—Clovis will be there with his rifle. We made another one across the lane over at the stand of trees. That's where Wayne will be stationed. Pa will be in the hayloft with me. Roy will be in the parlor so's he can shoot from the house. And if ya want, ya can be firing from the second floor."

Trace was going on about his plans, his body tight with energy. But it all went in one of Robby's ears and out the other.

"*Trace.*" Robby said it loud to get Trace's attention. Trace looked at him. "Maybe . . . Maybe we should send Marcy and Emmie and the kids away."

"Where?" Trace asked doubtfully.

"Well . . ." Robby thought. "What about that boarding house in Flat Bottom?"

Trace gave it a moment's thought but shook his head. "We need all the men here, and I don't trust Stan and the others to guard them in town. If the Bowery Boys knew who they were, they might grab one of 'em for a hostage."

"But they wouldn't know," Robby insisted, rising to his feet.

Trace shook his head sternly. "It's not worth the risk. No, they'll be safer here in the house. I can't watch them both places."

"But we'll be outgunned! Seven to six. The Bowery Boys are good, Trace. And heartless. And I bet those men in the Durby Gang are damned good shots too. Right?"

"No doubt," Trace conceded.

"Well? Your Pa and brothers are ranchers, Trace. And I'll shoot as best I can, but I'm not that good."

"Robby." Trace put his hands on Robby's shoulders, his face serious and his voice soothing. "Try to calm down. I was in lots of skirmishes in the army, and I know it can be hard facin' your first one. But trust me. All right? We can do this."

Maybe if his voice hadn't wobbled just a tiny bit on

"we can do this," Robby would have felt more reassured. But the truth was, Trace didn't know that for sure. He couldn't.

"There's still time for me to leave," Robby said quietly. "We could go tonight, you and me, take two horses and ride north."

"*No*. Then it would be just the two of us out there, without cover or backup. No, Robby. Our best chance is right here. We know the layout; we'll have the entrenched position." His face softened, and he took Robby's face in his hands. "Ya gotta know that I will do anythin' to protect you."

He kissed Robby then. And Robby let himself be kissed. Hunger rose inside him like a flash flood, obliterating his fear, arguments, and all his words, sweeping them all away like water from a burst dam. They clung together, pressed as tightly as two human beings can be pressed, kissing so deeply they might have been trying to crawl into each other's bodies.

Robby felt Trace's need hot and hard against him and he wanted it—wanted to feel every bit of this man, needed to have him inside and over and smothering him and—

He tore at Trace's clothes, not stopping until they were both naked. He begged Trace to take him and Trace did, slicking Robby up and filling him with possessiveness that was a little too frantic, a little too shaky.

Robby was unable to be passive. He rolled Trace onto his back and sat up, riding him with slow, rolling hips. Trace's expression was pained, and he grabbed Robby's hips to stop him. Robby stopped. They stared into each other's eyes, panting.

Robby reached behind himself to feel where they were

joined. He tried to memorize the sensation, inside and out. He wanted this so badly. His body was desperate to move. But he knew why Trace had stopped him. Because once this was over, it was over. And they might never—

Robby pushed aside the thought and the hot ball of sorrow that accompanied it. Not now. He didn't want to think about that now.

"I just want you to know," Robby said, his voice thick. "That I love you, Trace. I really do. And I know that doesn't change the way things are. But I just . . .wanted you to have that to keep. However, you want to keep it. And I thank you from the bottom of my heart for helping me."

Trace didn't reply. He pulled Robby down and buried his face in Robby's neck. But Robby felt the emotion in his hands as they petted his back and ass, grasped his hips. And he felt the heart of Trace when he began to move, driving up into Robby, and working them both so slowly and carefully, up and up, on their journey to the sun.

Chapter Twenty-Eight

"I've been thinkin' a lot about them fences," Pa-Pa said.

Robby jumped. He'd quietly let himself into the house after leaving Trace. It was dark, and Pa-Pa's voice scared the crap out of him. He looked around and saw Pa-Pa was sitting at the dining room table by himself. In the dark.

"Hey, Pa-Pa," Robby said.

"Them fences you were talkin' about. I never thought of it like that. But you're right. When I ride by a place where the fences are in bad shape, I feel sorry for the man who can't keep up his own land. And I feel all kindy proud that I *ain't* that man."

Oh.

"Only I never thought about it like ya said, with the kids and gals and all. Guess I see the point now."

"Well," Robby said philosophically. "Different people see different things. And that's why we're better off in a group."

Pa-Pa scratched his neck. "I was thinkin' maybe that could be your job around here. Ya can make sure the Crabtree . . . *fence posts* . . . never get too shabby-lookin' again."

It made Robby feel like the lowest of the low. He wouldn't be here to do any such thing.

"Though it shouldn't have to cost twenty damn dollars every time!" Pa-Pa said with more bite.

Robby smiled in the dark. "Yes, Pa-Pa."

"Yup. Guess we got into some bad habits after the boys' mama left. God rest 'er. And Marcy and Emmie, they're so soft-spoken, they wouldn't say boo to a lamb." He looked thoughtful. "Ya remind me of her a bit. Not that she was fancy. But she did have a way of talkin' a man around."

"The boys' mama?"

Pa-Pa nodded.

Robby wondered if he should be so bold, but he figured he had little to lose. "What happened to her?"

Pa-Pa said nothing, but his face pinched like he didn't like the conversation.

"You said 'God rest her'. She passed away, didn't she?" Robby pressed gently. He went and took a seat next to Pa-Pa.

Sadness washed over Pa-Pa's countenance, clear as day even in the unlit room. "Yeah."

"Why didn't you ever tell the boys?"

He hesitated, prodding around his mouth with his tongue. "My wife, Anne . . . her mother had that typhoid fever. And Anne got it nursin' her, and she died out there." He shook his head. "How do you tell four little boys that their mama's dead? I figured it'd be easier if they expected her to come home someday. And maybe I wanted to pretend she would. But that's the kindy lie that can get away from ya."

Robby felt angry for Trace's sake. "Trace, Clovis, and the others—they think their mama abandoned them. That she didn't love her little boys enough to come home. Something like that, it can make you go your whole life believing love has no more substance than . . . than a dandelion puff. It can poison you inside."

Pa-Pa scowled at Robby. "Hellfire. You sure talk a lot of bunk."

Robby shrugged. "You need to tell them."

Pa-Pa said nothing, just heaved an unhappy sigh. "Ya know, Rowena, sometimes I like ya. And sometimes you're just a big ol' pain in the behind."

Robby laughed. "Oh, believe me. I know."

He got up to go to the back porch, but Pa-Pa put a hand on his arm. "Just so's ya know, ya don't have to worry about tomorrow. Me and my sons, we'll take care of it. You're marryin' Clovis, so you're part of the family now."

Robby took a deep, shaky breath. "Thank you. Good night, Pa-Pa."

AFTER ROBBY WENT BACK to the house, Trace lay awake. He knew he should sleep. He'd need all his strength tomorrow. But he was so filled with thoughts and feelings, he felt like a young colt, unable to slow down.

I love you, Trace.

Robby had been emotional, that was all. Men said and did a lot of things that they wouldn't normally say or do when they were getting ready to go into battle. In a few weeks' time, Robby might forget all about him.

Except . . . Trace believed him. Robby didn't say things he didn't mean.

It surprised the hell out of Trace. He'd never expected to hear a man say those words to him. *I love you, Trace.* No, he surely hadn't. But then, he'd never met anyone like Robby Riverton. He didn't even know such a person could exist.

Robby was bigger than life. When he was in a room, he took up all the space. When he was speaking, or moving, he was mesmerizing. And it wasn't just Trace who felt that way, out of lust. Everyone else was just as taken with him.

His straight-shooting, lively essence was infectious. Marcy and Emmie had blossomed since Robby arrived. The kids loved him. Clovis looked like a different man. Even Pa-Pa was charmed. No one had ever gotten around Pa-Pa like Robby did. It was because, Trace realized, Robby always acted from a place of utter conviction and confidence, from a sense of fairness. When he spoke, he meant it. And he was smart, so he was always right too.

It was funny. Robby often apologized for being afraid. But he was the most courageous person Trace had ever known. Trace had simply grown disgusted with his father, with the way things were done at the ranch, and he'd run away. Twice. But Robby had looked at the situation, pushed up his sleeves, and he'd changed it. He'd stared Pa-Pa down, and Wayne and Roy and even the gals, and he'd made them do—*be*—better.

Now Robby said he loved him. The idea was terrifying. Trace admired Robby to hell and back. Heck, it was the first time Trace had really *had* a lover, not just someone to slake his lust with quick and fast while hiding in the shadows, but a true lover.

But being *in love*? To Trace's mind, that had always been a state close to madness, and it only existed between men and women, some crazy hoodoo nature put on folks to get them to marry up. Trace figured it had more to do with the backed-up lust of courting a lady than anything else. But whatever it was, it wasn't for him.

Sure, Robby made Trace's chest ache and his body yearn. He made Trace do stupid things, take chances, feel on fire with purpose again, filled him with an energy he'd believed he'd never find again. But that was lust, surely. He lusted for Robby something terrible. And he admired him. And he liked him. But all that didn't add up to love.

What was love, anyhow?

Whatever it was, it wasn't for men like him. That was just how it was.

Funny, though, he could imagine love being for a man like Robby. He was so good with the family. He deserved one of his own. And he'd make a wonderful roommate or partner or whatever they'd call it—he was good at all that household stuff. He'd be the person you'd want on your side in a crisis. Or when you got old. Or were injured, as Trace had been. Because Robby knew how to get things done and make burdens light. Plus, Robby had the strength and confidence to thumb his nose at society's expectations. He'd do what he wanted to do, regardless.

Yeah, Trace bet someday Robby would meet a man he could live such a life with, maybe in a city somewhere, where they could get lost in the shuffle of bodies and goings-on. Have their own private home and . . . be happy.

That would be one lucky man.

The idea that Robby might find that someday, with someone else, caused such an awful, crushing feeling that Trace had to stop that line of thought dead.

No. No point dwelling on shit that he couldn't change. They had enough troubles right here and right now. Trace had to focus on the next twenty-four hours and keeping Robby and his family safe. And for that he needed a few hours rest at least.

Chapter Twenty-Nine

Wednesday morning

R obby couldn't sleep. He went back and forth in his mind about what he should do, a frustrating loop that ground down his spirits and gave him a temple-throbbing headache.

The Bowery Boys were coming, and they'd hired gunmen. At least six hardened killers were coming to the ranch, and they'd attempt to cut down anyone who got between them and Robby.

Trace said he had a plan. He said the women and children would be safe. But Robby didn't see how they could be. If bullets were flying at the ranch, everyone was in danger.

Robby tried to imagine it. The intruders would be in the open, Trace and Pa-Pa and the others arrayed around the lane. But what if the men split up and went in six different directions? What if one of them circled back around? Approached the house from near the privy and woods? Robby could be in a back window with a gun. But what if the man saw him there and took him out without the men in front being any the wiser? Who would protect the women and children then? Robby was willing to fight to the death, but he knew in his heart he was no match for a professional gunslinger.

A deep sense of fear and foreboding grew inside him, spreading out from the region of his bowels. Dread caused bits of ice to prickle in his stomach, in his throat.

He was afraid for his own life, of course he was. He didn't want to die. But he couldn't imagine the guilt he'd feel if Marcy was hurt. Or young Billy. Or baby George . . .

Or Pa-Pa. Or Clovis.

Or Trace.

The idea that *any* of them might die for his sake was unbearable. A noose of guilt tightened around his chest. They didn't even know who he was. Only Trace knew. If the Crabtrees fought for Rowena, died for her, they'd be doing it under false pretenses. They'd be doing it to protect Clovis's wife, a daughter-in-law, a fellow sister, a person who was an illusion, a ghost. Robby's life would never be on the Crabtree ranch. He'd never be that person.

He'd tried to express that to Trace multiple times, but Trace just acted like he had it all under control, that this was the best option. But how could he *know* that? He couldn't.

And if Robby caused the death of a member of Trace's family, how long would it be before Trace began to hate Robby too?

It was around four a.m. when he got out of bed. He lit the lantern and went through the house noiselessly, his bare feet cold on the chilly floor. There was a small room where they kept the laundry supplies—a tub, wringer, and clothesline, as well as a basket of castoffs and items to be repaired. Robby found an old gray dress and tattered apron of Emmie's. He also grabbed an old pair of chamois gloves used for dusting and found a mob cap. From the row of pegs in the front hall where coats were hung, he took a beat-up old cane he'd noticed before, one Trace had used when he'd come home from the army wounded.

Back in his room, Robby took out his stage makeup and set the lantern next to a mirror. He looked himself in the eye for a long moment. This was it. Once he did the makeup, it would be hard to back out.

He nodded at his reflection and began to work. He used spirit gum to pucker the flesh around his eyes and on his cheeks. Light and dark pencils created the illusion of deep wrinkles from his nose to his mouth, around his eyes, and on his forehead. A gray tint hollowed his eyes and disguised their bright youthfulness. Finally, he threaded his hair with white powder and put the mob cap in place.

An old woman looked back at him from the mirror. *Mother Harper*, he named her. In the lantern glow, she was convincing. But he would have to sell her in the broad light of day.

Robby put a few items in a carpetbag—his own clothes, his makeup kit, his remaining cash. He wrote a letter with some stationary from Rowena's trunk. He absolutely did not shed a tear over it. He left the back porch and circled around the outside of the house to the barn. This was the trickiest part. He had to get a horse saddled and out of the barn without waking Trace. The bunkroom was on the other side of the barn, but Trace was probably a light sleeper.

Robby now knew where they kept the key to the tack room—at the top of a tall doorway. He found a saddle and took Bella from the barn and tied her to the corral, then went and got the saddle as quietly as he could. He put back the key.

Out in the pre-dawn air, he saddled the horse and led her through the soft dirt at the side of the lane until he was far enough away to risk mounting her.

As he rode away, he looked back. There was no sound or movement anywhere. The Crabtrees slept. Robby felt a pang of regret that Trace hadn't caught him, hadn't stopped him. But it was only a moment of weakness. Robby rode away.

When he reached Flat Bottom, the little town was not yet stirring. The glow of a lantern lit only one solitary window. Robby tied up Bella at the general store where the Crabtrees would find her and walked to the schoolhouse at the end of town. He sat on the steps to wait for dawn. A strategically placed willow tree kept him from being too obvious to anyone who might walk about the sleepy town, while allowing him to keep a lookout for the stagecoach. And if the Bowery Boys rode in, he'd see them and be able to slip around the side of the building and find someplace to hide before he was noticed.

He just prayed no one at the Crabtree ranch discovered his letter too soon—and that the stagecoach showed up on time. His stomach was in knots and he was filled with doubt. Was he doing the right thing? Or was he making a huge mistake?

But it was too late for second thoughts now. He had to have confidence in his plan.

The sun was rising when the stagecoach rolled out of the livery stable and over to the general store. Robby got up and walked toward it with his shoulders hunched over. He faked a hobble and leaned heavily on the cane. He shrouded himself in Mother Harper, becoming the role. Before he reached the coach, he saw a young couple cross the street from Mrs. Jones's establishment with several bags.

Robby waited until the couple had settled their fare and their bags had been secured on top of the coach. The driver, an older man with exorbitant blond mutton chops, an old blue army cap, and a tweed coat, hopped down and turned to Robby.

"Yes, ma'am, and how can I help you?"

"One way to Silverton, please," Mother Harper said, her voice shaky with age.

"Sorry, ma'am. This coach is goin' to Santa Fe."

Robby's heart gave a meaty *thump*. "But . . . it's Wednesday! I was told Wednesday's coach went east to Silverton."

"Well, now, it does normally." The coachman scratched his chin. "Normally, I would have taken the Santa Fe run *Saturday*. But, see, Saturday's coach was delayed, so it's leaving today."

"What about the Silverton coach?"

"Ah, I don't think that's gonna happen this week." The man sounded vaguely apologetic. "But they might go next Wednesday."

"Next—!" Robby stopped himself before he could go into a full-on rant.

"If you wanna go to Santa Fe, that's two dollars. I'm leavin' in ten minutes." The coachman checked his watch, then strolled off for a smoke.

Santa Fe.

Of course, Robby wasn't going to Santa Fe! But what other option did he have? If he went back to the ranch now, the Crabtrees would be stirring by the time he got there. And how could he explain the makeup, dress, and mob cap? Or why he'd left in the first place?

And besides, then he'd be right back where he started—endangering the Crabtrees.

Could he go to Santa Fe? He rolled it around in his mind. The Bowery Boys were heading to Flat Bottom. The stagecoach might not even pass them on the way—if the gang went off road, not wanting to be seen. Or if they did ride past, why would they stop the stagecoach? They expected to find Rowena Fairchild at the ranch. And even if they *did* stop the stagecoach, they were looking for Robby or Rowena. They weren't looking for an old woman.

It was a daring move to head right in their direction. Hiding in plain sight, as it were. Maybe that was smart?

No, it wasn't smart; it was terrifying. But Robby was going to do it. He had to trust in himself, in his disguise.

When the coach pulled out ten minutes later, Mother Harper was on it.

Chapter Thirty

Trace slept deeply. He figured the Bowery Boys and their thugs-for-hire wouldn't get to the ranch until eight o'clock at the earliest, and he'd get a warning from Carson Meeps they were on their way. He'd made his plans; everything was ready. So he set his internal clock for six. But it was Clovis who shook him awake around then.

After only a few seconds to orient himself, Trace sat up, anxious. "What is it? Is Carson here?"

"Rowena's gone." Clovis's expression was grim.

"*What?*"

"She left a note. Come to the house."

Clovis walked out. Trace yanked on his clothes as quickly as he could, strapped on his gun belt just in case, then jogged over to the ranch house. His mouth was dry, and his heart hammered an uncertain tune. Clovis couldn't be right. Robby wouldn't have done something that stupid. Would he? Trace glanced down the farm lane as he passed it. The sky was pink at the horizon and dim light was creeping across the landscape. But the air was clear and visibility good. No one was coming or going.

Inside, Trace found Clovis, Wayne, Roy, Marcy, Emmie, and Pa-Pa in the kitchen. They all looked worried.

"She left a note," Marcy said, holding it out.

Trace grabbed it and read.

Dear Crabtree family:

I will get right to the point. I am leaving to spare you the coming fight. This battle is mine and mine alone. You have offered me shelter—shelter and kindness and your friendship, and I will never forget it. But for that reason alone, I can't bring danger to your doorstep. I just can't.

Trace will no doubt say I'm being incredibly stupid. And maybe I am. But my parents raised me to know right from wrong. And bringing a gang of murderers onto your heads to save my own skin is wrong. And Trace, please understand that it's not that I don't trust you, or think you aren't the most wicked gun in the west. But I care too much to see you risk death for my sake. Or for your family to risk it. They would be fighting for me under false pretenses, and that's not right.

Please don't worry. I'll write to you as soon as I can, so you know I'm safe. I've grown to care about each of you, and I will always remember my time at the Crabtree ranch.

With abiding friendship,

Rowena (Robby)

"That gal up and left!" Pa bellowed angrily. "After all we done for her, and all the ways I tried to please her, that gal up and hightailed it outta here!"

"It's because of those men, Pa," Clovis said in a down-trodden voice. "She's just tryin' to protect us, I guess. But Trace, what the hell is goin' on? What does she mean by 'false pretenses' or this 'Robby' she added after her name?"

"Yeah," Wayne agreed. "I always thought there was somethin' fishy."

Trace was still numb with disbelief. *Goddamn it, Robby!* He'd been prepared last night for one catastrophe only to wake up to a different one. Why couldn't Robby have just *talked* to him for God's sake?

Clovis poked his shoulder hard. "Trace! Answer me! You'd best fess up right now, or I swear to God . . . ."

Trace looked up from the letter. Everyone was staring at him, angry and confused.

"I can't get into it right now," Trace said with an impatient shake of his head. "I have to go after Ro—Rowena. Before she gets herself killed."

Pa's eyes narrowed. "The hell you say! Ya ain't goin' nowhere until you answer Clovis's questions. What's goin' on with Rowena? Now, boy!"

Wayne, Roy, and Clovis crowded in closer. Wayne grabbed his arm and Clovis looked ready to hog-tie him if necessary. And knowing his brothers and pa, they would. Robby had left Trace with no choice. The letter laid too many hints.

"Fine! I'll tell ya. I just need to grab somethin' from the bunkroom."

"We'll *all* go," Wayne insisted.

So they did. The men trooped out of the house, leaving Marcy and Emmie to put on coffee. In the bunkroom, his brothers blocked the door making it clear no one was leaving until they were satisfied. So Trace pulled the WANTED poster from his saddlebag and grasped it for a moment, sighing. Then he held it up.

Clovis grabbed it. His eyes scanned the text and he stared at the picture in disbelief. The others crowded around him to see it. Then Pa snatched it and held it close to his face, squinting. Then Wayne and Roy had a turn, gawking at it like it was a mirage. There was a long, stunned silence.

Trace shook his head in frustration. "'Member I told ya about the fugitive on the wagon train? The man who'd seen a murder in New York by a big gang boss? Well that's him, Robby Riverton. As ya can see . . ." He swallowed. "Robby *is* Rowena."

"Are you tellin' me I contracted with a *man* to marry Clovis?" Pa-Pa said, bewildered. "What the ever-lovin' hell?"

"No, Pa. You contracted with a Miss Rowena Fairchild from St. Louis. She was on the wagon train with Robby. Only she decided she liked some other fella better, and she got off with him in Dodge City. Robby pretended to *be* Rowena when those Bowery Boys attacked the wagon train. If he hadn't put on a dress and fooled 'em, they'd have killed him on the spot. Then I ran into him in Santa Fe before he could change and . . ."

He looked at Clovis. "I'm sorry, Clovis. I hope ya ain't too disappointed. From what Robby told me about the real Miss Fairchild, she wouldn't have been the wife for you anyhow."

Clovis's face was slack with surprise. "Rowena ain't

my bride," he muttered, as if testing the idea on his tongue.

"She ain't even a woman!" Roy said in disgust. "I knew it all along!"

"You did not," Wayne snapped. "None of us did."

"Lemme get this straight," Pa said, his face flushing red. "You're tellin' me the gal I sent *two hundred dollars* so's she could pay her fare out here—*that* gal just up and ditched the wagon train way back in Dodge City?"

Trace closed his eyes and nodded, praying for patience.

"How did *you* know all this?" Wayne demanded. "And since when?"

Trace rubbed a hand over his face. "I figured it out that day we picked him up in Santa Fe. Look, I wired the U.S. Marshals, and they're on their way to Flat Bottom to take Robby into custody and protect him. But meanwhile, I . . . For god's sake. I just wanted to save his neck! I figured the best way was for him to sit tight here on the ranch and keep pretendin' he was Miss Fairchild. At least till the marshals got here. So that's what I told him to do."

"Ya told him to lie to us?" Pa bellowed, outraged.

"Pa," Trace said seriously, needing to make him understand. "Ya know if Robby had revealed who he was that first day, you'd have thrown him out on his rear. And if the gossip had gotten around about him, those Bowery Boys would have been on him in a flash."

Pa pressed his lips tight, but he didn't deny it.

Trace hesitated, wondering himself how this had all gone so horribly wrong. "Look, I didn't mean for it to go this way. I figured he'd be a guest in the house for a few days, and it would be no big bother. But Robby . . ." He shook his head with a growl. "It's just beyond him to be meek and retirin' and keep his nose outta things."

Pa grabbed the poster again and studied the drawing of Robby's face. "He played me for a fool." Pa's voice wobbled a bit. He sounded so honestly crushed that Trace felt sorry for him.

"Robby likes ya, Pa. All of ya. I am sorry for lyin'. But the person you took to your bosom is *still* a real person. Only she is a he, and his name is Robby Riverton. He left here tryin' to protect ya. And I need to go save him *right now* before he gets his fool throat slit by those Eastern gangsters. So, if ya wanna yell at me some more, ya can, but it's gonna have to wait."

With that, Trace's patience dried up and fear got the better of him. He grabbed his hat and stuffed his extra ammo into his saddlebags. His nerves were strung out like piano wire, and he was hardly aware of what he did. He had no idea how long Robby had been gone or where he was, but the first place to check was town.

When he turned to go, his brothers and Pa were still standing there, looking pole-axed.

Clovis spoke. "She—I mean he—Robby—was tryin' to teach me how to court Miss Stubbens, give me advice and whatnot, help me out. And I still didn't see it."

Trace paused to grasp Clovis around the neck with his palm. "I am sorry, Clovis."

Clovis shook his head. "Naw, I mean . . . Yeah. I guess I'm disappointed, but I ain't heartbroken. I told ya, Trace. I never could picture bein' married to Rowena. But—" His dark eyebrows furrowed, and he looked at Trace questioningly. "Is that why . . . I kindy got the feeling there was somethin' between you and her . . ."

Him, Trace thought. And that was the last discussion Trace wanted to have right then.

"I'm goin'." He walked to the door. "Ya can come with me for Robby's sake. Or ya can come with me for my sake. Or ya can stay here and be mad. But whatever ya decide, I'm leavin' now."

Chapter Thirty-One

The young couple sharing the stagecoach with Robby were Mr. and Mrs. Heller. They'd been visiting relatives in Silverton and were now heading back to Santa Fe. The young woman was especially solicitous of old Mother Harper, asking if she needed a blanket and plying her with questions. Robby invented a list of descendants, talking with an old southern twang. But his heart wasn't in it. Soon he pretended to nap to escape the conversation. Even with his eyes closed, he was as tense as a bow string and ready to snap.

He promised himself that once he got to Santa Fe, he would feel better. He'd check in at the *fonda* as old Mother Harper and hide in his room. There was no reason why anyone would suspect he was not who he claimed to be, or why anyone would expect Robby Riverton to show up in Santa Fe. He'd be fine.

But the journey itself . . . Robby was afraid. It was the kind of blood-level fear that caused a cold sweat to dampen the back of his dress and his heart to pound so forcefully in his chest he could feel every beat against his ribcage. This felt bad. This felt incredibly foolish. The coach was heading for Santa Fe at probably the exact same time the Bowery Boys were heading for Flat Bottom. Robby could only pray that this brass-balls feint would work, and luck would shine on him today.

Please God.

They'd only been on the road for about twenty minutes, the wagon jolting steadily beneath them, when shouts were heard outside. Men's voices.

"Whoa!" the coachman yelled. The coach slowed.

No, Robby, thought. *Keep going. Please.*

The wheels came to a standstill. Robby heard multiple riders, their horses circling the coach.

Oh God. Let it be some passing cattleman, bandits, curious Indians, anyone else. Just don't let it be them.

The wagon swayed as the driver disembarked. There was the sound of a flat accent as a man questioned the driver.

Robby's heart stopped. He'd know that voice anywhere. He heard it in his nightmares. It was the older of the two men who'd been chasing him, the one with eyes like shards of ice.

"What's goin' on?" Mr. Heller asked, pushing aside the curtain on the window.

"Maybe you shouldn't look," Mrs. Heller told her husband nervously.

Robby clenched his fists tightly, hunching up his shoulders as though he could draw his own head into his body, like a turtle.

The door was yanked open. "Out!" a man barked.

Robby dared a glance. Cold-Eyes was silhouetted in

the doorway, his black coat and stovepipe hat real, far too real, a bogey-man come to life.

"Who are you, sir? And what do you want?" Mr. Heller asked stiffly.

"We're checking the coach for a fugitive. Get out, all of yous. Come on."

The guns strapped to both hips discouraged argument. Grumbling, Mr. Heller moved to get out. Once his feet were on the ground, he held out a hand for his wife.

Robby was frozen on the far side of the coach. He tried to think of something, but there was nothing. There was nothing he could do. Nothing but brave it out. Nothing but *be* Mother Harper. Only he was so frightened, he didn't think he could move, much less perform.

Why hadn't he brought a gun? Stolen one of Trace's perhaps? Not that he'd be a match for a whole gang of gunfighters.

Cold-Eyes stuck his head back in. "That means you too, lady. Out!"

"Let me help her," Mrs. Heller said reproachfully. She squeezed past Cold-Eyes to look in the carriage. "Come along, Mother Harper. This will only take a few minutes. I'm sure these gentlemen won't hold us up for long."

She sounded nervous. She and Mr. Heller probably thought this was a robbery. If only it was. Mrs. Heller reached out her hand.

Move, damn it! You have to move. You're behaving suspiciously. At least try to act the part.

With a remarkable burst of self-preservation, Robby found the will to simper, "Thank you, dear," and take Mrs. Heller's hand.

Robby hunched his shoulders and hobbled his way

down the step of the carriage, holding tight to Mrs. Heller as though his bones were made of glass. The morning was warming, and the sunlight was rich but not yet blinding. He squinted into the light, trying to look around discreetly. It seemed as though a small army surrounded the coach. Three, four, five men on horseback. They trotted their horses around and around, like circling vultures.

One of them was the other Bowery Boy, the younger man with the blue feather in his hat. The others had to be the Durby Gang. They were hard-looking men with a range of guns and knife scabbards, wind-worn hats, beards, and flat eyes that flickered between the coach's inhabitants and the horizon, scanning for trouble.

Mother Harper, the Hellers, and the coach driver stood by the coach, completely vulnerable. Petitioners before a hostile judge. Cold-Eyes kept a gun trained on them while Blue-Feather jumped off his horse and hopped up on top of the coach, searching around the luggage. He came down again and looked underneath the coach at the underpinnings, then he went inside.

They were being very thorough.

Robby felt sick. He squinted his eyes and worked his jaw as if he were chewing something, pursing his lips. It was something his grandmother had done. Then again, she hadn't any teeth. He buried his hands under the apron as though cold and gave a shiver. But really, his odd chamois gloves would hardly pass inspection as normal wear, and without them his hands would give him away at a glance. He heaved a tired sigh.

"There's nobody else on the coach," Blue-feather said, reappearing. "Just these four."

"Well, all right then," Cold-Eyes's voice was bright, and it glittered with malice.

Let us go on our way. Please, God, Robby prayed.

But instead of waving them on, Cold-Eyes went up to the first of them in the line, the coachman. Robby watched as Cold-Eyes got within a few inches of the coachman's face and stared at him.

"See here," the coachman said, getting flustered. "We're not carryin' the man you're lookin' for. You can see that for yourself."

"Shut. Up." Cold-Eyes stared at the coachman's chin. He poked the roll of fat there and the one under his shirt buttons.

The coachman turned red, opened his mouth to protest, then thought better of it. He swallowed his complaint.

Slowly, Cold-Eyes stepped to the next in line, Mr. Heller. The young man was tall, thin and blond, with a pencil-thin moustache and black cowboy hat. His eyes widened with alarm and he pulled his wife closer, tucking her under his arm.

"What do you men want?" Mr. Heller asked, trying for defiance and missing it by a mile. "Is it money you're after?"

"We don't want your measly blunt, mister," Cold-Eyes said scathingly. "Just shut your gob."

Cold-Eyes moved on to Mrs. Heller. He gave her a loathing stare that made Robby's knees weak.

I'm done for, Robby thought. *I'm not going to pass this intense inspection. I'm not.*

The morning light was only getting brighter. From

such a close distance, the makeup lines of his "wrinkles" would surely be obvious.

Had he thought he was clever? He was an idiot. He should have stayed at the ranch. He'd been a fool to think he could do this on his own, that he could just slip right by them. And he was going to pay with his life.

His eyes watered with panic and terror filled his heart, but he made himself stand still. There was nothing he could do but brazen it out

Cold-Eyes stepped in front of Robby. He was so close, Robby could smell sour coffee and dirty teeth. Robby dropped his gaze, hoping to disguise his eyes. Even though he was hunched a bit, he was too tall, he realized, much too tall for an old woman.

Cold-Eyes spoke, a cruel smile in his voice. "You know, there's an old saying. 'Fool me once, and you're a smarmy son of a whore. But fool me twice? And you're a dead man.'"

His hand shot out and grabbed Robby's genitals through his skirts, pinching them hard enough to make Robby yelp.

"Ain't that right, Mr. Robby Riverton?" Cold-Eyes chuckled darkly.

Chapter Thirty-Two

"I'm not carrying his fooking head for two thousand miles!" Cold-Eyes said in a contemptuous voice.

"But Mose wants proof," argued Blue-Feather. "A hand could be anybody's hand."

"Not *his* hands. Just fooking look at 'em."

The horse Robby was on stopped. He was draped over the back of the beast, face down, bound and gagged. He felt the shift as Cold-Eyes's leg was swung over the horse's flank. The blanket covering him was removed, and he sucked in fresh air through his nose gratefully even though the daylight blinded him.

His hands, tied together behind his back, were yanked up. He let out a muffled yelp at the jolt of pain.

"Look. Tell me these ain't the hands of some prissy actor."

"I guess . . ." Blue-Feather hedged.

"Take his dick and bollocks too," one of the Durby Gang suggested. "His hands are probably used to their company."

There was much laughter at that.

Robby moaned around the cloth that was stuffed into his mouth. This was like something out of a Shake-spearean play, cutting off body parts to send to kings and emperors. Only it was real, and it was happening to him.

What had he done to deserve this fate? Killed at the tender age of twenty-four and cut up like a slaughtered lamb? But feeling sorry for himself was useless, as was lingering on the tragic drama of it all. He'd made mistakes, bad ones, and now he was going to die. If only he could find resignation. Or unconsciousness. Uncon-sciousness would be a welcome friend. But no, he was fully alert and terrified.

The red dirt beneath the horse grew blurry as his eyes filled with tears. Would Trace find his body? They weren't that far from Flat Bottom. Robby pictured birds circling in the desert air and Trace riding up on what was left of his remains. Minus his hand, cock, and balls. God, he'd spare Trace that if he could.

"You're payin' us the same, even though we never went to that ranch. Right?" Robby didn't recognize the voice. It was probably one of the Durby Gang. It sounded a bit high and broken, like there'd been damage to the man's windpipe.

"Yeah. That was the deal," Cold-Eyes agreed.

"Then just kill the damned molly, and let's get back to Santa Fe."

"I think we should question him," Blue-Feather said insistently.

"What for?" Cold-Eyes asked.

"See if he told anyone."

"So what if he did?" Cold-Eyes scoffed. "The lawyers

want an eyewitness. It ain't the same if you just heard a story. You have a point, though. I'm not eager to end the bastard. Chased this lousy foxy all the way from New York. Then he makes a fool out of us with that dress trick. Maybe I want to take my time with this one."

"So, take 'im along," the Durby Gang member said. "We got a hideout not far from Santa Fe you can use. You can kill 'im real slow there."

That seemed to settle the matter. Cold-Eyes tossed the blanket back over Robby, swung up onto the horse, and they started out again. The riding was hard. Robby's stomach and ribs hurt from taking all his weight over the horse's backside. And he wasn't secured either—with his arms tied behind his back, and his ankles bound, he had no way to hold on other than try to clench his body around the horse. It was exhausting.

Then he wondered: why bother? There was no way he could fall off and not be noticed. But maybe he could manage to break his own neck. That would be a cleaner death than whatever Cold-Eyes had in mind.

Could he bring himself to do it? His goose was cooked anyway. But there was still a chance. The smallest chance . . .

He was trying to build up his nerve when he heard a distant *pop*. He felt Cold-Eyes jerk, heard him expel a low gasp, then his body slid sideways off the horse.

It was all Robby could do not to go with him. He tightened himself around the horse as it danced and whinnied, fearful because—

Gunshot. Cold-Eyes had been shot. It had to be Trace!

The men around Robby started to fire. Round after round blasted in Robby's ears. He was still covered by the blanket, so he couldn't see a damned thing. Hoof beats pounded close to his head as another horse came up alongside him.

"Shit! Shit!" shouted Blue-Feather. "We're under attack! Make a circle."

"No! Make for those rocks!" the man with the high voice shouted.

Then they were galloping. Someone must have grabbed the reins on Robby's horse because he was jolted, could scarcely catch his breath as his chest and stomach pounded against horseflesh. He fought to stay on the animal, digging in his chin and knees. A moment ago, he'd been contemplating how best to fall off in order to break his neck. Now it was the last thing he wanted.

Trace had come. Robby had a chance of surviving this.

Please don't let him be shot.

They must have reached the rocks because the horses stopped abruptly. Robby's horse spun around, making him slide off the side. He tried to slow himself with his chin, but his feet, and then his knees, hit the ground and he fell in a heap of blanket. He was jarred, but it didn't feel like anything was broken.

A hoof kicked his thigh hard, and Robby choked on a scream. He fought to dislodge the blanket, so he could see where he was and avoid getting trampled. He managed to free his head and blinked to get his bearings.

They were at a mound of dirt and sharp-pointed stones. At the top of a mound was a cluster of tall, brown, pillar-like rocks, pitted with age. The Durby Gang had taken cover behind the rocks and were shooting into the distance.

Blue-Feather shouted at the other men to cover him

and ran back for Robby. He grabbed Robby's arms, still bound, and yanked him on his back up the hill. The stones cut into Robby's shoulder blades, his hands. There was a deep jab in his hip. Robby yelped but couldn't get away. The gunfire was deafening, and Blue-Feather cursed like a drunken sailor. Then Robby was behind the rocks and Blue-Feather let him go.

"How many are there?" one of the Durby Gang shouted.

"At least four. Maybe more." That was the man with the high voice. He sounded utterly calm. He wasn't firing wildly like the other men. He squinted into the distance, looking for his targets. He fired off three shots in a row then hunkered down as bullets hit the rock where his head had just been.

"Who is it?" Blue-Feather demanded. "Who the fook would come after this waste of skin?"

"Probably them ranchers he was stayin' with," High-Voice said coolly. "Guess we're gonna earn that money after all." He looked around the rock, aimed, and fired.

"They killed Ronnie!" Blue-Feather whined.

"Roscoe too. They got a dead shot out there. Now shut up and shoot!" High-Voice snapped.

Blue-Feather drew his gun and joined the fight, positioning himself behind a rock on Robby's other side. There were only three Durby Gang members left. One of them had been killed.

You got two, Trace. Only four more to go.

Robby lay there, panting up at the sky. If he could get his feet free, he could make a run for it. Maybe they wouldn't notice with all the shooting. He concentrated on his bindings. Cold-Eyes had tied his ankles and wrists with a rough twine rope. The rope was tight and the knots secure. The fibers dug into his skin, tearing into his flesh. Still, Robby worked his ankles, hoping to loosen them. But there was no give at all.

A bullet hit the rock high above his head, sending fragments of stone and dust down into his face. Shit.

Giving up on his bindings, Robby worked his way to sitting and started worming backwards, pushing with his heels and sliding on his ass. If he could just get out from behind the rocks. If Trace *saw* him . . .

But it was Blue-Feather who saw him. He turned to look at Robby, enraged. He clutched his arm, blood crimson against his white shirt and blunt, stocky fingers. He must have been shot—or hit by a rock fragment. The look he gave Robby was one of pure and utter hatred.

"*Riverton*. You ain't going anywhere but to *hell*."

He pulled a long, wicked-looking knife from a scabbard at his side and stalked toward Robby, his eyes wild.

Chapter Thirty-Three

Trace was in pure battle mode. He was a black storm cloud on the horizon—heavy, menacing, and ready to let go. He was prepared to do anything, anything at all. Whatever it took. Robby was in the hands of the Bowery Boys, and that was all Trace needed to know. He would rend heaven and earth. He would spill acres of blood. There was no possible outcome other than *getting Robby back.*

With his first shot he took out Cold-Eyes, because he had Robby on his horse. Trace hoped the horse would spook and run away, separating from the group. Then Trace could take out anyone who went after the horse while one of his brothers grabbed it and Robby. Only it didn't work out that way. Instead, one of the Durby Gang had grabbed the horse and they'd galloped for cover. He'd taken out one more as they rode.

Now they were sheltered in a group of rocks.

Trace, his brothers, and Pa had no cover. They stayed

just out of bullet range, pacing back and forth on their horses in the open landscape.

"Well?" Pa asked Trace. "We got 'em cornered, but that ain't a hell of a lot of use. We could be here all day. You're the army man. What do we do now?"

"The longer they have to think about it, the worse her chances are. Er—*his* chances," said Wayne, sitting anxiously upright in the saddle.

"I know that, Wayne," Trace said impatiently. "Let me think."

There were four men left—one of the Bowery Boys and three hired guns. Against five Crabtrees. Those were good odds, but now their opponents had the protected spot. Trace should have foreseen it. He should have noticed those rocks in the distance, but he'd been too anxious, too het up after seeing they had Robby.

Robby—under a blanket, slung over the back of a horse. Trace hadn't even been sure Robby was alive until he saw him move. There was a part of Trace, deep inside, that screamed and raged. But he had to lock that part away. He had to be smart now—deadly but smart. Anything less would get Robby killed.

He searched the landscape. What he wanted was higher ground, a vantage point from where he could shoot down into the rocks. But there was nothing like that. The rocks were the highest point for miles.

He looked them over, wishing he had General Armstrong's seeing glass. The rocks appeared to be a single upright row, tall but flat. The gang was *behind* the rocks—they only had cover on one side.

"You four put up a distraction," Trace ordered. "Ride

in and out of range. Fire at them. Keep their attention. And try not to get yourselves shot."

"Where you goin'?" Wayne asked.

"I'll circle around behind 'em. Got it?"

Clovis brought his rifle up to his shoulder, holding the reins of his horse with his other hand. "We'll keep 'em busy. Ya go take 'em out, Trace. Shoot 'em good for me."

The four of them rode closer and started firing. Trace waited until the men at the rocks were engaged, then turned to the right. He rode Jasper hard, making a wide circle.

He cleared the side of the rocks, now well to their south, and got a sightline on the men. *Got 'em.* As he'd suspected, the rocks provided a single barrier line. From behind, his targets were out in the open, set-up nice and easy for him on a hill. And they'd be focused on firing at his pa and brothers. If he rode up from behind them, and shot fast, he could take out two before they even turned around, and the last two before they drew sights on him.

He studied the layout as he rode. The remaining Bowery Boy was the closest, on the south end of the rocks. Robby was on the ground, possibly hurt. Possibly dead. Trace couldn't think about that right now.

He squeezed Jasper hard with his knees, bent low over his neck for speed. He needed distance, needed to hit them dead straight from behind. Finally, he turned Jasper toward the rocks. Gunfire covered the sound of his hooves as he galloped. Closer. Closer. One hand reached for his gun—

That's when the bottom fell out of the world. Robby was no longer lying on the ground, ignored. He was sitting up, arms bound behind him, and a Bowery Boy was leaning over him with a huge knife..

With a shouted, *"Ha!"* and a clench of his knees, Trace pushed Jasper harder. His own body strained so intently, it felt like he could leave the horse and fly. Every second was too long. *No. God's sake, no.*

The Bowery Boy raised his arm.

Trace was pure instinct now. He grabbed his right-hand six-shooter and took aim even as Jasper's hooves pounded the dirt.

ROBBY ROLLED AWAY FROM BLUE-FEATHER, pushing with his heels. The knife ripped through his left shoulder instead of his heart. He screamed at the bright, blinding pain, the violent invasion as steel entered his flesh, slicing through delicate tissue that should never see the light of day. A gush of warm liquid soaked his dress.

Pure survival instinct made him flail. He was on his stomach, his body jerking, back bowing, as he tried to scoot across sharp-edged rocks. *Get away!* It was pure, animal panic.

Blue-Feather grabbed Robby's bound hands and, using them as a handle, jerked him backward, nearly dislocating his shoulders. He was flipped over. A fist crashed into his face.

"I'm gonna carve you like a turkey," Blue-Feather promised, his voice dark and gleeful.

Robby tried to roll again, but Blue-Feather sat on his ribs, smashing his bound arms behind his back. A scream of pain got stuck behind the gag in Robby's mouth, choking him.

Blue-Feather raised the knife.

Robby was about to die.

Then a black dot appeared in the middle of Blue-Feather's forehead. At first, it seemed like a trick Robby's eyes were playing on him. Then a trickle of red spilled out of it like candle wax as Blue-Feather's eyes widened with shock and glazed over.

The knife dropped, nicking Robby's arm. Blue-Feather toppled like a leaded weight, landing on top of Robby's chest and head.

Relief flooded through Robby's veins, but it was short-lived. He couldn't get enough air around the gag, not with Blue-Feather's weight covering his face. His shoulder screamed as he tried fruitlessly to shift the body. Fresh blood gushed over his skin, onto his neck.

Please, God, he just wanted one clean damn breath! And maybe to scream. He could scream for *hours*.

But the breath wasn't there. Things went fuzzy and the world fell away.

Chapter Thirty-Four

Robby woke to the sight of Trace's golden-brown eyes. They were damp with worry and something more, something Robby couldn't quite trust. His mouth was blessedly free of the gag, and he gulped in air—huge, fresh, wonderful lungs full.

"You're all right," Trace said, cupping his face. "You're all right."

"The— the—" Robby tried.

"They're dead."

"All of them?"

Trace nodded solemnly, his gaze roaming Robby's face as if he couldn't quite trust that he was alive.

"Yo-you?" Robby managed, trying to sit up. He hissed at the sharp agony in his shoulder.

"No, now just sit tight." Trace's voice cracked a little. "Ya got a nasty wound in your shoulder."

He put an arm behind Robby's back for Robby to rest on and Robby gratefully relaxed into it. His vision sparkled with black dots and his head felt like it would float away on its own. He closed his eyes.

The next thing he knew, he was riding pillion behind Trace on a horse, slumped against Trace's back. His hands were fastened around Trace's waist in an effort to keep him upright. And he was drooling. It probably looked damned undignified, him with his tattered dress and apron hitched up to his thighs so he could sit astride, with his old-lady makeup and mob cap, and the bloodstain soaking one side of the dress. But Robby was perfectly content. If he had to be tied, being tied around Trace was a vast improvement. He felt quite smug about it just before falling asleep against Trace's back.

When he woke up again they were in Flat Bottom and Clovis was sliding him off the horse. Robby wobbled on his feet, blinking in the hot sunshine.

"We're gettin' the doctor," Clovis said, not meeting Robby's eyes. He looked ashamed or embarrassed or both.

Shit. Clovis knew.

"I'm sorry I lied to you, Clovis," Robby said earnestly.

"Aw, don't worry about that right now. Honest. I ain't mad."

"You're a nice man. A gem—no, a paragon. Truly. I don't deserve you. None of y'all." His words were slurred, and his head felt funny. He thought he heard Trace snort a laugh.

The ground rose up suddenly, but Clovis and Trace were there to catch him. They each took an arm and helped him into the sheriff's office and up a flight of stairs.

"I'm fine," Robby muttered.

No one was asking his opinion.

A few minutes later an older man came in—the doctor, Robby surmised. His wound was cleaned with alcohol, which stung like a bitch. The doctor gave him laudanum then stitched the long gash and wrapped it. Between the laudanum and his already woozy head, the pain of the stitches was remote, distant. That was nice.

He heard the doctor say he'd lost a lot of blood and needed to rest for a week or two. Whatever else he might have said, Robby didn't process it. He figured he'd be on a stagecoach out of Flat Bottom as soon as possible. Now that the Bowery Boys were dead, he needed to move on before anyone else got any ideas or Mose McCann sent reinforcements. And anyway, he didn't want to face the Crabtrees. They'd hate him now.

When the doctor left, Robby forced himself to sit up on the bed, using his good arm to push himself upright.

"Mrs. Jones's house?" he asked, blinking up at Trace. He was so exhausted. He just wanted a bed he could stay in for a while. Preferably one where the room didn't spin or stink so badly of wood smoke.

Trace frowned down at him. "Ya can't even walk."

"I can walk," Robby insisted, getting to his feet.

Whoo! The room went round, swoop-de-doo. Sounds were fuzzy, including the sound of Trace saying, "He's goin' down!"

The next time Robby opened his eyes he looked up at a gray ceiling. The bed beneath him felt familiar, as did the quilt beneath his hand. He was on the porch at the Crab-tree ranch.

His shoulder had woken him. His arm was in a sling and the shoulder hurt like a son of a gun.

He groaned and, a moment later, Marcy sat beside him

on the bed. "Does it hurt? Doc said ya could have some more laudanum for the pain."

Robby shook his head. He needed to be able to think clearly. "What time is it?"

"It's almost noon."

"What day?"

"Thursday," Marcy said with a hesitant smile.

Thursday. He'd slept for twenty-four hours. He went to reach for his hair to see if his bonnet was in place and was rewarded with a stab of pain in his shoulder. He gritted his teeth and switched to his right hand. There was no bonnet, just his own hair, still tacky with powder.

Seeing the flash of hurt cross Marcy's face reminded Robby that his secrets were out.

"It's almost time for lunch," Marcy said, rising. "Do you want me to bring a tray, or do ya feel up to sittin' at the table?" Her words were kind but reserved, stiff, like she didn't know Robby at all.

He swallowed. He might as well face the firing squad now rather than later. "I'll come out."

Marcy nodded and left the room.

Robby got up slowly. He felt incredibly weak and his body hurt everywhere. He found his mirror in Rowena's trunk and looked himself over. His skin was pale and his eyes dull. There were big black-and-purple bruises on his thighs, hips, and ribs. His face was still lined with makeup that had been smeared with dirt and blood. Between that and the white powder in his hair he looked downright spectral, like a ghoul risen from the grave.

In a way, he supposed he was. Rowena Fairchild was dead. Long live Robby Riverton.

He found warm water in the pitcher and a clean rag

and towel. He washed his face with soap and water, scrubbing the makeup off with his one good hand. He brushed his hair as best he could to remove most of the white powder. Then, finding the carpetbag near the bed—*thank you, Trace*—he put on his own clothes. He had to slip the sling off long enough to get his shirt on, which caused a fresh wave of pain, but he was determined to do this right.

When he was finished, it was startling to look at himself in the mirror. Even he wasn't used to this Robby—just an ordinary sort of young man, really. Yet so out of place in this room, in this situation.

God, Pa-Pa was going to kill him. And Trace would be angry that Robby had run. Well, hiding wouldn't change any of that. Robby squared his shoulders and left the back porch.

When he walked into the dining room, everyone was at the table, including Trace. They all looked at him.

Billy was the first to speak. "Oh my gawd!" he exclaimed. "Rowena, you really *is* a gosh durn man!"

No one bothered to yell at him for cussing.

"I can go back to the porch if I'm disturbing your lunch," Robby said. His face was burning.

Pa-Pa waved a hand. "Get your ass over here. Ya ain't gettin' off that easy."

He didn't sound happy, but Robby supposed it was an invitation of sorts. He walked to the empty chair next to Pa-Pa and sat gingerly. Wearing pants again felt downright liberating, but he had to remind himself to drop the feminine mannerisms and not sway as he walked.

He raised his eyes once he was seated. Everyone was still staring at him. If this was weird for him, he couldn't imagine how weird it was for them.

Pa-Pa crossed his arms with a grunt. "Well. Guess ya thought you'd never have to face us again."

"I guess I did," Robby admitted. "But I'd like to say . . . I'm sorry." He looked around the table. "I never set out to deceive you or hurt you. I guess . . ." He glanced at Pa-Pa. "I guess some lies just get away from you."

Pa-Pa huffed. "We already know the whole dang story," he said in a disgusted tone. "What with that murder in New York, and ya bein' chased, and hidin' out here, and all that hullaballoo. I wouldn't have believed it if I hadn't seen the bodies of them Bowery Boys. They sure looked like some kindy Eastern criminals."

Pa-Pa spat on the floor to show his opinion of anyone who came from New York City. Robby was half of a mind to copy Pa-Pa and do it himself.

"Did ya really see a famous gangster kill a man?" Billy asked, his eyes big.

Robby nodded. "I did. It sure turned my life into a mare's nest."

Marcy handed Robby a mug of hot coffee. "Well, I think you're very brave to have gone through all that."

Robby gave her a grateful smile. She was trying, bless her heart.

Trace spoke up, his voice dry. "Ya know what turned *all* our lives into a mare's nest? Ya takin' off like ya did, runnin' right into the Bowery Boys' hands at the last minute. Stupidest damn thing I ever saw."

Robby took a deep breath to keep calm. He sipped his coffee, saying nothing.

"I swear to God, Robby. One more minute and you'd be dead. *One more minute!*" Trace was flat-out angry now. It

255

had probably been simmering for hours. He jabbed at his potatoes with his fork.

Robby pressed his lips together tightly and gave Missy, to his right, a tiny smile. "Would you pass the milk, sweet pea?"

She nodded and reached out with her chubby hands for the little milk pitcher on the table. "Aunt Rowena—do I still call you Aunt Rowena?" She wriggled her nose like it itched and handed Robby the pitcher.

"You can call me Robby. Or Romy. That's what my baby sister used to call me."

"How come?" Missy giggled, finding that hilarious.

"Oh, I suppose she just found it easier to say."

"Uncle Robby," Paul said to himself, chomping on a piece of bread. He peered at Robby with a tilted head and a frown as if trying to see Rowena in his face.

"And *these* guys—my so-called family!" Trace ranted on. "There they were, yackin' away at me, demandin' explanations for this and that, holdin' me up. I could *easily* have been a minute later. But for the grace of God!" Trace jabbed his fork in the air. "*Or* ya coulda broken your neck falling off that horse when ya were hogtied. What kind of idiot wouldn't *secure* ya to that damn animal? Or they could have killed ya right there at that stagecoach. Just shot ya dead! Dressing up like an old woman. Christ on a goddamn crutch, Robby!"

Robby pressed his lips tight and gave Emmie a wide-eyed look as if to say, *They do go on, don't they?*

Emmie, who'd been sitting in her seat doing her quiet vanishing act, choked on a laugh.

But the truth was, Trace's scolding made Robby's heart full to bursting with happiness. Trace *cared*. He really did.

He'd been scared to death. Robby took a shaky breath and took a bite of potato. "You're right, Trace. Completely," he agreed sincerely. "And thank you for saving my life yesterday. And thank you Roy, Wayne, Clovis, and Pa-Pa too, for fighting alongside Trace. I don't know how I could ever repay you."

Trace just glared down the table at him.

"Well," Emmie spoke up, straightening her back. "I agree with Marcy. It was awful brave to try to protect us by leavin' the way ya did."

"It was *stupid*," Trace said. "Idiotic!"

"Ya wouldn't have had to take the time to explain it to us, brother," Clovis said testily, "If ya'd told us about it days ago, like you oughta."

"Potatoes?" Marcy asked, passing the platter to Robby from the other side of Pa-Pa.

Robby reached for it with his left hand and winced.

"I'll get it," Pa-Pa grumbled.

Pa-Pa held the bowl while Robby spooned some potatoes onto his plate.

Pa-Pa looked at Robby side-eyed, his gaze moving up and down, his expression hurt. "Shoulda known. Never have met a woman with your kindy gumption."

"You'd be surprised," Robby said. "My friend Jenny Daley in New York? She's a famous actress. That woman can send a man to his knees with a few choice words." He waggled his eyebrows at Marcy.

"I wanna meet a famous actress!" Billy said, pronouncing it "act-less." Which Jenny would *not* find amusing.

"Ya sure the Bowery Boys didn't kill the *real* Miss Fairchild?" Wayne asked, his face closed off.

Robby shook his head. "No. Thank God. They caught up with the wagon train long after she'd left."

"I spent two hundred dollars on that gal!" Pa-Pa huffed bitterly. "Was she at least *pretty*?"

Robby nodded. "She was very pretty. Actually, I have a letter for you."

Robby felt guilty that he'd forgotten all about Rowena's farewell letter. He'd stuck it behind a bit of loose lining in her trunk. He went and fetched it, and Pa-Pa read it over with a scowl. Then it got passed down the table to Clovis.

Clovis read it warily then scoffed. "True love! Well, Pa. So much for findin' me a wife." His attempt to sound bemused didn't quite come off.

"I can tell you about her," Robby suggested. Because, well heck. Rowena was happily married hundreds of miles away. It wasn't like she was ever going to visit Flat Bottom. And Robby didn't want Clovis to feel too badly. So Robby told them how he'd met Rowena, about her bun in the oven, the bible salesman, and some of the amusing and silly things she'd said and done. He liked Rowena, but he wanted the Crabtrees to see she wasn't cut out for the ranch.

Soon most of the people around the table were laughing, Wayne and Roy included.

"Oh, good Lord! Ya dodged a bullet there, Clovis," said Roy.

"Geez, Pa, told ya. Ya can't just go around buyin' a woman you never even met," Wayne said, shaking his head.

"Your brother wanted a wife! It's not my fault we got took for fools. Took for fools more than once."

Pa-Pa's words were harsh, and Robby didn't know what to say. The rest of the meal was eaten in silence.

After lunch, the men and Billy went out to work and Trace left with them, saying something about needing to go into town. He shot Robby a foreboding look as he left. Robby tried to help clear the table, the way he used to do. But with his sling it was awkward and the laudanum from the day before had him dragging.

"You go rest," Marcy insisted. She started to push his back, the way she might have done with Rowena. But then she seemed to think it was inappropriate to touch a man that way. She dropped her hands, blushing.

Marcy and Emmie gave each other a bewildered look.

"I'm sorry this is so strange," Robby said. "But you don't have to be different with me."

Emmie's eyes watered, and she turned away.

"Aw, Emmie, what's wrong?"

"It's all right." Emmie sniffed. "I'm not mad. Only . . . I liked Rowena so much. I'm sad she won't be my sister."

Marcy nodded in agreement, her eyes tearing up too.

Robby heaved a sigh, guilt eating at him. And sadness too. "Maybe I won't be your sister. But can I be your brother? I'd like to be."

Emmie blinked at him, thinking about it. "I never had a brother."

"Well, not one like you anyway," Marcy said with a quirk of her lips. "If you're my brother then I can tell ya to get your butt back to bed and rest."

Robby nodded. But he gave them each a hug before he went.

Chapter Thirty-Five

When Trace got back from town, he couldn't wait to see Robby. Marcy said he was sleeping, but Trace didn't care. He needed to make sure Robby was all right. So he let himself onto the porch, quietly, and sat in a chair next to Robby's bed.

He looked so young lying there. It was hard to believe such an innocent-looking creature could have caused all the havoc he had. Or gotten under Trace's skin so deeply.

Robby opened his eyes, cool as day, and looked at him.

Trace licked his lips, feeling unsure of himself. "Sorry I yelled at ya at lunch."

"You should be sorry," Robby said, but he didn't sound mad.

Trace sighed. He wanted . . . He didn't even know what he wanted.

"Get over here and hold me a minute," Robby demanded.

Trace glanced at the door. "I shouldn't."

"No one's coming in here. Come on. I'm a wounded man. I'm in dire need of comfort."

With an exaggerated huff, Trace got up and sat on the edge of the bed. He put his arm out and Robby snuggled under it, lying on Trace's lap. God, it felt so good. Why did it have to feel so good? Why did he want Robby like this?

Why did Robby have to *love* him?

Love.

Last night, Pa had told Trace and his brothers about their mother's death all those years ago. Trace had been fit to be tied, but it seemed like the wrong time to yell at his pa about lying to the family, so he'd let Wayne do the ranting and raving. Wayne, who remembered more about those days than any of them, said he'd stood at the end of the driveway looking for their mother to come home every day at sunset for a whole year. And his voice had broke. Pa admitted he'd done wrong and said he was real sorry. Seeing both Wayne and Pa emotional like that shocked the hell out of Trace.

He didn't know how to feel about his mother's fate. Of course, it meant a lot that she hadn't left them on purpose. She never would, Pa said. And maybe that would take some time to sink in. But on the other hand, it just went to show that a body could ride off on a whim someday and never come back, like Robby had nearly done. And Trace wasn't sure how much more of that his heart could take.

"I know ya thought you were doin' the right thing. But it would have ruined me if I'd found you dead out there," Trace said finally, his voice thick.

"Yeah?" Robby tilted his head to look up at Trace.

Trace touched Robby's jaw. "Yeah. Idjit."

Robby yawned and smiled. He looked up at Trace with warm, happy eyes, gazing at him as if just the sight of him was wonderful. It made Trace feel awful.

He cleared his throat. "Ya must be in pain."

Robby's smile faded. "*Yes*. I feel like I was run over by a wagon train. A long one."

"Well. Just rest. Doc says it'll get easier."

Robby shifted in his lap, frowning. "You know I have to leave, right?"

"Ya don't have to. My family knows about ya now, so you could stick around."

Robby barked a laugh. "And do what? Muck out the stables?"

"Actually, Carson Meeps has that job," Trace said, with a hint of a smile. "I dunno. Maybe you could be a deputy or something."

Robby shook his head. "My dearest darling, I'm an actor. There's too much life out there waiting for me. But . . . you could come with me."

Trace gave him a long, measured stare. He couldn't make himself say the words—*I can't*. But he didn't have to. Apparently, it was written all over his face because Robby's expression closed up. He sighed and turned into Trace's shirt.

"Ya have to at least stick around till the marshals get here. Ya should give 'em your testimony. Then ya won't have to worry about the Bowery Boys comin' after ya again."

Robby fiddled with one of Trace's buttons, not meeting his eyes. "When do you think the marshals will get here?"

"Shouldn't be too long now. Week or two?"

"All right," Robby said slowly. "Maybe I should move

to Mrs. Jones's place. I don't want things to be awkward for your family."

Trace thought about it, his hand soothing Robby's back. "Maybe it'd be good for them to get to know ya as Robby."

"Why?"

Trace didn't have an answer, only that he wanted it. He didn't want their last memory of Rowena to be one of confusion and betrayal. He wanted them to know Robby the way he did.

Well, not *exactly* the way he did.

"Why don't ya stay a day. If it don't feel right, I'll take ya to Mrs. Jones."

Robby nodded. *Okay.*

Trace wanted to kiss Robby, wanted to climb into bed where they could hold each other, skin to skin. Pull the blanket over their heads and shut out the rest of the world. Forever.

Trace dropped his voice to a whisper. "You could come to the bunkroom tonight, just so's I can hold ya."

"As long as I'm here, Trace, nothing could keep me from you," Robby said with quiet gravity.

Trace nodded. He felt the same. As for the pain in his gut, sometimes life hurt. And a man just had to live with that.

Chapter Thirty-Six

R obby stayed at the ranch for two more weeks. He had an interesting position in the family, not quite family and not quite a guest anymore. Not quite one of the men, nor one of the women any longer.

Sometimes he helped Marcy and Emmie in the kitchen or with sewing braid or buttons on the new clothes. Sometimes he helped with barn chores along with the boys. The children were fascinated by Robby's life on the stage. He organized a play, such as it was, the way his mother used to do when he was small. Trace and his brothers insisted on being "the audience" but Pa-Pa took a part and played it with gusto. None of the Crabtrees kids would ever be star talent, bless their hearts, but they had fun.

Robby stayed long enough to meet with two U.S. Marshals in the Flat Bottom sheriff's office. They told him Mose McCann was in custody and faced a slew of charges including the murder of a banker Robby had witnessed. They wanted Robby to return east with them for the trial.

But Robby was tired of being tossed around by the fates and letting that one night rule his life. So they figured out a compromise. He wrote a detailed statement and signed it in front of three witnesses. And that was the end of it.

Robby stayed long enough to see Clovis begin a formal courtship of Miss Harriet Stubbens. They could be seen most evenings sitting on the steps of the schoolhouse or on the porch at the ranch trying to catch the evening breeze. Clovis tried his best to look presentable and Robby, Marcy, and Emmie all helped by sewing him new clothes and encouraging him to, for the love of God, *keep shaving*. Robby was happy for Clovis, and it helped assuage his own guilt. But the more time Harriet spent at the ranch, the more Robby felt he needed to move on. Not that there had ever been anything between he and Clovis, but he wanted to spare the new couple any awkwardness.

The story quickly got around town about the fugitive eyewitness from New York, and how he'd hidden out at Crabtree Ranch in the guise of a woman. The Crabtree men, led by the town's own dear sheriff, had taken down those bloodthirsty Eastern killers along with the infamous Durby Gang. They became the talk of the territory.

Robby let out a few hints to Mrs. Jones that the Crabtrees had been in on the subterfuge the entire time. It was about then that Pa-Pa began to like the story. A lot. Everyone said he'd never been seen in town so often, nor with his head held quite so high. Pa-Pa embellished the story each time he told it, until you'd have thought Clyde Crabtree was on friendly terms with President Hayes, and that he'd agreed, as a personal favor to the president, to give sanctuary to Robby Riverton before he ever left New York City.

Pa-Pa took to ribbing Robby at mealtime, and Robby ribbed him back. The smarter Robby's mouth was, the more Pa-Pa was tickled by it. His cackle—and it really was a cackle—became commonplace.

During those weeks, Trace stayed in the bunkroom in the barn. Robby snuck over there every night when the house was asleep and later snuck back to the porch, sated and warm and missing the feel of Trace's arms. They didn't talk about Robby leaving again. It was too painful a subject. But each time they touched they made love with an intensity that said it might be their last.

Eventually Robby bought his stagecoach fare, heart in this throat, and packed the small carpetbag with the few items he had left to his name. He gave Rowena's things to Marcy and Emmie, including an old gold-plated locket that had been in Rowena's trunk, the one he'd used to convince Pa-Pa he wouldn't run away. And then Robby found himself with nothing to do but leave.

He said his good-byes at the ranch on a Tuesday afternoon. Everyone gathered on the porch, including Clovis and Harriet. There were a lot of hugs and good wishes and promises to write. Robby felt a hole open inside him as he and Trace rode on Bella and Jasper toward town. The Crabtrees weren't perfect. Or even close. But, much like his own large family back in Pennsylvania, the family unit had an energy, a pull all its own, like being part of a pack. They were honest and had no airs and graces. He would miss them.

But the worst part of leaving Flat Bottom by far was leaving Trace. They didn't talk about the future. Not in those last two weeks of late-night rendezvous, not in the quiet moments they'd caught together at the ranch, and not on that final ride to town. It wasn't until they were within sight of the brown buildings, riding side by side, that Trace spoke.

"Where ya headin'?" he asked, breaking the unspoken agreement.

"Pete said if you travel south from Santa Fe, you can take the Gila Trail to California. It'll take a while, but eventually I'll reach San Francisco. Maybe it won't be what I think it is. But it's been in my head long enough, I figure I should give it a try. After all, I've come this far west."

"Yeah," Trace said, his face solemn. "Ya should."

"You can still change your mind and come with me." Robby glanced over at Trace. He looked for some sign in his expression that he was at least sorry.

Trace glowered. "Christ on a crutch, Robby. I've only known ya a month. I can't just up and leave a good job, and my family, and everythin' I've ever known."

"No that would be risky. Though not as risky as running off to be a sharpshooter in the army."

Trace glowered harder. "Well, maybe I've learned better since then."

Robby nodded solemnly. "Maybe you have. No, you're right. You should stay here. Sit on the porch all by yourself. Nice and quiet. For years. Nothing to worry about except the flies. And you can spend lots and lots of time with your family."

Trace narrowed his eyes. "Don't think ya can talk me around, the way ya do Pa."

"I wouldn't dream of it," Robby sniffed.

"This ain't the same as the gals' clothes or table manners or fake archways in fake castle walls. This is a serious matter. A man's life. *My* life."

"I know," Robby said sadly. "Really I do."

"I don't have a thing in San Francisco."

"You'd have me."

Robby could have said a lot more—about adventure and taking risks and about how it wouldn't be the first time either of them had run away to the great unknown. But what was the point? Trace knew all those things. But he chose to stay. Robby had to respect that. He owed Trace his life. The least he could do was not make this more difficult for him.

They reached Mrs. Jones's boarding house, and Trace went upstairs with him. Robby put his bag on the bed and they stood in the small bedroom looking at one another. Robby felt heartsick, an ache deep inside him. Trace licked his lips. "Wanna come next door for a bit?"

Robby would take any opportunity to postpone the inevitable. "Sure."

His hands shaking, Robby shut the door to his room and they trooped downstairs, over to the sheriff's office, and up to Trace's apartment above. Robby had only been there once, after he'd been saved from the Bowery Boys, and he'd been half-delirious at the time. He looked around at the plain space.

This is what Trace chooses over me? It hurt. It was irrational, but it hurt.

Trace looked at him, his eyes tormented. Robby undid his pants and pulled off his shirt. Soon they were both naked in Trace's bed. They came together with a heat born of sorrow.

Robby couldn't bear to think that he'd never be with Trace again. He wrapped his legs around Trace's hips, hardly able to let go long enough for Trace to prepare him. Trace filling him up was exquisite pain. The ache stemmed from his chest and not from the invasion, but it was unbearable all the same. So Robby took over, rolling Trace onto his back, riding him relentlessly, squeezing Trace's chest with strong fingers—hard. Hard enough to hurt. Trace's fingers, in return, dug into his hips. It was as if the pain needed somewhere to go, some outlet in blood and flesh. As if bruises were all they'd have left of each other tomorrow.

I love you, Robby said with his eyes. He'd said it out loud once before, and it hadn't mattered. He wasn't going to say it now, when it mattered too much. He didn't need to.

I love you and I hate this, Trace's eyes said back, or so Robby believed. But it wouldn't change anything. Because Trace believed a man simply had to accept things, things like two men being unable to share a life. And Robby hated that too.

Afterward, they lay sweaty in each other's arms. It hurt more than the knife wound Robby had taken, but he would have stayed the night anyway. Trace was the one to push him gently away and sit up on the edge of the bed, his back to Robby.

"Want me to go?" Robby asked.

Trace sighed then nodded. "I have to take care of some things tonight."

"Right," Robby said, feeling the cold creep into his heart. "Right."

He got up and put on his clothes slowly, feeling like he might shatter.

He went to the door. "I'll write to you," he said

without turning. "Maybe you'll decide to come visit sometime."

"Yeah. Let me know where ya are. Okay?"

Robby nodded and ran down the stairs before he could do something stupid, like beg or cry like a little child.

He hesitated before heading next door to Mrs. Jones's. He went into the saloon and bought the cheapest bottle of whiskey Stan had. He took it up to his room and drank until the despair floated away.

IN THE MORNING, Robby felt like something stuck to the bottom of Clyde Crabtree's boots as he washed his face and packed up his few belongings. The coach was on time this morning, thank the Lord. And it was going in the direction it was supposed to, toward Santa Fe. This time he actually wanted to go there.

He got on board. It was still early, and the streets were quiet. Robby laid his head back and closed his eyes. No one had come to say good-bye. It was just as well. He'd said his good-byes the day before, and it was too hard to have to say them again.

The coach swayed as someone stepped onboard. There was the feeling of a heavy body landing beside him on the bench seat.

Too close. Robby opened his eyes to glare at the new passenger.

"Sorry," Trace said, shifting over a little. "Don't mind me."

He was freshly shaven, his shirt was clean, and his hat had been brushed. He wore a long canvas coat. He gave

Robby an assessing look from the side, the corner of his lips quirking up. "Good mornin', sunshine. You goin' to San Francisco too? What a coincidence."

"What are you doing?"

"I am accompanying you on your journey West," Trace said with formal politeness. "I'd have thought that much was obvious."

"But. But you said . . ."

"Aw now, it's not very Christian of ya to throw a man's nonsense back in his face."

Robby stared.

"Truth is, I was scared to try to hold on to ya. I couldn't see how it would work. So I dug in my heels. But, Robby—" Trace swallowed, his golden eyes intent on Robby's face. "Turns out, I'm more scared to let ya go. I don't seem to be able to bear it. So. Looks like you're stuck with me."

A bubble of happiness rose in Robby's throat, threatening to burst out as a laugh. "Do you mean it?"

"Sure looks that way. Already spent two dollars on the fare, and ya know how tight we Crabtrees are. Told ya I always wanted to see San Francisco. I figured this was the best motivation I was ever going to get to move my lazy behind in that direction. That is, if ya don't have any objections."

Robby shot a quick look around, but they were the only two in the coach so far, and he didn't see anyone out the windows. He threw his arms around Trace's neck and gave him a kiss. Trace returned it, patting Robby's back. But then he straightened up.

"We'll have to be a tad more circumspect on this trip," he drawled.

"I can't believe you're coming with me!"

Trace's expression grew serious. "I didn't have much choice in the matter, since you're so all-fire determined to go. Hard to imagine my life without ya. Don't really want to. I've never felt that way about anyone, and I doubt I ever will again. So. Here I am."

Robby swallowed hard. It was the best "I love you" he'd ever heard, and it was coming from the heart of the best man he'd ever known.

All the love Robby had tried to push down and put in a box, just to survive this parting, came bursting out to fill his being, tightening his chest and throat with unbridled joy. He wanted to shout. He wanted to dance in a spotlight in a top hat and tails. But seeing as how they were in a stagecoach, he just squeezed Trace's hand. And Trace squeezed back, his eyes warm.

Robby settled back on the seat. He had a dawning sense of brightness and hope. It was made all the brighter in contrast to the darkness and fear he'd lived with for the past months. There'd been so many times he'd thought his life was over, that he'd lost everything. Now it was as if someone had turned on the light in the world. He couldn't ask for anything more.

"I don't have much money left," Robby said. "But I will charm the shirts off those people in San Francisco. I'll find work."

"I don't doubt that for a second," Trace said. "And I'll find a job too."

Robby raised an eyebrow.

"Not that I'm the most ambitious son of a bitch in the world," he grinned. "But you're worth it, Robby Riverton."

Epilogue

Two Years Later
Maguire's Opera House, San Francisco

"Hell of a show, fellas! Hell of a show!" Mr. Thompson grinned and patted Robby and Trace on the back as they left the stage.

They got cheery greetings from people backstage as they made their way to their dressing room. Once inside, Robby fell onto a settee and poured himself a glass of water. "Lord, all the racing around in that third act does me in."

He took a long drink, then raised his sweaty shirt to peel off the bloody wound. It always made men gasp and ladies shriek when it was revealed in the kidnapping scene.

Robby was in men's clothes at the moment, but he only got to wear them for the first scene and the last. It turned out Robby was not through with Rowena's gowns or bonnet. In fact, he now made a handsome living wearing them.

Rowena and the Bloodthirsty Gangsters, a comedy-drama written by Robby—and edited extensively by Trace—had been a rip-roaring hit at the Maguire for six months. It showed no signs of slowing down.

Robby, of course, played himself. Or rather, he played a hapless New York bookkeeper who witnesses a murder and is forced to go into hiding as a mail-order bride. Trace played the sharpshooting sheriff who comes to Rowena's rescue.

Trace had taken to the stage like a duck to water. Women adored him. They were constantly sending him love letters, undergarments, even hotel room keys. Robby was grateful Trace couldn't care less.

All the papers had written that the play was based on a true story of the Wild West, and that Robby had been instrumental in bringing down the notorious gangster Mose "the Terror" McCann, so people flocked to see it. Honestly, Robby would rather be playing Hamlet. But as a way to get established in San Francisco, the play was a godsend.

It was also a hell of a lot of fun acting with Trace.

Trace was examining himself in the dressing room mirror, turning this way and that, with a slight frown. "The applause didn't seem as big for the shootin' scene tonight. Did you notice that?"

"No," Robby said honestly. The scene where Trace did some fancy trick shooting with stacks of fruit cans always got a standing ovation. "The audience ate it up."

"You sure? I felt a little slow on the draw. Does it look like I've put on weight?"

Robby rolled his eyes but couldn't stop a fond smile. "No, darlin'. You get better-looking each day. Now help me with these boots."

He held out a leg and Trace tugged off one boot and then the other. With a lazy smile, he took a moment to knead Robby's toes. "Feel better?"

Robby winked back. "Yes, but you're giving me ideas. Did you lock the door?"

They felt comfortable at Maguire's, and Robby figured most people knew he and Trace were more than "friends." But they preferred to keep their private business private.

"Not yet. I'll get it." Trace walked over to turn the lock. While he was over there, he pulled an envelope out of the long, black coat that hung on the coatrack. "I forgot to mention we got a letter from home today."

He flopped down to sit beside Robby, tossing the envelope into his lap.

"Ooh!" Robby opened it eagerly and read out loud.

Clovis and Harriet's son Tyler, a chubby baby boy with oodles of black hair, had started to crawl. Marcy swore he was the "cutest thing you ever saw."

Missy had a new front tooth.

Billy bested Killboar three-to-one the previous week.

Emmie and Roy were expecting again.

There was news that the Atchison, Topeka and Santa Fe Railway would soon lay tracks to Santa Fe. Pa-Pa said that once it was in, he expected them both home for Christmas or "they was no kin of his."

Marcy sent her love.

Robby and Trace chuckled over the letter. When it was done, Robby let it drift to the floor and snuggled up to his stage-sweaty beau.

Trace carded fingers through Robby's hair. "Ya know, it's only a matter of time before the railroad goes all the way to Omaha and hooks up with the line to New York. Mr. Thompson wants to finance takin' *Rowena* on the road."

"Umm-hmm." Robby kissed Trace's chin.

"Wouldn't you like that? Goin' back to New York City as a big star?" Trace wrapped his arms around Robby and pulled him close.

Robby thought about it. The idea of taking *Rowena* on the road, seeing new places, and showing Trace the sights of New York City, had its appeal. But then he thought about the two-bedroom bungalow they'd bought in the Western Addition, a new section of the city, and about the vibrancy of the town, and how fast it was growing. There was the Maguire and the Dramatic Museum and the Jenny Lind. The theater scene in San Francisco was bawdy and booming, seats packed every night. It exceeded all of Robby's wildest dreams. And they'd made friends here. Good friends.

"Honestly?" Robby said. "I'd like to visit your family someday and mine. And God knows, my mother will be the first in line for a ticket west when the train does go through. But as for going on the road for years with a traveling show—it doesn't appeal. There's no place I'd rather be than right here."

Trace smiled against Robby's forehead. "Honey, I'm just as happy to sit in this here town with you until we grow old."

And so . . . that's what they did.

THE END

Dear Reader

Thank you so much for reading "Robby Riverton: Mail Order Bride". I've always loved historical Western romances, and I've long dreamed of writing books in this category myself. I have lots more ideas for stories set in the Old West. If you'd like to see more books like this one, you can help Robby Riverton succeed by sharing about it online, reviewing it on Amazon and Goodreads, and recommending it to your friends.

Thank you! Your reviews really make a difference.

I appreciate my readers so much. It is awesome to hear from you and to know that I made someone smile or sigh. Feel free to email me: eli@elieaston.com.

You an also visit my website: www.elieaston.com. I have first chapters up for all my books and some free stories too. And you can sign up for my newsletter to get a monthly email about new releases and sales.

www.subscribepage.com/ElisNewsletterSignup

My facebook group is a place to chat about Eli stories and get opportunity to read ARCs, excerpts from works-in-progress, and other goodies.

www.facebook.com/groups/164054884188096/

Follow me on Amazon to be alerted of my new books.

www.amazon.com/Eli-Easton/e/B00CJUKM9I/

I can promise you there will always be happy ending and that love is love.

Eli Easton

About Eli Easton

ELI EASTON has been at various times and under different names a preacher's daughter, a computer programmer, a game designer, the author of paranormal mysteries, an organic farmer, and a profound sleeper. She has been writing m/m romance since 2013.

As an avid reader of romance, she is tickled pink when an author manages to combine literary merit, vast stores of humor, melting hotness, and eye-dabbing sweetness into one story. She promises to strive to achieve most of that most of the time. She currently lives on a farm in Pennsylvania with her husband, bulldogs, and a cat.

Her website is elieaston.com
You can e-mail her at eli@elieaston.com

facebook.com/100008994061782
twitter.com/EliEaston

Also By Eli Easton

Unwrapping Hank

Midwinter Night's Dream

Merry Christmas, Mr. Miggles

Desperately Seeking Santa

www.elieaston.com

Howl at the Moon

If you enjoyed the humor in this book, check out the author's "Howl at the Moon" series—gay romances featuring dog shifters in the little mountain town of Mad Creek, California.

LEARN MORE HERE

www.elieaston.com/howl-at-the-moon-series/

A Second Harvest

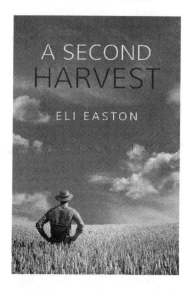

A Second Harvest – a love story between a Mennonite farmer and a man from the city who inherits the house next door

www.elieaston.com/men-of-lancaster-county/

75597968R00180

Made in the USA
San Bernardino, CA
02 May 2018